MURDER AT THE HORNY TOAD BAR

&

OTHER OUTRAGEOUS TALES OF THAILAND

D1529512

Also by Dean Barrett

Fiction

Hangman's Point – A Novel of Hong Kong
Mistress of the East – A Novel of China
Kingdom of Make-Believe – A Novel of Thailand
Memoirs of a Bangkok Warrior – A Novel of Thailand
Skytrain to Murder – A Novel of Thailand
Murder in China Red – A Novel of New York

Non-fiction

Don Quixote in China: The Search for Peach Blossom Spring
Thailand: Land of Beautiful Women

Children

The Boat Girl and the Magic Fish

Published in the United States by
Village East Books, Countryside, #520, 8775 20th Street, Vero Beach, Fl. 32966

E-mail: VillageEast@hotmail.com
Web site: http://www.deanbarrettmystery.com

ISBN: 0-9661899-8-1

Printed in Thailand by Allied Printing

Cover and interior design:
Robert Stedman, Pte., Ltd.

Cover Photo: Robert Stedman
Cover model: Panida

Publisher's Cataloging-in-Publication Data
(Prepared by The Donohue Group, Inc.)

Barrett, Dean.
    Murder at the Horny Toad Bar : & other outrageous tales of Thailand / Dean Barrett.

    p. cm.
    ISBN: 0-9661899-8-1

    1. Barrett, Dean—Journeys—Thailand. 2. Americans—Thailand. 3. Thailand—Social life and customs. 4. Thailand—Description and travel. 5. Thailand—Fiction. 6. Mystery fiction. I. Title.

PS3552.A774 M87 2004
818.6

2004102444

A few of the articles in this publication first appeared in FCCT *Dateline, The Big Chilli* and *Sawasdee magazine*.

This book is dedicated to all *farangs* (foreigners) who washed up on Thailand's shores and who at some point came to realize they are far beyond hope of redemption. And especially to those who have yet to realize it.

"Each new excess weakening me further – yet what is an insatiable man to do?"
— *The Dying Animal,* Philip Roth

"Abroad, he had lived as exclusively as he possibly could, among women whose characters ranged downwards by infinitesimal degrees, from the mysteriously doubtful to the notoriously bad."
— *Basil,* Wilkie Collins

"She got up to get the potatoes. Her dress fell open for a second, so I could see her leg. When she gave me the potatoes, I couldn't eat."
— *The Postman Always Rings Twice,* James M. Cain

MURDER AT THE HORNY TOAD BAR

&

OTHER OUTRAGEOUS TALES OF THAILAND

DEAN BARRETT

VILLAGE EAST BOOKS
FLORIDA

CONTENTS

MURDER AT THE HORNY TOAD BAR
&
OTHER OUTRAGEOUS TALES OF THAILAND

Fiction

Non-Fiction

Harry Boroditsky, Private Eye

CONTENTS

Memoirs of an Oversexed *Farang*

MURDER AT THE HORNY TOAD BAR

&

OTHER OUTRAGEOUS TALES OF THAILAND

Fiction

"Because only when you fuck is everything that you dislike in life and everything by which you are defeated in life purely, if momentarily, revenged. Only then are you most cleanly alive and most cleanly yourself. It's not the sex that's the corruption – it's the rest."

— *The Dying Animal,* Philip Roth

.

The Death of Ron Adams

There are times when I blame myself for Ron's death. And there are times when I don't. I mean, I wasn't the one who wanted to install a fancy fish tank in our go-go bar. He was. OK, I was the one who insisted we fire Dang. And that led to the hiring of Pla. But I wasn't the one who fell in love with Pla. *He* did. And I warned him about her several times. You don't run a bar in Bangkok and fall in love with one of the dancers and think it's all going to have a happy ending. That dog won't hunt. But something about these Thai women, once they got you, they got you. And common sense, the well-intentioned advice of a friend, a lifetime of experience — it all don't mean a damn thing.

Sorry. I'm getting ahead of myself. But it still makes me angry and I suppose I still feel some guilt. Wouldn't be human if I didn't. After all, I was the one who convinced him to visit Bangkok.

Ron had been a happily married man and the proud owner of two stores in Baton Rouge, Louisiana, selling Goodyear tires and tubes. He seldom traveled from the neighborhood where he went to school and grew up. If you had asked him why not he would have asked you "What for?"

Except for a bit of fishing in his spare time, his wife of 29 years had been the sole joy of his life, and once the cancer took her, he had little in life except his business. He worked hard, sold an amazing amount of Goodyear products and before long had won a Goodyear incentive trip to Hong Kong.

I had dated his wife in high school and known Ron fairly well. We'd been on the same basketball team together and almost got into a fight in a gym locker room over something but I can't remember what. It wasn't over her because I'd stopped dating her by that time. Might have had something to do with the Vietnam War.

Anyway, after I'd moved to Bangkok, I kept in touch with both of them so when he said he was coming out to Hong Kong, I reminded him that Thailand was a mere two hours and twenty minutes' flying time away. It took three letters to convince him to add Thailand to his itinerary but in the end he did.

But after several days in Hong Kong, Ron decided the former British colony was all money and no fun and he was looking forward to getting back to Louisiana. Then he landed in Bangkok where I met him at the airport.

He had changed very little from when I had last seen him years before. He had not an ounce of fat on him and while his auburn hair had thinned considerably, his tiny bald spot could easily be covered by a five-baht coin. He had a clean-shaven, weather-beaten face with craggy, angular features and not quite hollow cheeks. But he had a ready smile and bright cornflower blue eyes and he moved with the vigor and purpose of a much younger man. Although his face could not be described as handsome, it was an interesting face, intelligent and alert.

Despite mild protest on his part, the very first night he was in town I took him to some of the bars of Nana Plaza. Pinching himself to make certain he wasn't dreaming, Ron found himself surrounded by nearly naked, incredibly beautiful and miraculously available women. Women who practically begged him to take them to his hotel. And just as the song's lyrics warned, Ron soon found the devil walking beside him.

He flew back to Louisiana but only to sell his business as quickly as possible. Ron told me later that his neighbors and friends shook their heads and clucked their tongues but Ron assured them he knew right well what he was doing and prepared to fly back to Thailand to stay. The preacher of his Southern Baptist congregation made a trip to Ron's house and informed Ron that he was shocked at Ron's decision and not a little worried about his soul. But he left in a hurry once Ron explained that it was simply a case of "the Bible belt discovering the bikini belt and discovering that 2000-year-old scriptures ain't quite as comforting as 20-year-old flesh."

Ron soon saw an opportunity to buy one of the very bars that had attracted him to the city, and before long he was the proud owner (with me as a minor partner) of the Feminist Nightmare bar. The Feminist Nightmare was one of those which had been around for a very long time and — rarity among rarities — over the years various foreign owners had actually made a bit of money out of it. Its symbol was a flashing neon sign with a caricature of a balding, big-bellied Western male surrounded by Thai go go dancers in skimpy bikinis.

Many of the girls who worked at the Feminist Nightmare came from the northeast of Thailand, and almost all came from the countryside. And I could tell right away that Ron was fascinated by them. Well, who wouldn't be; several of them were good looking and one or two were stunning. Wearing only the tiniest of bikinis, the girls gyrated on stage to the latest western songs and threw themselves wholeheartedly into the incessant and throbbing rhythms.

Ron got himself an apartment not far from the bar and we appointed a couple of former bar mamasans as managers. I had had some small share of a bar before, so finding the right disc jockey was left to me. And I knew just the man for the job.

I had been in Bangkok since the late 60's when I'd been stationed here with the military. One of my best friends had been a dark-skinned, humor-loving, Thai mechanic named Wichai.

Wichai had worked for JUSMAG and had flown to American Army and Air Force bases all over Thailand in a C-130, wherever and whenever the Americans had a vehicle to fix. He could repair anything the American Army gave him: jeeps, trucks, vans and, by the end of the war, helicopters.

I had met him at an air base in Udorn where I was spending several months TDY (temporary duty). Wichai and I hit it off right away. The incredible din of American warplanes taking off at night to pay their nocturnal visits to Vietnam and returning to base early the next morning allowed us so little sleep Wichai began working part of a night shift in the American clubs as a disc jockey. He often made up to twenty dollars a day in tips from Air Force pilots and crew chefs who had (sometimes accurate) premonitions that they might not be returning to spend the money.

Wichai had done real well and like many Thais working with the American military during the war, had thought the good times would go on forever. He gambled at dice and card games and lost heavily and lost most of the rest in a failed business venture with a dishonest Thai-Chinese partner; and when we'd finally lost our own gamble in Vietnam, he'd been left with no job and a wife and two young children to support.

For over two years he drove a ten-wheel truck between Bangkok and Chiang Mai, hauling soybeans from north to south and Sony television sets from south to north. He'd worked in auto repair garages, then began driving his own taxi during the day. Then, eventually, he'd found nighttime jobs as a disc jockey in various bars and once he'd heard about my involvement in the Feminist Nightmare it wasn't difficult to recruit him.

Ron and I finished our renovations, hired a publicist, and, before long, the bar was packed with customers. Our beer was cold, our women were gorgeous and our music was popular. Despite a recent government crackdown on showing too much female flesh, we were doing well and would have continued doing well; until one day Ron made the first of his two serious mistakes. He decided he wanted his bar to be a bit classier than the rest and that he would add class to the bar in the form of a fish tank. He had had a tank in his office in Louisiana and it had added class there and he was certain it would add class here. Besides, he had always liked fishing and enjoyed being around colorful fish.

He made several trips to the exotic fish section of the Weekend Market and was pleased that he was overcharged less than the average foreigner. And so it came to pass that every night in the Feminist Nightmare all the colors of the rainbow displayed themselves for dazzled customers who chose to sit near the fish tank. Unlike the more convenient plastic aquarium, the standard glass-and-metal tank kept the visual distortion of the brilliantly colored specimens to a minimum.

Elaborate and impossibly graceful dorsal fins, caudal fins, pelvic fins, pectoral fins, and anal fins swayed languorously back and forth while slim bodies enclosed in magnificently colored scales of perfectly symmetrical designs were propelled by fantails, sword tails, round tails, speartails, pintails and flagtails. Yellow eyes, green eyes, black eyes and orange eyes stared out at customers and bargirls alike; for they too were observers.

The excitement and pride surrounding their collection of fish quickly spread to nearly all the girls in the bar (except for one or two who resented competition of *any* kind) and their income from ladies' drinks, "casual stays" in hotel rooms and all-night stands — money which once went to buying dresses, cosmetics, jewelry and the latest cellphone — now often went for buying still more resplendent fish. Regular customers began to joke that they were pushed a bit harder for drinks whenever the "fish fund" was in need of more money for a still more exotic purchase. And they were right.

Out of a sense of generosity and also due to a shortage of

garbage bags, the bargirls were unselfish in sharing their own food with the fish; but in their exuberance, the girls had bought the fish with the most brilliant colors and exotic shapes without too much thought as to how the specimens would co-exist with one another in a community tank. Customers would often stop watching the dancers to observe several fish with nipped fins and tails, involved in deadly pursuits and fatal chases. It wasn't until the girls learned something about incompatible species and employed a trial-and-error method that most of the mistakes were finally eliminated.

Ron had planned on placing one of his mamasans in charge of the fish tank but Dang, one of the dancers, used her not inconsiderable charms on him and Ron finally succumbed to her pleading and placed her in charge of the fish. Dang's obvious attractions made her popular with Ron (a bit too popular, I thought) although unknown to him she was unpopular with the other girls in the bar as she was suspected of stealing money from another girl's purse in more than one bar. But as her dancing and her figure were cynosures of nocturnal interest, no bar manager was willing to throw her out without absolute proof; and either because she was innocent or extremely clever she had never been caught at anything more serious than hustling drinks from someone else's regular customer.

In my opinion, Dang was a disruptive element in the bar and I wanted to let her go; Ron didn't. That led to the first time Ron and I had heated words.

One night I told him I needed to see him in our office. And I had it out with him over Dang. I told him I was aware that I was only a minor partner in the bar but I was still a partner. Furthermore, I had been a minor partner in a bar before and knew a bit about the many pitfalls in the business. More important, I was his friend. I told him Dang stole money, upset other girls by stealing their regular customers, and wasn't to be trusted. She had to go. I also pointedly reminded him that it was bad form for bar owners to show favoritism to one of the dancers.

He gave me a few limp arguments about why she shouldn't be fired but finally, very reluctantly, he gave in. And that was the last night Dang worked at the Feminist Nightmare. I felt a sense of relief at knowing the bar's bad apple was gone.

I also felt a sense of relief at hearing Ron speak of his medical report from a local hospital. Something about Bangkok seemed to energize him and I thought he looked fine. Except he had a small lump on his neck which I had been telling him should be checked out. He'd finally agreed to have a sample taken and also an MRI. The result was negative, nothing was malignant, and whatever was on his neck was little more than a harmless cyst. As he put it, it was just one of many unsightly things that men our age might expect to come along. We went back into the bar and drank to his good health.

Dang's departure left an opening in the bar and word got around quickly. The next day, several dancers stopped by and applied for the job. But one stood out above the rest; and I mean *way* above them. She was from somewhere near Surin and there was no question she was beautiful. Glossy, jet-black hair down to her waist, an oval face with large dark eyes, full lips, high cheekbones and perfect features. And a way of looking at a man that could cause him to forget there were other women in the world.

Ron reacted as if he'd been struck by Cupid's arrow right on the spot. She danced for us on the stage and she was terrific; better than Dang had ever been. She used the brass pole in a way that gave erotic dancing new meaning. We looked at each other, smiled and nodded. We had our new dancer.

A few nights after that, I saw Ron put his arm around her and take her into the office. And I knew then beyond any doubt she had already ensnared him just like a fish in a trap. I also knew that her nickname, Pla, meant "fish," and while I wasn't superstitious about that, looking back, perhaps I should have been. In fact, she later told me that when she'd heard about the fish tank she had decided that, with her nickname, it would be lucky for her to work at the Feminist Nightmare. Ron's fish tank had attracted Pla and now Pla had ensnared Ron.

The months passed and, by the end of the first year, we had made a good profit. Ron was strict with the girls in prescribing the way they acted toward customers and even in insisting that if they put on too much weight, they be fired. All except, Pla, of course. Pla had such a hold on him that she could have burned the bar down and I'm sure Ron would have made excuses for her.

I had already heard rumors of Ron buying her expensive gold jewelry and other gifts, and I had seen her new "absolutely red" Toyota Camry Solara SE sport coupe parked outside the bar, but it was Wichai who first alerted me to the fact that she had moved in with Ron. At the time I said nothing, but it did worry me that Ron wasn't even telling me about it. It also worried me that he gladly took her onto his lap or in other ways showed affection and favoritism to her right in the bar. The few times I broached the subject with him, his attitude was quite clear: his relationship with Pla was his business; nobody else's.

By the end of our first year in business, the bar remained popular and the fish tank had undoubtedly become one of the most colorful in all of Bangkok; and the fish seemed as fascinated with the girls as the girls were with them. And, as Ron loved to point out, like the girls themselves, each fish had its own personality. Some nervously darting, hugging their fins close to the body, like a schooner caught in a storm, some gracefully swimming with all fins and tails coordinating like a galleon with full, billowing sails, some using their pelvic fins like oars propelling a rowboat. A world full of constantly moving fins and tails, lips and gill covers. And always the imperfectly round staring eyes, continually rotating in their sockets with quick, abrupt, almost furtive, movements.

The kaleidoscopic underwater spectacle provided the girls in the bar with such delight that not only did they look forward to coming to work, on occasion, they preferred gazing at the fish to being bought out and jumping into bed with a customer. Although their enthusiasm for the fish was great, and they paid an enormous amount of attention to them, how much the girls actually knew about proper care of tropical fish remained a problem. The staple diet of the fish consisted of slender and threadlike worms — both white and red varieties — tiny fish, chopped liver and mosquito larvae, lettuce and ground shrimp. Despite my warnings, the girls were unselfish in sharing the leftovers of their own meals, and the fish were often inundated with the remains of fried bananas, slices of pineapple, pieces of durian, partly crushed locusts, piscicidal bits of red-and-green chilies and the down-on-his-luck cockroach.

After each new display of generosity, several bloated carp and other abnormally large scavengers got to work and cleaned up. Of all the specimens of fish in the tank, the carp and other scavengers were the most frequently replaced.

Among the favorites with the girls were the extravagantly colored goldfish with their sinuous swimming movements and darting splashes of red, gold and yellow, particularly those with bulbous eyes such as the Telescopic-eyed Moor and the protuberantly globular-eyed Celestial Goldfish.

The fish were appreciated for brilliant color, unusual shape, humorous activity and even curious sound. The sole Lionhead Goldfish boasted a fluffy, red-orange head covering resembling a lion's mane; the Indian Algae-eater employed its sucking disc to remain anchored in strange positions and served well as the aquarium's janitor; the Glass Catfish was favored for its two prominent whiskers and its transparent, skeleton-revealing body; the Croaking Tetra gulped air and gave the girls enormous pleasure with its soft croaking sound caused by tiny bubbles expelled through its gills.

Without doubt, the most favored of all were the Kissing Gourami which would usually be surrounded by girls who should have been dancing or entertaining customers, the remonstrations of Ron and the mamasans, Ning and Noy, being only reluctantly heeded.

A few fish had been chosen by nomenclature regardless of looks. All of the girls could identify with such names as Celestial Goldfish and Angelfish, but no amount of money was spared in keeping at least one specimen known as Slippery Dick in the tank. And, indeed, the long and slender Slippery Dick did at least resemble a male organ more than other fish which diverted attention from their basic phallic shapes with large and exotic fins and tails.

Unfortunately, despite the best of intentions, in addition to overfeeding, providing improper temperature and mismatching community members, the girls had made other mistakes. Fish with fragile scales and swaying fins soon ripped themselves to shreds on the sharp edges of stones a few of the dancers had placed at the bottom of the aquarium for shade and decoration. These were replaced by smooth, round stones as soon as the mistake (in the form of dead fish) was discovered.

Pla (herself a Pisces) enjoyed watching the antics of some of the fish swimming to the surface and opening and closing their mouths in what she imagined was their way of saying, "Hello, you buy me drink!" It was only later that she realized fish which tend to gulp repeatedly at the water's surface are suffering not from lack of ladies' drinks but from lack of oxygen usually from overcrowding or polluted water. Such fish, she decided, were in fact saying "goodbye" rather than "hello" and she belatedly thinned out the tank.

And those goldfish which kept to themselves lurking alone behind rocks — those most admired by the dancers for their "independence" and "non-conformity" — were, on closer examination, found to be in extremely poor health rather than off contemplating the state of the world (or tank). Nevertheless, the girls learned from their mistakes and their piscine community stabilized and prospered.

Three nights before Ron died, Pla and a few other girls were dancing on the stage. Suddenly, Wichai rushed from behind his enclosure, jumped up onto the stage, and pried open Pla's fist. He grabbed something from it and held it in front of her face as proof of her guilt. Pla tightened her chin and folded her arms across her chest, which she thrust out in defiance. Ning, the older of the two mamasan's, began scolding her, and, while bearing the brunt of her scolding, Pla looked more sullen than ashamed. She stared at a point off to the side of the stage as if she might suddenly jump down and leave. Finally, though, she nodded. Ning said something and Pla nodded again. The mamasan leapt from the stage and the girls resumed their dancing.

Ning threw the offending object onto the table of our booth and continued to grumble in an angry voice as she walked off, still upset by what had happened. Ron picked up the object and handled it as a scientist might examine a slightly unusual specimen — curious but calm — and handed it to me. I leaned forward to examine it in the light near the fish tank. I placed it near my nose, sniffed, and wrinkled my face. "A ball of cotton-wool soaked with enough paint thinner to supply all the artists in Thailand."

He seemed about to respond but grew silent so I continued: "Some girls sniff it while they're doin' their dancin'; relaxes them; makes them forget about the angry boyfriend, unfaithful husband or some other trouble. Good at first, but then they keep it up. Pretty soon they don't want to eat, and then they turn as yellow as a piece of pineapple and then the fumes from the thinner destroy their nasal cartilage and pretty soon they're young-old hags back in the ricefield or worse yet in a Chinatown brothel." I threw the ball of cotton-wool onto the table. "If they want to mess with *yaba* or paint thinner or whatever, they all know better than to do it here."

I looked at Ron. We had a no-nonsense policy in the bar toward any kind of drugs and had already fired two dancers because of their use of amphetamines. Pla's use of paint thinner had been seen by everyone in the bar. Both of us knew what had to be done.

I spoke to him quite matter-of-factly. "Pla has to go, Ron." He stared at me for several seconds then turned to stare into the fish tank as if looking for a way out of the dilemma. Whatever the reason, in the year that he'd been in Bangkok, Ron had visibly aged. Almost alarmingly so. His blue eyes were dimmer, his wrinkles deeper and his attention less focused. He had gained no weight but moved as if he had. His manner — once confident and resolute — was now hesitant and uncertain. Even the once warm and ready smile had been replaced by one far less genuine.

Wichai had stopped the music, and the gulps of the Croaking Tetra punctuated the room's silence like an exhausted percolator. Finally, Ron turned back to me. In the light of the tank, it looked as though he had become a very weary old man. "I'll let her know after work."

Three nights later, the night he died, Ron still appeared to me to be either in ill health or else sick over what he'd had to do. He hadn't said a word to me about how Pla had taken the news of her dismissal.

I sat with him in the bar as he began speaking about his concern for the girls who came from upcountry farms and small villages and who were suddenly confronted with the bright lights of Bangkok. I remember he kept emphasizing that a lot of them had had very bad experiences, and while they might be tough on the outside, inside they were very vulnerable. It seemed to me he was to some extent using metaphors to defend Pla.

As he spoke, I leafed through the dual-language English-Thai edition of *Tropical Fish Care*, a well worn and heavily stained book, kept near Ron's position at the bar. "You see, when these girls first get to Bangkok, some of them are taken straightaway to the bars and they start workin' right off! Which ain't right!" *A fish should never be plunged suddenly into a new environment.*

"The problems come when a girl just in from upcountry starts workin' and right away some drunkin' slob starts pawin' her and she don' know how to handle it." *Hands have been known to damage even the toughest specimen by tearing off scales.* "And if they're pretty, which lots of them are, some of the older girls get jealous." *In a properly maintained aquarium, care must be taken to ensure that various species can co-exist peacefully.*

He smiled at remembering some of the dancers we'd had. "Then again, we have had one or two gals up from the south who were hot-tempered as hell, haven't we?" *Naturally pugnacious and naturally vulnerable fish should never be kept in the same aquarium.* "Remember the one from Surat Thani? Went after everybody's boyfriends and all hell broke loose." *Some species are particularly disruptive in community tanks because of their fin-nipping proclivities.*

"Well, I'll say this for our staff, Ning and Noy do a damn fine job teachin' 'em about avoiding pregnancy and what to do if they do get pregnant." *The breeding habits of certain species are the subject of considerable controversy; some are amazingly quick to breed.* "We've seen every type, haven't we? Some just come to dance and make some money," *largely nocturnal and rather shy specimen,* "some seem to love to get it on," *small but very active sexually,* "and some are just dick teasers," *an amusing fish to watch as it devises elaborate games.*

As I ordered my fourth beer, Ron pointed at the fish tank. "You see that sorry looking son-of-a-bitch? That's a celestial goldfish. It is the only livin' thing that can stare into its own eyes. If a bar owner ain't careful, he's gonna' end up lookin' the same way."

For a few minutes we just drank our Singha beer and silently stared at the fish tank in which our tropical fish swam amid coral formations, colored stones and vegetation. I gazed at the small plastic figure of a diver trapped in the tank bed's compost. Molded in the form of the traditional hard-hat variety, the diver had one foot permanently poised to take his next cautious step. He peered out from inside his cumbersome helmet and constantly emitted bubbles which expanded gradually as they slowly, gracefully made their way to the surface of the water.

The tubing from the closed air valve attached to its plastic connector was unbroken, and the diver functioned perfectly as the tank's aerator; yet, something in the ornament's mechanism had malfunctioned and the diver remained forever motionless, with arms outstretched, unable to bend over and pick up the treasure chest of jewels and gold bars which lay at his feet. He reminded me of foreigners who come to Thailand and buy a bar and reach out for profits which are never quite there. But he especially reminded me of what was happening to Ron — right before my very eyes.

I had not seen Pla since she'd left the bar that night. I thought she might show up to say goodbye or to clear out her locker, but she hadn't. While we sat talking about the fish, Wichai stopped by our booth and whispered into Ron's ear. Ron gave him an uncertain smile, then nodded. He looked at me then glanced away. His lips stretched into one of the saddest smiles I'd ever seen. And I knew Pla was gone. With Ron's money.

I decided the best thing would be to let Ron bring the subject up and if he didn't bring it up in a few days, I'd sit down and talk with him. Find out how much of his savings was gone. Maybe if I hadn't waited I could have done some good; but I doubt it.

Later that night I found his handwritten note inside an envelope on my office desk; an elderly vendor of fried bananas
found his body on the small *soi*, the side street below his 14th
floor apartment balcony.

To my partner & best friend,

When I was selling stuff in the States, I wasn't even living. Nothing more exciting had ever happened to me than getting a best sales-
man award. It wasn't until I came here that I came alive. This has
been the best year of my life. And I want to thank you for that. If it
hadn't been for you, I'd have ended up retired somewhere playing
shuffleboard and eating early bird specials without ever having had
this incredible experience. I have no regrets and you sure as hell
shouldn't have any.

Most Thai girls are lovely; you should find the right one for yourself some day. Pla had a bad life and she had lived in poverty far too
long to trust a man or to really believe she didn't need to reach out
and grab anymore. By the time fortune got around to favoring her,
she just couldn't make the leap. Please don't blame her and above all
don't try to find her or have her punished. Her ex-husband did a lot
of that while she was still married. I've seen the scars.

The irony is I was leaving my savings to her, anyway. I lied, my
friend. The cancer is malignant and they found more clusters inside
my skull than bar girls have excuses for being late. So I think you
can understand that I have no interest in hanging on for a slow,
painful, death.

Take care of the fish tank, my friend. And the bar. It's all yours
now. And thanks again.

Ron

Later that night, Wichai and I headed for the building known
as the police hospital morgue near Siam Square to identify the body.
It was Ron, all right. And I still wish to this day that that hadn't
been the final image I had of him. I kept remembering what he'd
said about the Celestial Goldfish looking into its own eyes.

29

I'd known the manager of the local Bank of Ayuthya for some time and kept my own accounts there. He was cooperative and friendly. What he told me was exactly what I suspected. Ron had set up a joint account with Pla. The account had been emptied. I had Wichai check with a few of the car dealerships in Bangkok. He found the one Pla had taken the Camry Solara to. She had sold it the day after she was fired for six hundred thousand baht.

One of the regular customers in the bar worked with a Thai lawyer/detective and asked if I wanted Pla found. I just shook my head and smiled. To an extent, I knew exactly how Ron felt: when a man reaches a certain age it's pretty difficult to blame a woman in her early 20's for making mistakes; even bad ones. If there's no fool like an old fool it's because the old fool is happy with what he's getting in return for being thought a fool. And I knew that for most of his time in Bangkok Ron had been a happy man.

I chipped in what money was needed and, thanks to the assistance of the American Citizen Services section at the US embassy, Ron's body was sent back to Louisiana for burial. I wondered if the preacher there used Ron's fate as a perfect example of what happens to good Christians when they are tempted by the devil and head off to a sin-filled city like Bangkok. I didn't mind; I knew Ron would have laughed his head off.

The Fish and the Interpreter

Bill Spencer had flown to Bangkok on business several times without once having ventured outside the often unbearably hot city. Everything he needed was right there in the capital and he had no interest in touring the countryside of the Land of Smiles. In fact, he seldom ventured from the luxurious, air-conditioned splendor of the Oriental Hotel except when accompanying his Thai agent to a factory. This, he supposed, would have continued indefinitely had it not been for something directly related to his export business.

He had braved the heat long enough to search for an ATM machine when he noticed a display of teakwood carvings far superior to the run-of-the-mill type he had been exporting. As usual, there were the pedestrian carvings that flooded the city: fighting elephants, water buffaloes and bowls of various shapes and sizes; but at the back of the store, he came upon foot-high carvings of Thai women which displayed expert craftsmanship. Women at the market, women on elephant back, women paddling in *klongs* (canals), even a few go-go dancers. Bill studied them carefully and realized that even the facial expressions had been meticulously delineated. He had never seen anything in any type of wood from Southeast Asia so well carved.

Although feigning only polite interest, Bill had soon managed to charm the vendor into giving him the address of the man who had carved the women. A block from the shop, Bill waved a taxi to a halt, showed him the directions the man had written down, and set out on his journey.

Somewhere north of the city it became clear to Bill that the driver had trouble following the directions and they spent over two hours fruitlessly searching back roads until the taxi developed engine trouble. The driver protested when Bill paid partly in American currency, the value of which he did not understand. But Bill just shrugged and slung his jacket over his shoulder.

As he began his walk, he loosened his tie and wiped the sweat from his forehead with his already drenched handkerchief. A child's head appeared above the grassy bank at the side of the road. Two children rode slowly toward him on a water buffalo. The animal glistened in the heat as it climbed out of the small canal. The two children stared at Bill from beneath their wide straw hats until they were two small dots against the green rice fields and areca palms. Bill was surrounded by the clean flat land and nearly even vegetation on all sides. And only the deep blue of the cloud-streaked sky challenged the color dominance of the lush green fields.

A large, gaudily-decorated truck sped by loaded with Thai workers. One pointed to Bill and yelled the only English word he knew: "You!"

They all laughed and waved. Bill wearily waved but his sweating features refused to smile. How, he wondered, could anyone actually live day after day in this heat and humidity?

A small bright spot of reflected sunlight to the west soon revealed a temple's orange-and-green tiled roof rising from the surrounding bright red-orange blossoms of a dozen flame-of-the-forest trees. But as these trees advanced westward beyond the temple toward the city, now directly under the sun, they became imbued in a bluish-gray tinge, bereft of individual color and pattern.

The rice field on his right began to give way to large trees separated from the road by a small canal. Just as the canal began to wind in a northerly direction away from the road, Bill saw a small vegetable store with the omnipresent faded Coca-Cola sign. As he walked along the narrow path to the store, he heard the soft murmured sounds, "*farang, farang,*" which, somewhere Bill had learned, meant: "foreigner."

Three motionless, naked children stared at him as he cautiously crossed the unsteady wooden planks of the small open porch. One white-haired woman, unmindful of the chunk of betel nut held precariously between blackened teeth, spoke quickly to another, a woman about forty, whom Bill guessed to be the owner of the store. No men were present. The younger woman spoke to him in Thai. He smiled and pointed to the sign: "Coke," he asked, "Cola."

"Ah, Cola," they remarked to one another, stressing the second syllable of the word. This successful communication animated the woman and children toward the soda. The woman smilingly opened the bottle while the old bare-breasted woman, with lips stained a bright purple from a lifetime of beetle nut chewing, brought a straw and pointed to a small, wooden stool. Bill sat smiling at the staring children. He turned to watch the Thais paddle the small boats upstream and downstream. Some would stop at the store and buy or sell vegetables and fruit. All would talk about the *farang* on the porch.

For a while Bill watched the younger woman cut fruit by rolling the sharp edge of the knife toward her fingers. He wondered how long it took to learn to control this movement and why she didn't move the knife in toward her thumb as is done in the West. Something about the action reminded him of his fiancee in New York. And the heated arguments they had had in the kitchen of her Midtown apartment before he'd left for Thailand.

Bill decided to finish his Coke and continue hiking toward the highway, or until he could hail a taxi. He had almost stood up when he noticed an attractive young Thai woman paddling from upstream approaching the store. About fifty feet from the porch, she stopped paddling and stared intently at him as her boat drifted out of the tunnel of overhanging trees. She reached out to the porch and steadied her boat before getting out. She looked again at him with a slightly bemused smile, them smiled broadly.

Her light brown skin was drawn tightly and smoothly over her slender body. A beautiful mane of long black hair cascaded downward, hanging freely in front and in back of her well-worn white blouse, reaching the top of the bright red and black sarong-like *pasin* wrapped around her waist and legs. Perfectly rounded cheeks formed by her smile gave even greater depth to the natural beauty of her dark brown eyes. Bill stared in silence at her delicate features even as the children continued to observe him.

The girl left several small green mangoes on the old woman's table and talked swiftly to the owner of the store. Bill strained his ears to hear the sound "*farang*," but heard nothing he could understand. As the barefoot girl returned to the boat, her *pasin* showed clearly, and, to Bill, provocatively, the graceful form of her slender waist and legs. As she began to paddle away, she looked at Bill and again beamed an innocent, unaffected smile. This time, Bill smiled broadly and waved promptly, almost knocking the Coke bottle into the canal. Only after she disappeared around the bend of the canal did he notice the women and children smiling at him. Despite his embarrassment, he felt a strange sense of exhilaration. This, he knew, was the most beautiful woman he had ever seen.

Bill made careful notes on his location and the next day, he met with Somnuck, his partly American-educated agent in Thailand. Somnuck listened without comment to his story about the women he had seen, smiled wryly, but agreed to accompany him to act as interpreter.

As they walked from the road to the store, the same hot sun burned into Bill's reddening skin. "*Sawasdee*," Somnuck shouted, placing the palms of his hands together before him in a Thai *wai*. The two smiling women returned the gesture and also the verbal greeting.

Again Coke was brought to the small wooden table. Sliced areca nuts lay on a cracked porcelain plate drying in the sun. Bill shifted uncomfortably on his low teakwood stool and turned to Somnuck: "Ask her the name of the woman who brought the mangoes here yesterday."

Somnuck complied. "Her name is Vilaileka Rangavara. The people here call her Miss Thailand because she is from Nakorn Chaisri. It is believed that area of Thailand has the whitest rice, the sweetest pomeloes, and the most beautiful women."

After a moment's silence Bill said: "Ask them if she will come today."

As Somnuck spoke to the woman, one of the children, bald except for his topknot, peered around the corner at Bill. Bill turned and watched the canal.

"Yes, they expect her to come very soon. She lives with her mother and sister about two kilometers downstream. She has already gone upstream to market so she will return soon. They say she is very poor but has a good heart."

"I have seen many beautiful women since I came to Thailand, Somnuck. But I never wanted one until now."

"Yes," Somnuck answered quickly. "This one must be like your fiancee, I think. Not the carbon's copy."

"How do you know about my fiancee?" asked Bill sharply, looking directly into Somnuck's startled black eyes.

"Her picture is on your desk in your hotel room. I noticed it during our last meeting. She is beautiful, is she not?"

Bill returned his attention to scanning the canal and spoke as if to himself. "Yes, beautiful." And, thought Bill, educated. And

an ardent feminist who loves to babble for hours about empowerment and relationships and every other American cliché; the
type of American gender wars cliché which as time passed Bill
found more and more boring.

After a moment's silence Bill said: "A carbon copy."

"Excuse me?"

"You said before this woman is not the carbon's copy. You
mean she is not a carbon copy."

"Oh, yes, of course, thank you. American idioms still cause
me some trouble."

Bill watched a middle-aged woman, clothed in a long red *pasin*,
walk to the opposite bank of the river. White foam began to
appear on her hair as she walked into the canal to wash. In a
moment, a toothbrush appeared between her dark fingers and
she began brushing her teeth.

As Bill watched for the girl, the women offered the two men a
bowl of what to Bill looked like dead cockroaches. Bill refused
the offer; Somnuck accepted. Bill had shared drinks and Western cuisine at the Oriental with Somnuck and now he watched in
morbid fascination as the man he thought he knew expertly and
with obvious relish devoured the beetle.

Sunset produced a twilight in almost complete stillness. The
gray hue he had seen in several sunsets did not appear. The
colors of the boats, trees, grass and water seemed to fade within
themselves without merging. Bill could hear only the distant
sound of a dog barking and the occasional sound of a paddle
slicing the water. Conditioned by the familiar sounds of his
own world, Bill felt such profound silence all but unnatural
and unnerving.

Somnuck motioned to Bill. "The woman says you should
relax and eat."

Bill smiled briefly and lit another cigarette. "If the girl doesn't
come soon we'd better go," he said.

"She will come, *Khun* Bill, Somnuck said softly. "You must be patient. 'A white elephant,' we say, 'is found only in the deep forest.'"

"And a white elephant is a good find?"

"The best of all."

Directly across from Bill a woman walked out on a horizontal wooden ladder that protruded over the side of the canal. A large fish net, hanging from the ladder, dipped into the water as she walked. After a few moments, she moved slowly toward the shore. The leverage again raised the dipnet above the water. She began pulling the ropes attached to the sides of the net.

"Only one fish for all of that work," Bill said.

"Ah, but it is a beautiful fish; well worth the trouble," Somnuck replied. "Although I hate to see a beautiful fish in a net, I think one can forgive the woman when catching for necessity." After a pause he continued: "Fish are intriguing, aren't they? Their environment throughout their lives is water. Yet, lacking a conceptual level, they do not even realize such a thing as water exists. It is so close to them they cannot see it. They even fail to realize that to leave it is to die."

In the darkness that was steadily devouring the canal's bright colors, Bill saw the light from a small fire behind several trees on the opposite bank. Soon the lights of many cooking fires appeared along both sides of the canal and into the countryside beyond. The same countryside that had seemed nearly deserted during the day now had flickering eyes from all directions. Bill was about to ask for some fruit when he noticed several flies alighting on almost every variety. As he replaced a mango his arm knocked his Coke bottle off the table. Only Somnuck's quick catch prevented it from pouring into the canal. For a moment Bill sat silently, then turned to Somnuck. "Do you think I could live with her?" he asked.

"Excuse me, *Khun* —"

"You heard me. Would she come into the city?" He noticed the women staring at him and he stopped talking and turned to the canal.

Somnuck allowed a full thirty seconds to pass before answering. "You know, *Khun* Bill, some day all this will be gone. The canals, the peasants, the small boats. The government is quickly filling the canals to build roads. And it is good. This poverty cannot be allowed to remain in an age of progress. These conditions and low standards of living cannot continue for long. In twenty years, perhaps thirty, in the Bangkok area, it will all be gone. But gone with it will be the innocence of the people, the ready smiles, the unique customs, the quaint setting. It will be easier then for us to be with one another. Yet, I fear, easier because so many of the attractive differences will have disappeared."

Somnuck tore off the legs and head of a beetle but, seeing the shock on Bill's face hesitated. "Progress demands so much of human relations." He threw the beetle into the *klong*. "You see, *Khun* Bill, once a fish has gained the ability to conceive of the existence of water, it has lost the ability to communicate with those who have not; for it is no longer a fish."

A small child leaned over the low railing. Suddenly he darted across the porch and pointed upstream. He spoke softly but excitedly to his mother.

Somnuck turned to Bill. "She is coming," he said.

Bill tossed his cigarette onto fresh red splotches of beetle juice staining the rickety wooden porch and watched the red blotches extinguish it. He rose. "Let's go. We're leaving."

"Leaving? I don't understand."

"You damn well understand!" Bill stared into Somnuck's unsteady gaze. Then with a slight trace of a smile he added: "There's a new bar at Nana Plaza. We're going to drown our cultures in drink while I curse you for helping the one that got away."

Somnuck walked quickly behind him. "Yes, *Khun* Bill," he smiled. He waved goodbye to the children, then walked quickly to Bill's side. With a grin large even by Thai standards, he said: "Drown in drink. This idiom I understand."

Obsession

It is impossible to describe the bewitching charm, seductive grace, and erotic nature of a Thai woman to men who have never experienced them. And that is why it is impossible to get friends from 'back home' to understand how a man can become so obsessed with a Thai woman that he will not merely unwittingly play the fool but even wittingly play the fool. And once a man has fallen under the spell of a Thai woman's sexual power, he does things he might not be especially proud of. Particularly if he is an older man and she is a beautiful young woman. I should know: it happened to me when I quarreled with a Bangkok bargirl I was head-over-heels in love with.

Sukanda was the most beautiful woman I had ever seen and it was immediately obvious to both of us I had no defense against her charms. The sensual and lascivious way she danced on stage, the way her waist-long hair fell across her smooth, bare shoulders, the knowing smile on those perfect lips, the dark brown apricot eyes that rendered me helpless — it was as if a goddess had descended to earth and, for whatever reason, had chosen to take me as her lover.

We made love at her apartment, at mine, in Pattaya hotels, in Phuket hotels, and on a deserted beach at Ko Samui. But to say simply that we made love is to misrepresent the frenzied passion of our encounters. If she had simply attempted to be sexy I don't think she would have fascinated me so much; but there was a completely natural eroticism about her that I found irresistible.

On those nights when I had had too much to drink, or when I felt uncertain about my sexual prowess, I disappeared into the bathroom to take a Viagra, never letting her see me do it. And shortly after we became lovers, I began dyeing my salt-and-pepper hair. I have no doubt I was every bit as ridiculous as van Ashenbach chasing after Tadzio in Mann's *Death in Venice*, but I was constantly afraid of losing her to someone younger.

It was nearly three months after I had first seen her that we quarreled. I was upset that she still refused to quit dancing in the bar and move in with me, and the night before our quarrel she had spent the night with a girlfriend, or so she said. I, of course, accused her of having had a one-night stand.

After drinking too much Mekhong whiskey, I made quite a scene at the bar, almost getting into a fight with Boonsom, the disc jockey and a very nice guy. Sukanda left the bar suddenly and disappeared before I could sober up and apologize. She never answered her cellphone or the phone in her apartment and she had no answering machine.

Like some lovesick schoolboy I went to the bar several times over the next few days practically begging for news of her. Finally, her best friend, Dao, took pity on me and, provided I would take her with me, and pay the bar whatever they said would compensate for her absence, she agreed to tell me where Sukanda went. Once I agreed, she opened her purse and removed a pack of matches advertising the Pattaya beach resort a short drive from Bangkok.

Thanks to my generosity, the bar had allowed Dao whatever time off she needed to aid in my search for Sukanda, and as Boonsom had to run an errand in Sattahip — just south of Pattaya — the mamasan had asked him to give us a lift. Boonsom had arrived at the bar at eleven in the morning, an hour later than we had agreed, and was now apparently trying to make up for lost time.

As he maneuvered his Datsun back into line narrowly avoiding an oncoming, horn-blaring, pick-up truck, I glanced again above my head at the three gold leaf squares and white Sanskrit lettering, which I remembered with nervous gratitude, were symbols affixed by Buddhist monks for protection of drivers and, I hoped, for passengers as well.

The three of us sat in the front seat — Dao squeezed in the middle — and sped along the highway toward Pattaya at a speed which I found excessive to the point of suicidal. I couldn't be certain but I was pretty sure Boonsom had been briefed on why the two of us were hitching a ride with him. In any case, he concentrated on his driving, chatted with Dao in Thai and broken English and asked me nothing of a personal nature.

I could sense a certain excitement in Dao's attitude toward my search for Sukanda. She seemed to cherish her involvement in a romantic attempt to reunite two lovers. A situation which, for me, represented an embarrassing, obsessive and puerile pursuit of a girl nearly half my age seemed to provide Dao with a sense of drama, purpose and determination. Hers was an amatorial mission in which the successful rescue of an endangered *affaire de coeur* might well depend on her tact and diplomacy not to speak of her ability to locate the object of my affections in the first place.

While Boonsom and Dao chatted merrily over aspects of bar life, near misses on the lottery, the relative merits of the latest albums and the peculiarities of various regular customers, I made several determined attempts to avoid thinking of my situation or of evaluating my own actions. But I knew I was acting like the stereotypical, immature, out-of-control, *farang* chasing an alluring and much younger Thai woman. I felt that my being under the spell of Sukanda's seductive power was yet another cliched act among thousands of other similarly cliched acts; those sad, yet funny stories bandied about in bars across Thailand — sad unless they are about you. I knew all this and yet I knew I was helpless to turn back.

After a mid-way stop at a highway fruit stall, Boonsom insisted I move to the back seat where I could spread out in relative comfort. For a while I concentrated on simply watching the fields and distant houses fly by. I had gotten very little sleep the night before, drinking and talking with friends until early in the morning. Despite my best efforts my eyes began to close and the voices from the front seat sounded farther and farther away.

In an attempt to stay awake, I shifted my gaze from the monotonous scenery to the interior of the car. But there too the surroundings seemed to have been arranged to induce sleep. A garland of jasmine with a dying rose attached hung from the car's mirror and, beside it, a large Buddha amulet hung from a strap. Both moved slightly back and forth in unison, as captivating as a hypnotist's metronome. Above the driver's seat, on his broken visor, Boonsom had tucked various green and yellowing leaves: *ngern lai ma*, *nang kuat* and *sonnai jahn*, all reputed to bring in customers or to induce good luck. And in the unlikely event that these failed, dangling soporifically from the mirror was a miniature fish trap with a bit of money inside for good fortune and good business.

When I finally gave in and leaned against the side of the seat I must have dozed off in less than a minute. And when I awoke, I could see Areca palms clustered about small houses set back from the road, and just beyond them, late morning sunlight wove bright golden patches across the blue water of the Gulf of Thailand.

I placed my half-empty bowl of fruit and yogurt to one side and looked up at the green palm fronds stretched out against a deep blue sky. We had reached Pattaya just after one in the afternoon and, now, almost finished with a quick lunch beside a hotel swimming pool, were about to set out in search of Sukanda. As

Dao busied herself with her fried rice and squid salad, I wondered what she must think of my pursuit of a woman so much younger than myself — a woman who had, for whatever reason, run away from me.

Sukanda had told her she was fleeing to Pattaya and would stay for several days, but she had not said which hotel she would be in. She might have checked into a tiny hotel or bungalow somewhere on the outskirts of Pattaya itself and I knew if she didn't want to be found it would not be easy to find her. I had also made the decision not to stay overnight; we would find her by evening or else we would return to Bangkok. As if that made my pursuit any less humiliating.

Immersed in my thoughts, it was several moments before I noticed the missing coconuts. In order to ensure that no dining, sleeping, sun-bathing or cavorting tourist was inconvenienced by falling coconuts, all surrounding trees had had their coconuts removed. Tourists were protected by spayed, neutered, castrated coconut trees — trees as bare of their fruit as if a blight had ravaged them.

I looked about as nonchalantly as possible, all the while hoping against hope I could spot Sukanda. Pampered, slothful tourists beside the swimming pool even now glistened with their fragrance-free, oil-free UVA/UVB sunscreens and sun-tanning lotions, steadfast allies enlisted seasonally to change skin hues from tourist-white to coppertone-brown. Tourists served chartreuse green drinks in aborted coconut shells on gleaming hotel trays by diffident Thai hotel staff attempting to avoid the sun; Thais who would dearly love to exchange their natural brown skin color for the greatly admired, always desired, tourist-white.

I felt Dao's hand playfully tug on my arm. "Why you so quiet?"

"Just thinking about Sukanda. Maybe this is all a waste of time."

Dao took her last spoonful of fried rice, pushed the plate aside and sighed contentedly. "I think you think too much. No can be happy if too many thinking too much. You no worry. Dao will find her."

"I wish I had your confidence."

I paid the bill and together we walked down the path leading beside palm trees, around a small garden with brilliantly colored flowers, into the quizzical gaze of a hotel security guard and onto the street facing the beach.

In tops, shorts and sandals, together we walked to one end of the beach road, crossing back and forth several times, searching the beach area to the left and then strolling into hotel lobbies, restaurants and swimming pools to the right. I shaded my eyes with the bill of my cap and scanned the bodies lined up along the sides of several swimming pools. Thin, just-arrived white stomachs from Hong Kong; huge reddening stomachs from Frankfurt; trim brown stomachs from Bangkok, and, occasionally, the flat brown stomach of a local Thai girl positioned near a fat reddening one. All inquisitive hotel receptionists, restaurant waiters and poolside servants received the same reply: "No, thank you, we're just looking for a friend."

As we neared the end of the narrow beach, we passed a large wooden shrine draped with garlands and colored strips of cloth, and stocked with oranges, orchids, bowls of rice, wooden elephants, tiny figures of Thai dancers, gold leaf, incense, candles, both Lipton and Chinese tea and a peacock feather. A long line of scurrying ants energetically and methodically carried rice from the shrine onto the trunk of a tree.

Beyond the shrine we came upon a group of women — American and Thai wives, Thai girlfriends and Thai bargirls — awaiting the imminent arrival of American sailors. The women sat patiently and silently along a low stone wall beneath coconut palms, eyes shaded and gazes fixed on the approaching line of small single-decked, Thai boats ferrying their men in from ship to shore. Despite the almost certainty that Sukanda would not be among them, I made certain I saw the face of each woman before moving on.

A boat with a dozen Naval officers in immaculate dress whites landed and the men descended a metal ladder in orderly fashion, carefully clutching leather briefcases and good quality suitcases. On the beach, they embraced and kissed their wives and moved off.

A few yards away, American sailors in colorful civilian dress ignored a tiny wooden ladder placed against the gunwale of their boat and leapt onto the sand. Some, in their enthusiasm, let out loud yells and threw their duffel bags over the side onto the beach ahead of them. Some held wives or girlfriends in passionate embraces while others knelt on the beach and ecstatically tossed handfuls of sand into the air or at one another. They had been at sea for over two months and, despite the half hour briefing they had received before leaving their ships, it was certain that girls in numerous bars were in for five days of good business.

We crossed the narrow strip of sand to the water's edge and began walking slowly toward the other end of the beach. As we walked, Dao fended off vendors of beach massages, manicures, pedicures, coconuts, soft drinks, newspapers, sandals, hats, hammocks, teakwood elephants, flowers, shirts, semi-precious stones and beach chairs. A very tanned young Thai in a wet bathing suit, red baseball cap and soaking "I Believe in the Power of Positive Drinking" T-shirt approached us. "Water scooter?"

I was about to refuse, then suddenly stopped. I spoke to Dao: "A scooter isn't a bad idea. I can ride it slowly near the shore while you walk along the beach halfway between the water and the road. Between the two of us, if she's on the beach we'll find her."

Dao squinted up at me from under her bangs and from under the floppy hat I had bought for her. Her round face glistened with sun blocking oil. "OK. But if Dao have to walk whole beach Dao get thirsty. Maybe hungry."

I smiled and handed her four hundred baht. "OK, bandito. Here's ten dollar's worth of drinks. That should quench your thirst."

She threw her arms around me and kissed my cheek, nearly toppling me into a beach chair. "You number one!"

I followed the boy into the water and while he held the scooter and started the Suzuki outboard motor, I climbed aboard. He shouted to Dao who seemed to be paying more attention to food stands near the road than to any serious search for Sukanda. "Bandito! Pay attention!"

I turned the scooter out toward the open sea, and braced myself for each shock as the small craft bounded over the choppy green water. I passed other water scooters steered expertly in show-off fashion by their young Thai owners and slowed my machine to stare into the distance where I could just make out the faint forms of off-shore islands. Beyond a shuttle boat returning from one of them I could see a speed boat used for towing para-sailers, its huge Yamaha engine towing a water scooter with yet another Suzuki outboard motor. Nearer the beach several wind-surfers with colorful sails were gliding over the water with surprising speed.

The thought occurred to me that Sukanda could have decided to spend a day on one of the islands and, if so, I wasn't about to find her. But the futility of the search made me confront the unpleasant and humiliating fact that a young and petulant Thai woman had such a hold on me that I would neglect my work in a demeaning and almost certainly futile attempt to find her. And when I found her, then what?

To escape my thoughts I gunned the scooter in toward the beach, skimming over the white caps and wavelets, narrowly avoiding the lines of fishing boats anchored near the shore. I moved slowly and steadily along the shore observing the swimmers and everyone on the long narrow beach, searching for the familiar face and figure. I moved completely down the beach and then turned and began back, still intent on my search. I could see neither Sukanda nor Dao and I began to wonder if Dao had given up.

Tourists relaxed on beach chairs under thatched-roof shelters and swam in the ocean. Thais renting inner tubes with 'love' painted on each one sat under trees chatting and snacking with friends. Middle-aged masseuses gave massages to tourists lying face down on their hotel towels. I wondered what all of them would think if they understood that my obsession with a Thai bargirl had sent me on a fool's errand.

I had become the modern version of Don Quixote: a fatuous, older man undergoing useless trials in a silly, fruitless search; and although a bargirl had replaced Sancho Panza as squire, and although Pattaya Beach had replaced the Spanish countryside as the field of battle, I was every bit as addled and pathetic as the Spanish knight-errant had been.

The last of the day's sun began to set, reducing the Thai show-offs on water scooters to two-dimensional cardboard cut-outs, black figures against a golden ocean. As the sky turned from dark blue to gray, it left only a patch of pink over one of the off-shore islands, as if the island had burst into flames.

I began moving along the beach for the fourth time, with less hope and growing anger at myself and my obsession. I watched a teenage Thai flirting with a beach sweeper who pretended to chase him with her broom. It was then that I heard someone call me.

"Hello! Richard!"

My eyes swept the beach but the voice seemed to come from the sea itself. "Hellooo! Here I am!"

Then I realized the voice was coming from above. Above my head, strapped securely into a harness and dangling from a red-and-white parasail, Dao grinned broadly and waved down to me.

"Dao no drink! Parasail better!" As the speedboat towing her line sped ahead, the tow line became taut, and Dao was quickly pulled in toward the beach.

I shook my fist at her in mock anger and motioned for her to land on the beach. I waited as she splashed into shallow water and three Thais expertly helped her out of the harness, then rode the scooter onto the sand. Neither of us had caught a glimpse of Sukanda.

Our search continued into the evening. I decided to concentrate our efforts along the 'strip,' the main road and small lanes of South Pattaya where bargirls and tourists sat on stools watching passersby.

We climbed into the rear of a small covered van with two rows of seats known as a *song-taew* and headed south along the beach road toward the even more touristy area of South Pattaya.

The *song-taew* sped past several open-air bars, gaudy jewelry shops, money-changers, small hotels and guest houses, balloon sellers, bar girls and transvestites, tourist coaches arriving from Bangkok, German beer gardens, Indian tailor shops and American fast-food outlets, and jerked to a stop almost directly under a huge white banner with red letters welcoming the US Navy to Pattaya.

As we alighted from the *song-taew*, a family on a motorcycle careened wildly around a corner and barely missed hitting Dao. A young husband with a headband was driving and a young mother straddled the pillion. Between them were three small children hanging onto each other. Their mother's arms were their only safety belt. No one wore helmets. As the motorcycle sped off down a lane and disappeared in a roar, Dao favored it with some choice Thai epithets.

A blue Toyota van with two speakers drove slowly past blaring loudly over the noise of bars and motorcycles that a clinic for AIDS was available for those who would like a free test. Another pick-up with a stenciled "Go Orgy Go" slogan across the upper windshield pulled up near the curb. A man got out and began passing out leaflets. He handed Dao a diamond-shaped piece of paper advertising a wet T-shirt contest at a local bar where "sparkling girls" would "astound" guests at "every-night orgies."

We walked past a confused jumble of stalls and shops selling cuttlefish and fried locust, ivory and jade, recently antiqued Buddha statues, stuffed mongeese and cobras, Nepalese thunderbolts, silk kimonos, coral necklaces, Indian sarees, snakeskin purses and belts and woodcarvings of elephants making love.

Inside an enormous room with several bar counters open to the road, beneath a sea of yellow and pink fluorescent lights, two boxers were boxing Thai-style with fists, elbows and feet, while on yet another stage behind them amateurish local musicians performed. Young men standing near the entrance had draped fat, drowsy pythons around their necks ready for tourists who wanted to be photographed with fat, drowsy pythons draped around their own necks. Customers bored with the sights and sounds of Thai boxing turned to watch musical performances, legions of loose ladies in tight clothes, or any of several television sets installed along the ceiling for easy viewing.

Yet another entrepreneur down the street with a hawk on his shoulder lured tourists into being photographed with the bird. The man had draped a cloth on his shoulder and on his arm to protect himself from the bird's talons. The bird posed motionlessly on the boy's shoulder, erect, dignified and slightly indignant, and stared at me like a priggish butler serving a guest who does not quite come up to the mark.

Bargirls reveled in shocking, colorful and revealing outfits, and in speaking to the world through slogans emblazoned across the front of their T-shirts: 'I love you more than I can Pay,' 'The Chicago Pizza Pie Factory,' 'Sleep with the Best,' 'I've Just Been to Copenhagen,' 'If it's not in Pattaya you don't need it,' 'Scuba

Divers do it Deeper,' 'I'm Home: Take Me Drunk,' 'Middle East Oil Man.'

In the midst of this rakish display, not unlike a lotus rising from the mud, a young Thai woman in a conservative blouse-and-skirt outfit passed out religious leaflets to passersby. I reflected on how wholesome she looked and how completely that incongruent quality of wholesomeness stood out in a place like Pattaya.

I remembered the Pattaya I had once known in the 60's: a still unspoiled Pattaya, a nearly deserted, tranquil, unpretentious fishing resort with only one hotel. Far beyond the normal progression of fishing village-into-tourist attraction, it had now become a flashy, gaudy destination, specializing in nightlife shows for tourists with a craving for sensual pleasure. In stark contrast to its languorous past, Pattaya was no longer for the demure, the shy, the innocent, or the reserved.

Like the girls themselves who had left the rice fields to become bargirls, Pattaya had changed too quickly, too erratically, too haphazardly, and in both sad and humorous ways had adapted itself to accommodate, to stimulate, to satiate. Here, aging and toughened bargirls with headbands and bold outfits straddled 1100 cc Suzukis, 1000 cc Hondas and 900 cc Kawasakis to roar through South Pattaya's main street either alone or with their latest foreign boyfriend holding on behind them.

Outside a bar on a small promontory by the bay a crowd gathered to watch transvestites in glittering costumes sing and dance and act on stage. An inebriated member of the cast, in a tight woman's bathing suit, and with a flower in his hair, took uncertain steps before colliding with three sailors and their Thai girlfriends. He sat down beside a roadside wall covered with a phantasmagoric drawing of a naked green goddess with long golden hair riding a giant four-winged insect in a flamboyant, surrealistic green forest.

Dao grabbed my hand and kept me moving along the narrow sidewalk. "Why you walk so slow?"

"Sorry, sweetheart, but I think I'm being overwhelmed by images and memories. And maybe a touch of sunstroke." Outside a small wooden police station an old woman held a long stick in both hands and spat a stream of beetle-nut juice into the dirt. Anger and self-righteous indignation suffused her wrinkled, nut-brown face as she watched two policemen interrogate a contrite young boy who had obviously committed some offence against her.

A skimpily dressed and possibly stoned bargirl listened dreamily to her Sony Walkman, and walked in the protective arm of her well-built, bearded and colorfully tattooed boyfriend, her head not quite reaching his shoulders.

A few feet from them, a farmer on a bicycle with a rooster under one arm pedaled leisurely out of a small lane onto the main road directly into the path of a motorcycle just as it sped past a patrolling pick-up truck with four policemen riding in the back. The motorcycle rider — a bargirl on a fat, gleaming Suzuki — was dressed in tight leotards and red headband. A white bandage hung loosely from one arm.

In an attempt to avoid the bicycle and the bearded man, she smashed into a cart with layers of fried squid hanging in rows. Squid of various sizes were flung in all directions and landed on the bearded man's expansive chest, smack against the slogan, 'If You Can't Fly with the Eagles, Go Pick Shit with the Chickens.' Flying squid landed in the laps of two policemen, hit Dao on the shoulder, and fell beside my shoes. Among the laughter and heated arguing and growing audience of tourists, bargirls, sailors and fishermen, we turned a corner and began searching the bars and restaurants along the smaller lanes.

Just inside an open-air bar a drunken European held tightly to a ten gallon hat while riding a noisily creaking mechanical bull.

The interior of the bar had been done up Texas-style yet the bar's ceiling remained painted in what must have been the preferred style of a previous owner: A Viking ship — its bow painted as a leering face with wide eyes and lascivious, fanged smile — sailed in the direction of a sexy and voluptuous mermaid reclining on a rocky islet.

Two local girls emerged from a changing room wearing over-sized boxing gloves, T-shirts, shorts and sneakers. They passed incuriously by the bull rider, and entered a small roped-off area to prepare for the bar's 'All Girl Champion Boxing Match' designed to attract Pattaya's voluptuaries.

As we left the bar, we passed several Arabs in flowing robes and head-dresses walking out of a money exchange. I turned to watch them enter a bar with its façade painted in unintended caricatures of desert scenes — sand dunes, camels and an oasis.

I wondered how the Sukanda I knew could possibly fit into this raucous combination of Sodom and Gomorrah. She had always said she disliked Pattaya; noisy and dirty, she had said. I wondered if her coming here to Pattaya, her strange choice of destination, was deliberately chosen to display her irritation and anger toward me. I decided that if that were the answer, it at least indicated she still cared what I felt and how I felt. And I couldn't help but wonder if she had expected me to pry her destination out of Dao and chase after her.

My circle of friends was equally divided into those who loved Pattaya and those who loathed it. I remembered the night in my apartment when I held on to Sukanda, nearly asleep in my arms, while several of us had debated it merits and demerits. Ken, a newcomer to Thailand, described Pattaya as a lewd, lascivious destination with wall-to-wall hookers and water too filthy to swim in. Bill, an old Asian hand, countered that Western ideas of romance are just products of a bourgeois middle class adept at game-playing, glorifying sexual attraction and elevating it to give dignity to human existence, and that Pattaya was "too honest" for pretense, for affectation, for polite conversation. According to him, Pattaya was the Asian beach-bar-beer resort "where the libido had stopped hiding behind the tuxedo, and where ego and superego had fucked their brains out leaving a barefoot id to run amok."

I had told both that I was going to Pattaya and why. Ken, still the newcomer, had thought I was nuts. Bill, wise enough and experienced enough to understand the inexplicable, irresistible hold a beautiful Thai woman exerts on certain men, simply shook his head, sighed and wished me good luck.

My head was throbbing and my feet were sore from walking, so I asked Dao to stop for a drink at a carrousel snack bar — a hexagonal-shaped bar constantly turning. On the bar's sloping roof, a weather-beaten Thai flag drooped its five horizontal stripes of red-white-blue-white-red then flickered to life in a sudden breeze only to droop again a moment later.

With the rainy season over, the bar's canvas shutters had been rolled up and lashed to the top of the mushroom-shaped roof. At the center of the bar, shelves were stacked with bottles of liquor, foreign and local cigarettes and cans of juice. Several speakers blared out the latest vocal selections while, simultaneously, on a television perched above the bar's counter, a pudgy hobbit from the celluloid version of the *Ring* trilogy spoke with a pseudo-Irish lilt. Ceiling fans were left off because of the breeze and the Christmas decorations had been taped to them. On one a Thai lizard made its way cautiously across a Santa Claus with one eye closed in a good-natured, conspiratorial wink. The lizard's tail rested as a heavy eyebrow just above Santa's wink.

By the time I finished my beer, I was feeling feverish. The Singha, the spinning of the carrousel and the day's overexposure to the Thai sun had rendered me enervated, exhausted and spent. In the reflection of the bar's mirror, I appeared as I felt: haggard and fatigued and as bedraggled as the bar's flag.

The bar made continuous, sluggish, soporific rotations and into my febrile vision passed a deserted Chinese shrine, a hotel façade, go-go bars, an Indian tailor shop, a Chinese jewelry shop, a go go bar with dancers in the doorway beckoning to customers, and then, once again, the Chinese shrine. I began to feel sleepy, dizzy, nauseated and a bit high and wondered if I was getting more than just a touch of sunstroke.

I looked again at the conspiratorial wink of the Santa Claus and feeling more listless and tired with each revolution of the bar, speculated on the meaning of the wink. Was it that Sukanda had returned to Bangkok hours ago? Was it that I was acting like an immature fool? Or was it that I was searching for something other than a seductive young woman?

I suddenly remembered Jack Kerouac's quest of his surname in Paris — a dignified search for his real name while I traveled with one Thai bar girl to search for — for what? What was I really searching for? As both my head and the carrousel continued to spin, I felt my elbow slip and my beer glass go over. I stood up quickly and avoided most of the spilled beer. A few drops appeared on the crotch of my slacks. Dao wiped my trousers with a napkin. "What you do? I think you dlink get dlunk too much."

I took a deep breath and let it out slowly. "No, sweetheart, I'm just weary and upset and angry at myself for coming here and for acting like a schoolboy smitten by the charms of his first girlfriend. And I'm angry with Sukanda for being able to make me act this way." I wiped my brow with a second napkin. "And I've had too much sun today." I squeezed her hand. "Come on, let's look for Sukanda one last time. Then we get a taxi back to Bangkok, OK?"

Dao's eyes lit up as she spotted an outdoor shooting gallery and she looked up at me and smiled coquettishly. I handed her two hundred baht. "All right, all right, you deserve a break. Enjoy yourself for ten minutes. But stay here; I'll come back to get you." Even before I had finished speaking Dao had run to the gallery, thrust the bills at the young attendant and picked up a rifle.

"Get one that shoots straight!" I yelled. Dao was too engrossed in aiming her rifle to hear. During a volley of several shots, I could see a small, stationary cutout of a rabbit sluggishly flop over.

I walked around to the rear of the gallery past a nearly deserted open-air bar and came upon an enclosure with bumper cars. Near the ticket booth a rooster tilted its head and stood motionlessly watching me. I walked closer to the ring to watch the cars — driven mainly by male tourists and their local girlfriends — as they sped across the area in every direction; collisions — head-on, rear and along the side — produced only shrieks of laughter even as the occupants' cars were jolted several feet backward.

Suddenly the cars stopped and people clambered out while those who had been sitting along a bench jumped up and rushed to take a car. I was about to turn back when I saw her. Dressed in a white blouse and blue shorts, Sukanda jumped quickly into a nearby red car, and sat with her hands gripping the wheel, in anticipation of the battle. It was then that our eyes met.

For just a few moments her expression was one of confused emotions. I could see the anger cloud her eyes just before she abruptly turned her head away. But I thought I had seen something else: pride of conquest. She now knew that I would humble myself even to the extent of following her here. That my need for her could make me neglect my work and travel to a beach resort so that I could apologize and beg her forgiveness. And if we did get back together it would be on her terms, and from then on, my fear of upsetting her and losing her again would make me as much her slave as her boyfriend. And as she turned back to stare at me, there was no doubt from the expression on her face that she took pride in her victory. And that made me furious.

Even as I hurriedly bought my ticket and ran along a line of empty cars against the far side of the arena, I knew my anger was from the hurt I felt, and at the realization that she now had so much power to hurt me. I jumped into a blue car just as an attendant with an open shirt and a tiger tattoo on his chest turned on the power. My car was almost immediately hit by that of a sailor and his girlfriend and then by an Arab driving alone. As my car jumped backward I felt my anger grow toward Sukanda still more, and a blind, irrational, puerile need to use power to hurt her overwhelmed me.

I pushed the gas pedal and followed the majority of the cars in their imperfect circle and then again spotted her. She glanced back at me and then quickly turned away. I moved closer but just as I was nearly alongside, she steered away and the Arab veered in sharply, careening me into the path of several other cars each of which inadvertently collided with me. I realized the Arab had begun to follow Sukanda's path as if trying to protect her from my wrath. I could feel an intense anger flooding my head and settling in a forehead already flooded with sunstroke-induced pounding.

I drove on, swerved away from several cars and made my way back into the mainstream until I saw Sukanda just across the center of the circle. The Arab's car had been blocked by others and the Arab was desperately trying to wheel his car around to shelter Sukanda. I veered my car sharply away from the circle and well ahead of my target so that by the time I hit her car broadside I had gathered enough speed to send it backwards several feet. Seconds before impact she had turned toward me and stared into my eyes in recognition of my anger and frustration.

From the shock of the impact I realized that the cars were not properly built or maintained to absorb collisions at that speed. I avoided another two cars and then turned to see that Sukanda's car had stopped near the edge of the arena. Smoke poured out of it. As I saw her tears and her face contorted in pain, I jumped out of my car and ran to her. All anger immediately left me and was replaced by guilt, remorse and fear.

Brushing by the confused and fuming Arab, I was at her side holding her and repeating her name as if invoking a religious incantation. Her breathing was labored and she complained of sharp pain in her ribs. And as one dream impinges on the mood and texture of another, through her sobs and above the disembodied sound of my own apologies I could hear the Arab shouting, and could discern the crowd of onlookers and the fact that the cars had been stopped. I understood that a middle-aged Thai woman was talking to me, trying to persuade me to do something, and that I was then walking Sukanda gently, and then holding her in my arms in the back seat of a taxi, the Arab in the front seat.

Despite the driver's careful maneuvering, occasional bumps jolted the car and Sukanda groaned and her pale face grimaced in pain. I knew my own forehead was bathed in sweat; the byproduct of fear and remorse.

As the car pulled up to the front of a small, brightly-lit clinic, a staff member in white physician's coat opened the door. He listened to only part of the driver's words before disappearing inside. He immediately reappeared with a nurse and together they pushed a wheelchair to the car. They wheeled her through the small waiting room and behind the closed doors of the examination room. A receptionist seated behind an old-fashioned cash register directed me to fill in a form.

I calmed my mind enough to fill in the form and to respond to the girl's questions, then sat down beside the woman. The Arab sat sullenly looking at no one, staring at the Chinese shrine or the television set propped on a counter close to the low ceiling. The set's sound was off. An elderly Thai woman with white, short-cropped hair and a mouth stained a blackish-red from beetle-nut chewing sat beside a girl in her early teens. The girl was handing her a cup of water from a cooler on which someone had pasted a sticker with the word, "Love."

The walls were bare except for gold-framed pictures of the Thai king and queen and a row of four colorful posters with cartoon figures explaining in Thai the benefits of proper sleep and exercise. On the television, the heroine of a low-budget, locally-made film fired a machine-gun to scatter several villains searching for her in a jungle.

I glanced at the Arab sitting stiffly in his Arabic robe and head-dress. Beside him, the green fronds of a bamboo palm reached over him framing his head and shoulders. The Arab, the palm and the bare wall behind them gave me the impression of exotic props in the studio of a photographer too impoverished to provide proper setting or lighting. The Arab constantly squeezed the back of his right hand and wrist with his left hand, as one might work with worry beads or a rosary. He stared back at me with an accuser's directness.

I spoke to him in a somber voice. "It was good of you to accompany us." His eyes narrowed into an inflamed glare. I spoke again but I knew my words sounded like an excuse. "I think the cars aren't built well enough for collisions."

The Arab could no longer contain himself. "What do you expect? That was no accident!" He spoke his words quickly, then paused briefly to remember the right words for his next thought, as if the rhythm of his speech had been affected by the stops and starts of the bumper cars themselves. "You aimed for her. You . . . you tried to . . . I saw your face."

The man's thick lips were raised in anger and defiance and his long thin mustache drooped around the edges of his mouth.

He gripped the aluminum arms of his chair, glanced toward the TV and then back to me. "I saw your face." His glowing dark eyes — centered between the white of his long *jellaba* and his banded, shoulder-length *akal* — appeared as the angry eyes of an avenging ghost.

I sat facing my accuser trying to think of something to say in response to the man's anger but I couldn't. I *had* wanted to hurt her. Against my own will and common sense, I had fallen in love with her and she had made me vulnerable and I was ashamed of my own vulnerability.

Humiliation and self-disgust sapped my energy like a cancer and I felt extremely heavy, sick and lethargic. I stared at the man unable to refute his charges or to acknowledge them. He sat back and waited. Neither of us spoke again.

A phone rang. The receptionist spoke to her caller in a coquettish and teasing manner. Her soft voice and the roar of an occasional motorcycle passing were the room's only sounds. The television's silent jungle battles continued with still more villains and a dozen Thai police now added to the plot. I slowly placed my fingers inside my shirt at chest-level, held the Buddha amulet Sukanda had given me, and silently prayed that she would recover. Every second of waiting was unbearable but so was my fear that when she did appear she would leave with the Arab and never want to see me again.

A hallway door opened and as I stood up, a doctor came out of a cubicle helping a thin, elderly Thai farmer with a bandaged leg into the waiting room. I sat down and the man limped past me, slowly but with grace. I thought I heard the doctor say something in Thai about his having been bitten by something in a field. His wife spoke to her husband then to the doctor. The old man, his eyes watery and his step uncertain, merely smiled slightly, as if the answer to all questions could be seen in his missing teeth, and allowed himself to be helped out the front door by his wife and daughter.

The doctor entered the hallway, hesitated, then turned and walked back to face me. He was a moon-faced, middle-aged, Thai-Chinese with very narrow, heavily hooded eyes and a professional, almost sinister, smile. I guessed he was the owner of the clinic, hence the Chinese shrine on the floor rather than a Thai shrine on the wall.

His thin lips formed a slightly embarrassed smile as if he could see the passionate love scene between the heroine and one of her rescuers on the TV screen behind him. "I believe the girl you are waiting for has left already."

I stood up. "Left?"

"Yes. She asked that she be allowed to leave by the back door." With the full realization that any feeling she had for me was over, I could only stare at the man as he continued speaking.

"She is all right. The X-ray revealed nothing broken. She just had the wind knocked out of her. I told her to get some rest."

When I tried to pay the receptionist I was told Sukanda had paid herself. I walked outside, still trying to absorb the fact that it was really over. The Arab stood near the door smoking a cigarette. He stared at me and then turned away. I began walking along the road, ignoring the horns of *song-taews* cruising for passengers.

Just before a bend in the road I turned back to look toward the clinic. The Arab was walking slowly into the darkness, his spectral image receding and then disappearing beneath the sharp outline of coconut palms.

The Legend of Hard Bones Haggerty

Although I had flown with him as door gunner on several missions, and had gotten closer to him than any man in the unit, the truth is I never really did get very close to "Hard Bones" Haggerty. Nor did I ever discover exactly when and why he had been given that nickname. A crew chief told me it was a term connected with a throw of the dice, and, God knows, in his own soft-spoken, unassuming manner, Hard Bones enjoyed his beer and his gambling. Another door gunner (who wasn't to make it through the war) had flown several missions with him before I arrived from Bangkok, and he said Hard Bones had earned it by crashing his chopper several times without breaking any bones. I don't know. I never will know now. But of all the Vietnam-related images that return to haunt me in dreams and in nightmares, the thin, smiling, well-tanned face of Hard Bones Haggerty is the most vivid.

He had grown up in Dothan, Alabama, which he still remembered fondly as a small, slumberous, Southern town immersed in graceful pendent tufts of grayish-green Spanish moss and liberally sprinkled with playfully adventurous, well-endowed women. While in college, he married his high school sweetheart and stopped attending classes just before he would have received his B.A. in World Literature. He loved to read but resented having to read something prescribed as part of a course, and he was also anxious to see a part of the world which, rather than clustered with Spanish moss, boasted of mysterious triple canopy rain forests.

At the time his friends were donning caps and gowns, Hard Bones was undergoing basic training at Ft. Polk, Louisiana. His basic flight training was at Ft. Wolters, Texas, and he perfected his flying skills during instrument and advanced flight training at Ft. Rucker, Alabama. He graduated at the head of his class and was, at the time I first met him, one of the few survivors of those who did graduate.

His 92nd Assault Helicopter company left San Francisco on a battered WW II troop carrier and docked first at Danang and then at Cam Rahn Bay. Ten days later, news came that the unit's helicopters had arrived on an aircraft carrier at Vung Tau (the old French Cap. St. Jacques), on the coast some 60 miles from Saigon. Hard Bones and his unit flew down to pick up their choppers and fly them back to Cam Rahn Bay.

At his first station, Qui Nhon, the dislike between Hard Bones and the commanding officer, Major Reginald Johnson, was instantaneous and mutual. Major Johnson was deeply resented by officers and enlisted men alike for being a disciplinarian and a martinet. Any violation of regulations would bring punishment and men were often confined to base for no real reason at all. He was as petty and spiteful on the base as he was gung-ho and kill-crazy in a helicopter. Both traits would be his undoing.

The Major soon saddled Hard Bones with any extra duty he could think of which included the running of the base PX. Hard Bones quickly realized that when such desirable items as Sansui speakers and Kenwood receivers arrived they were snapped up immediately, and he soon learned to hold back the models the supply sergeant was after who in return would favor Hard Bones with several cases of top quality filet mignon and American beer.

In turn, Hard Bones would trade the steak to the lieutenant in Naval Supply in charge of gunboats cruising the harbor and also in charge of the 18-ft. fiberglass sloop which was available for recreation to the highest bidder. The lieutenant was a vegetarian but he sent the steaks to the base dentist which enabled him not only to jump the dental clinic's queue but also to display the best gold fillings filet mignon could buy.

When word reached Major Johnson that some of his men were enjoying their time off sailing around the bay and off to Paula Gambir island, he made certain that they were kept too busy to make any further use of the sloop. He, however, soon found ample opportunity to take it out himself. Unfortunately for the Major, although Hard Bones had no particular love for the Navy, he was not the type to give up his ship without a fight.

One bright and lovely morning, the Major and his bikini-clad Vietnamese girlfriend were sunbathing on the sloop. Beside them was the Major's recently purchased camera equipment and as fine a radio as the PX had ever stocked. The breeze was pleasant, the water calm and the sky a deep blue. With one hand on the tiller and one on a can of Budweiser, the Major concentrated at nothing more strenuous than deciphering cloud formations and felt at peace with the world. Beside him the Vietnamese girl consumed prodigious amounts of dried cuttlefish as she read, or more accurately, looked at the pictures in an American fashion magazine.

The Major took no notice of the distant sound of an approaching helicopter. As the green speck and the faint "whumping" sound of blades got closer, the Major still showed little concern: helicopters constantly flew over the area and the "whump" of the blade's tip as it broke the sound barrier with each rotation was a familiar, soothing and soporific sound for Major Johnson. It was only when it grew louder, loomed larger and continued to fly directly at him that the Major sat up and shielded his eyes to stare at what now looked and sounded like a behemoth. Whump. Whump. Whump! WHUMP!!!

Hard Bones was flying the chopper three feet above the water at 140 knots. Two hundred yards from the sloop, as the Major prayed for whatever it was to break away, the helicopter flared back, tail skimming the water, skids raised karate-style, and sent its rotor wash to fill the sloop's mainsail and jib, ignominiously dumping the boat, the Major and his girlfriend into the South China Sea.

Hard Bones pulled up on the collective and pushed the cyclic forward, abruptly sending the nose down, buzzed straight over the fallen sloop and streaked off into the distance. The last glimpse Hard Bones had was of a furious Major shaking his fist beside a beautiful young girl in a bikini frantically hugging an empty ice chest with what, Hard Bones supposed, was more passion than she had ever shown Major Johnson.

Despite his suspicions, Major Johnson was never certain which pilot had swamped him, but he soon tightened up restrictions and brought charges against several of the men whom he said were having intercourse with their hootch maids. Hard Bones realized yet more persuasion was necessary before the Major understood that men facing death every day do not appreciate chickenshit from a turkey.

II

P.F.C. Mathews had been the most reliable and industrious company clerk Hard Bones's unit had ever had. He had also managed to ingratiate himself into the good graces of Major Johnson. It was unfortunate for P.F.C. Mathews that he tended to gossip about the unorthodox missions Major Johnson assigned to him, and that that gossip often reached Hard Bones. Mathew's latest assignment was to pick up the Major's Vietnamese girl-friend, stop along the route on the way back to have the jeep washed, and to drop her off at the Major's hootch. A simple enough assignment and, in Vietnam, a fairly common one.

A Vietnamese roadside gas station was invariably a jerry-built shack behind which was a jerry-built brothel. Hence, to go out to "get the jeep washed" could mean any number of things depending on who said it and on what his priorities were at the moment.

P.F.C. Mathews, harboring no confusion whatever regarding his priorities, stopped the jeep outside the shack and quickly disappeared inside the brothel. The Vietnamese gas station attendants parked his jeep beside the stream and began pumping water up to wash it. The Major's girlfriend sat nearby on a fallen tree eating sugar cane and flipping through the pages of an American fashion magazine, wishing, perhaps, that she could trade her *ao dai* for whatever outfits the Bloomingdale models were wearing.

At the sound of the first "whump" she involuntarily shuddered. Already bathed in fear-induced perspiration, she jumped up and looked into the twilight to discern the steadily approaching and steadily growing shape looming larger and larger. She could see the helicopter was carrying something bulky underneath and, had she not already had one memorable experience with an American helicopter, she might have lingered longer to satisfy her curiosity. As it was, she fled into the jungle in panic, determined never to have anything to do with Americans in this or any other life.

As the helicopter hovered overhead, the Vietnamese servicing the jeep looked up, and Amerasian children in American baseball caps playing nearby looked up and P.F.C. Mathews pushed two Vietnamese sisters off a lumpy mattress to dash to the window and look up.

As soon as his crew chief had waved everyone away from the target, Hard Bones hovered at one hundred feet. The two thousand pound load of concrete blocks suspended in a mesh net beneath the chopper from the external cargo hook should rightfully have been delivered to the top of a nearby hill for the Koreans' new bunker.

Instead, Hard Bones followed the directions of his crew chief as he centered the load directly over the jeep, pressed the external cargo electrical release switch, braced himself as the lightened chopper abruptly bounded up, immediately swiveled and banked over to see the results. As P.F.C. Mathews hopped out of the doorway still trying to pull his trousers up above his knees, he saw the explosion of red dirt and jeep fragments as the end of his hopes of receiving a promotion — in any branch of the service — ever.

Although Major Johnson never saw his Vietnamese girlfriend again, he had gained new insights into the handling of men. In the face of Hard Bone's sustained defiance and unsettling harassment, the Major curbed his disciplinarian ways and the men of Qui Nhon were again free to come and go as they pleased and, incidentally, to get on with the war.

III

Whether harassing American military martinets or fighting communist armies, Hard Bones proved himself to be one of the best helicopter pilots in Vietnam. He was daring, innovative, skillful and often totally disregarded deadly enemy fire to support soldiers on the ground. And the men on the ground knew this. In more than one action, grunts facing a well-entrenched enemy were reliably reported to have cheered wildly when a voice over their field radio reported that Hard Bones's unit was the one sending assistance. But the same independent spirit which motivated him throughout his years of flying finally led to his being grounded.

One oppressively humid summer day Hard Bones assembled with his co-pilot, crew chief and myself as door gunner and received orders to support Korean Tiger Division infantry engaged in a vicious firefight with an enemy concentration that outnumbered them at least three to one. We climbed into the Huey UH1-C (Iriqois) chopper and Hard Bones waited for us to attach M-60 machine guns to the roof with bungi cords. Six thousand rounds of 7.62 ammunition were packed in two rows of three thousand inside permanently installed polished aluminum boxes just in front of the fire wall.

Once over the target, Hard Bones flew the helicopter speedily up to two thousand feet and paused long enough to enjoy the pleasant coolness of the altitude. He then made several intrepid dives in support of the Korean forces which brought him within easy range of communist rifle and machine gun fire. As usual, he ignored the bullet holes which appeared in the chopper, the sudden vibrations and the inexplicable engine noises and continued to concentrate on his work.

When the bright yellow chip detector warning light appeared, the co-pilot, crew chief and I agreed that there were scattered bits of metal chips in the transmission. As usual, Hard Bones attributed any such warning lights to a short circuit in the system and refused to pull out. When one of the red hydraulic lights lit up, indicating the number two hydraulic system was out, the crew chief stuck his head out the door into the slip-stream and announced over the intercom that he could see hydraulic fluid leaking.

Hard Bones banked his chopper to the left and spotted green tracers of the Vietcong automatic weapons coming toward us from a clearing in the jungle. He spotted a companion diving toward the target, its red tracers heading earthward in return fire.

Among screams from all of us that "We got too many bullet holes!" and "Head back!" Hard Bones maintained his insouciant attitude and near-suicidal dives. It was only when a piece of engine cowling slammed through the blades with a loud "Whoomph!" sending an incredibly strong vibration throughout the chopper, that Hard Bones reluctantly agreed to head back to base.

But as the disabled chopper limped homeward, it must have appeared an easy target to anyone on the ground with anything more powerful than a slingshot, and before long we could hear the sounds of small arms fire aimed in our direction. Below the chopper, surrounding a hut almost in the middle of several rice padis, several Vietcong stood out in the open, energetically emptying their AK-47's at the chopper. I think Hard Bones might have ignored their fire had an enemy bullet not ricochetted off his chicken plate to give his cheek a permanent shrapnel scar.

Proper procedure specified that when fired upon, helicopter pilots would immediately climb up to altitude, find the village on the map, call headquarters and request permission to return fire. Headquarters would call the province chief and assuming by that time the war wasn't over and that he was not a Vietcong plant, the province chief would give his permission or not.

Hard Bones knew from bitter experience that the province chief almost always reported villages in our area to be "friendly" even when American helicopters took fire from those same villages.

Not being in the mood for bullshit, Hard Bones didn't bother to radio; instead, he climbed slowly and not without difficulty to 1500 feet, wiped blood away from his cheek and flicked the switch arming the guns and rockets. He turned to his co-pilot with the unlikely name of McGeorge Bundy and ordered him to blow the hut away. The co-pilot said, "You got it," and pulled the minigun sight back down from its stowed position.

The chopper dove noisily and erratically toward the area like an enraged, wounded eagle. As we approached the target, still taking enemy fire, Hard Bones fired three pair of 2.75 inch HE (high explosive) rounds, while his co-pilot fired two 7.62 miniguns, their six rotating barrels slamming 4000 rounds per minute into the target area.

The hut, along with chickens, buffalo, cattle, trees and bits of Vietcong soldiers went up in a big boom of dirt, straw and wood flying in all directions. There would be no further enemy fire from that village. But the province chief reported the action to Major Johnson, and when Hard Bones limped the chopper back to base, he learned that he was temporarily grounded for ignoring proper procedure. In the face of his unrepentant attitude and sarcastic remarks, Major Johnson began to form a flight evaluation board to do what would hurt Hard Bones the most: ground him permanently.

IV

Less than a week after his grounding, just after midnight, Korean troops in the area reported to Major Johnson that they suspected some VC activity on a mountain near the base, and the Major personally joined one helicopter crew as aircraft commander and Hard Bones, "ungrounded" for the emergency, commanded another.

Once over the target, one helicopter would swoop down and make its gun run sending steady streams of red tracers into the Stygian darkness and total silence of the thickly clad mountainside. At the last possible moment, it would break off and swing around and climb to altitude while the other helicopter passed by making its gun run in turn.

After a few passes, Hard Bone's helicopter was coming back to altitude, and I had just turned to look toward the Major's chopper, when the sky turned orange, as if a flashgun had gone off. Hard Bones pushed the cyclic to the right, tilting the chopper to see what had happened. All we could see was a perfect circle of fire midway down the mountain where Major Johnson's helicopter had disintegrated, the results of his insane obsession to "get Charlie." At the risk of being shot at, Hard Bones turned on the landing lights but could see that nothing was left of the helicopter or the men.

Finally, we headed back to base. The next day a search party found two wallets and one jungle boot - all that was left of four men. Hard Bones was convinced Charlie had never been there in any case. They had been shooting at trees in a triple canopy jungle. Score: Americans 0 — Trees 4.

V

The following morning, I came down with high fever and chills, and, for several days, Hard Bones carried out his missions with a different door gunner. I heard that he was getting more and more daring and taking even greater chances than he had previously. The day when I felt well enough to rejoin him, Hard Bones gathered his crew, stared at me for several seconds, and then told me I wasn't ready for this mission.

When I started to protest that I felt well enough, he held up his hand and simply said, "This isn't your mission." Then he climbed aboard his chopper and flew off to lend fire support to American infantry.

By nightfall, his helicopter hadn't returned. It never did.

Every man in our unit checked and rechecked. Every man received the same answer: There had been no call for assistance and no one among Americans or our allies had sighted a lone helicopter — disabled or otherwise. Hard Bones and his crew had vanished.

For the rest of my tour, whenever possible, I spent time among helicopter pilots and crews asking anyone for a clue to what might have happened. Almost to a man they had heard of Hard Bones and his disappearance; but no one could solve the mystery. For months after his disappearance, I got very little sleep and whatever snatches of troubled rest I did get, Hard Bones made certain he was there.

I was reassigned to Nakorn Phanom, Thailand and there I served out the rest of my tour of duty. There too they had heard of Hard Bones's disappearance; but there too the mystery remained unsolved.

Years after I had returned to the States, during one of my bad periods, I joined a Vietnam Veterans support group, and it was there that I ran into a former co-pilot who had flown several missions with Hard Bones. The man was very pale, unresponsive to all attempts to reach him, and sat chainsmoking his way through the meeting.

When I felt able to speak about my Vietnam experience, I mentioned a bit about my encounter with Hard Bones and, from that moment on, I noticed the man's deepset eyes staring at me.

After the meeting, I had just walked out into the street when I felt someone put a hand on my shoulder. The grip was so tight I found it difficult to turn around and face him. The chainsmoker fixed me with his stare and whispered to me with a gravelly voice. I could smell whiskey on his breath. "I remember he always used to say how beautiful and peaceful Nam was from the air. He really loved the place, Hard Bones did. I think all of us did. At least from the air."

I started to interrupt but he continued: "Up there even the war could be beautiful: trails of brass cartridges tumbling out of the gunships onto the ground like rain, silhouetted black against the blue sky, light coruscating off 'em like dozens of little suns."

I asked him if he knew anything about Hard Bone's disappearance. He simply smiled enigmatically and pointed overhead. "I think Hard Bones would have hated to leave. The thing he loved most was flying. Maybe he's still up there." Then he turned and walked off. I never saw him again.

In my meetings with harried Veterans Administration psychiatrists, I assure them that I have at last come to terms with the fact that Hard Bones won't be returning. And that I no longer feel guilty for not having disappeared with him. Although I don't think I'm ready to visit the Wall yet; one day I know I'll run my fingers over the cold marble letters spelling out his name. One day. But not yet.

But, sometimes, even now, when a face in a magazine or on the street or in a bar bares some resemblance to him, Hard Bones appears before me as he always did: the boyish, almost innocent, Huck Finn grin on the face of the jungle-hardened veteran he was, and I feel an irresistible urge to ask him: "Hard Bones, just how did you get that nickname, anyway?"

MURDER AT THE HORNY TOAD BAR

&

OTHER OUTRAGEOUS TALES OF THAILAND

Non-Fiction

"No matter how much you know, no matter how much you think, no matter how much you plot and you connive and you plan, you're not superior to sex. It's a very risky game. A man wouldn't have two-thirds of the problems he has if he didn't venture off to get fucked."

— *The Dying Animal,* Philip Roth

In Search of Seri Court

In the glare of the afternoon sun, the fruit and vegetable sellers of Bangkok's Sapankwai (Buffalo Bridge) area gathered around the Thai driver and myself and stared as if we were from another planet. And, indeed, when none of the sellers — not the middle-aged lady selling durian, not the old man selling mangos, not the elderly rambutan sellers — remembered Seri Court or any American soldiers stationed in their area, I definitely felt as if I were from another world.

It had been the world of the sixties — where for over two years beginning in early 1966 — I had been stationed as a GI during the Vietnam War. American military personnel left Seri Court forever in 1970 and the war ended in 1975 but now, 34 years later, it was my intention to try to find some of the places I had known in a very different and far more innocent Bangkok. Especially Seri Court.

Seri Court, on Patipat Road, had been home to hundreds of American servicemen stationed with the Army Security Agency's 5th Radio Research and Special Operations Unit (RRSOU) and, with its name change just before I arrived, the 83rd RRSOU. It was my intention to see what, if anything, was left of what had been my home for two years. While our counterparts stationed in Vietnam had been concerned about survival, we had been more concerned about whether we could complete our basketball games without fainting in the heat, whether the creaking swimming pool gate would keep us awake during afternoon naps, or whether, on our slim paychecks, we could afford to go into "downtown" Bangkok on the weekend.

During our off-duty hours, our sanctuary from the heat and humidity was our dayroom which we had named Club Keemow (Club Drunkard). Inside the dayroom was the welcome sound of the always smiling Thai bartender putting cold bottles of Singha beer on the counter, GI's arguing over card games or embroidering their latest nocturnal adventures on Patpong Road, and, at the back, the incessant whirring sound of three slot machines.

One day while several of us were, as usual, losing money to these slot machines, it occurred to me that we might take a small portion of the slot machine profits each month and donate it to a worthy cause. After some discussion with a few buddies — you, dear reader, may have "friends" or, if quite successful, you may have "colleagues," but, in unwritten American law, GI's may have only "buddies" — that worthy cause turned out to be an orphanage on Sathorn Road.

Our fellow GI's not only agreed, but in their spare time, went down to the orphanage to cut grass, do some minor repairs and play with the children. In no time at all the money donated largely from the profits of Seri Court slot machines allowed the orphanage to build a wading pool for the kids and a medium-sized wooden building.

I had been transferred to Taiwan just before the completion ceremony but the sign placed on the side of the building had read something to the effect that the building had been financed by men of the 83rd RRSOU. A friend — sorry, I mean, buddy — had sent the article and photograph as they had appeared in the *Bangkok Post*, and there was our Commanding Officer, no doubt buoyed by the good works his men were doing and by the chances that his superiors would not fail to notice the favorable publicity his unit had achieved for Americans stationed in Southeast Asia.

So, now, 34 years later, I was off to Sathorn Road in search of the orphanage, expecting it would not be difficult to find a place I had visited so many times before. Over two frustrating hours later, I found myself in the hallways and driveways of modern buildings desperately trying to explain what I was looking for while my driver went off searching the area. No doubt I was perceived as a mad *farang* (foreigner), and, not unlike the Ancient Mariner, a bit tetched. But at last we learned the truth: sometime during the economic boom of the 90's, the orphanage buildings had been torn down and the children moved into a new building somewhere else in Bangkok. I was standing not far from a half-built building where, to the best of my memory, the orphanage had stood. Still, our building had probably survived and functioned for nearly three decades. I could ask no more than that.

It was then I remembered that this was not the first time my past had been wiped out. In 1970, while at the University of Hawaii, I had lived in Waikiki at the Coco Palms Hotel, more of a hippyish *motel* for laid-back college students and diehard surfers. When in 1980 on a visit I could find no sign of it, I asked a parking lot attendant if he knew where it was. He informed me that I was standing on it. As Thomas Wolfe said, "You can't go home again."

Still, I was not ready to give up. While a GI, several nights a week, in sweltering heat, I had taken a bus from Sapankwai, then changed busses, then finally arrived in an area close by the Temple of the Emerald Buddha. Here, secluded from nearby traffic and noise, was Dr. Chalao Chaiyaratana's English School. Dr. Chalao taught at nearby Thammasat University and was highly respected among students. During my year or more at the school, I had taught both adult and children classes and will never forget my first class of children, all on their knees with the palms of their hands pressed together, *waiing* me, their teacher. It was as if the musical, *The King and I*, had suddenly burst into life. They only did that on their first day but it was something I shall never forget. And, if that wasn't enough, once a year the wooden rooms were disassembled and the yard became the venue for the Miss Thailand contest.

But when the driver pulled into the side street, my heart sank. Where the wooden school had once been, a large Thai-style concrete building had risen. I walked from the car and inquired about Dr. Chalao's English School. I already knew that Dr. Chalao had died of cancer long ago and now I was told that the school had been pulled down and replaced by — if my rusty Thai served me correctly — the Ministry of Foreign Affairs.

The orphanage and the school were gone; and now I was in Sapankwai, on Patipat Road, somewhere close to where Seri Court was (or had been) yet I could find no trace of it and no one remembered it. Finally, a very old woman with short white hair and nut-brown skin mentioned that Americans had been stationed at the Capitol Hotel around the corner. Only officers had stayed there but at least I now knew I wasn't mad. Americans *had* been here before.

It was late afternoon when someone on the street pointed down a lane and suggested we ask the teacher who had lived here for many years. After a great deal of knocking and dog barking, a late middle-aged Thai woman appeared. My driver spoke to her at length and the woman nodded. "Wong Seri, Madame Seri." Yes, I remembered! The court had been named after a *khunying*, an upper class Thai woman, who owned it. The teacher informed us that Madame Seri had died but the court was very close. She would take us.

Within five minutes, we had walked to the driveway of the court which curved to the right making it impossible to see what was now inside. She said she would leave us here and I thanked her profusely.

As the driver and I followed the curve of the wide driveway, we passed by women who seemed to be maids, and finally Seri Court came into view. We passed small rooms on both sides with curtains covering car parks and then passed under the four-story concrete structure which had served as rooms for American servicemen. The wooden messhall — where we had pinched apples to give to taxi drivers and bargirls in lieu of money — had disappeared as had Club Keemow, as had the sleepy Thai guard and the wooden vehicle barrier. (The guard and barrier served less to check vehicles than to keep out young ladies who believed that one or another of the Cheap Charlie GI's inside had "done them wrong.")

But the three concrete buildings remained. Greenish-black streaks and blotches staining them like a horrible disease. Discolored with decades of dirt and partly overrun with weeds. Filthy, neglected, decrepit, weather-beaten; looking almost as forlorn and abandoned as the ruined temples of Ayudhya and Sukhothai. But there they were. And I could again hear the laughter of men waiting to get on the bus to go to our "site" in Minburi; I could feel the fear of not being ready for an inspection; and I could again see the tension in the Colonel's face when news of the Tet Offensive first reached us.

And the faces of those I would later write about in exaggerated form in the novel, *Memoirs of a Bangkok Warrior*, came back in a rush: Hogbody, Butterball, Blinky, Bumbles, Whore House Charlie, Noy the Laundry Girl, Corporal Comatose, Boonrawd, Lieutenant Pearshape, Corporal Napalm and Agent Orange. Memories of men and events I had forgotten came back as clear as the events of yesterday.

And then I walked past the old wooden water tower to the last of the three decrepit buildings where the Colonel's office had been. I walked up the stairs and I looked out o ver the top balcony upon a Bangkok that had changed forever. The Colonel's office

was where I had been called to account for some infraction of
military rules more times than I cared to remember. And yet, as
I exited the forlorn building, I suddenly turned, stood at attention, and saluted. Why I did that, I'm not certain. It might have
been a salute to simply acknowledge the joys and sorrows of the
past, or an attempt to put the past to rest, or a gesture of respect
to the men who had once lived at Seri Court, especially those
who had transferred to Vietnam and never returned.

I noticed the Thai driver saluting also. He smiled. "Big boss
was here?"

I nodded. "Big boss was here."

On the way out I inquired from one of the women working
there if she knew a Boonrawd, long ago the Thai assistant to our
sergeant who fixed things in Seri Court. She did. He still worked
there but wasn't in that day. She said, "He is very old now."

I gave her my namecard to give to him and then left. He
would not know my name but he would know that he had been
remembered.

As we again passed the small rooms with the curtains, I
understood why the teacher had left us at the gate. And I
noticed my driver's embarrassment. I smiled. "It's a love hotel
now, isn't it?"

He smiled. "Yes. Love hotel. People come here to be happy."

And so the Sixties with the students' slogan of "Make Love
not War" had come full circle. And here in Seri Court, at least,
the ideal had been put into practice. I found myself chuckling;
laughing. My driver laughed. And together we walked off into
the growing darkness.

Just One Beer

One of the things I most love about Thailand is the unpredictability of the place. It is possible to go out at night for a beer — just one beer — and have an experience you will remember the rest of your life. It might be wonderful; it might be not-so-wonderful; but it will be wild, wacky, humorous, vivid, perhaps poignant, perhaps dangerous. And you might just fall in love. But it will never be ordinary. I know. It happened to me more than once.

But the time I most treasure was when I entered Cambodia by mistake. Which was not a good idea as it was during the Vietnamese occupation in the early/mid-80's. How does one enter Cambodia by mistake? And fall in love, almost get killed, and get hoodwinked as well? Let me explain.

At the time, I was sharing a small wooden house in a quiet lane off Phaholyothin Road with an Australian photographer. The Aussie was somewhere on assignment and the Laotian maid next door who flirted with us over the fence had gone in for the night, so I decided, rather than swelter in the heat while swatting mosquitoes and listening to the cries of the lizards, I would go to Patpong for a beer. Just one.

I don't remember which bar it was. It may have been the Grand Prix or the one next door but before long I got into a conversation with two friendly Scandinavians. It turned out they were newspaper journalists from Norway, I think it was, and they were planning to hire a car and driver in the morning and head off to the Thai-Cambodian border — which at that time was a dangerous nexus of Thai police, Thai army, Cambodian refugees, bandits, Cambodian Khmer Rouge and the Vietnamese army. The area made the usual "no-man's land" seem like a walk in the park on a sunny day.

I tried to tell this to my newfound Scandinavian friends but they were in Thailand on assignment and they had no choice but to get a story from the refugee camps along the border. I did my best to explain that there basically was no border; and the Vietnamese army was firing on anything that moved because some of the refugees were in fact bloodthirsty Khmer Rouge (*Kamen Dang*) Cambodian Pol Pot communists who had killed one or two million of their own people. It was when they kept attacking Vietnam that the Vietnamese got fed up and chased them all the way to the Thai border. When shells landed inside what the Thais believed to be Thai territory, they fired back at the Vietnamese. Doing a story at that time in that place was a good way to end up having a story written about you–on the wrong page of the paper.

Nothing I said could dissuade the two intrepid journalists and, in fact, as the night progressed, they attempted to persuade me to go with them. I knew Thailand (somewhat) and could speak the language (somewhat), "so what do you say?"

I say, "no way in hell I would leave the peace and quiet of Olde Siam and the flirtatious, next-door Laotian maid with dark eyes and come-hither smile for the unrewarding danger of the very porous and very downright unfriendly Thai/Cambodia border."

Unfortunately, they were buying beers, and after a few Singha and just a shot or three of Mekhong, I heard myself saying what a great adventure it would be. And so the next morning found the three of us with our car and driver heading pell-mell for Aranyaprathet, the town which was the kind of stopping off point for refugee camp visits. Hangovers-be-damned!

I believe we arrived after dark, in any case, I remember nothing of that night or in which hotel we stayed. However, the events of the next day I shall never forget.

The journalists had finished breakfast ahead of me and gone out to do whatever journalists do. By the time I exited the hotel, they were heading back toward me. Now, however, they had someone with them. But not just someone. She was one of the most beautiful women I had ever seen. Almond eyes, a gorgeous mane of raven-black hair cascading to her waist, the grace of an antelope, the allure of a goddess, and the half-shy/half knowing gaze of the Asian woman.

I could also tell she was Cambodian. This I knew from the beautiful, impossibly full lips. Yes, Virginia, lips like those do not exist only on Cambodian Buddha statues and frescoes; some of the living, breathing women of Cambodia have them. In the West, women achieve such labial perfection only by several injections of collagen, but when it came to perfection, this Cambodian woman . . . had . . . it!

When they approached me, the journalists introduced us and she lowered her head slightly and smiled up at me. I responded by saying something not unlike Jackie Gleason in the *Honeymooners*: "Humahumahumahuma."

We spoke in English because it turned out she had fled Cambodia and now lived in Australia. She had got word that her mother may have made it out of Cambodia in the latest wave of refugees and could we in some way help her persuade the Thai police and the Thai army to allow her into the camp at Ban Tap Prik to search for her mother.

Well, two thoughts went through my head so fast it was almost simultaneous. The Thai police and army were incredibly busy and had their hands full with Cambodian refugees, the bloodthirsty Cambodian communists and the Vietnamese army; and they weren't about to allow a Cambodian from the Thai side of the border to enter and muck about in the camp. Second, she was absolutely gorgeous and whatever she wanted me to do was exactly what I would do. In fact, if she had said she would sleep with me that night and all I had to do was to torture and kill the two Norwegian blokes, well, let's just say, their newspaper would have been hiring. But I figured even if the Thais said no she would be suitably grateful to the man who did his best to reunite her with her mother.

So off we went — or, rather, off I went, to attempt to plead her case with the Thais. I *waiied* them and used every bit of whatever polite Thai I might have picked up from Dr. Chalao Chaiyaratana's English School in the late 60's to explain the situation and allakazam! They said yes! She could go in and look for her mother!

I gave her the wonderful news and she looked into my eyes with the adoration of one who (at least so I interpreted the look) would be suitably grateful when the time was right. You understand, I was not stupid. I knew the journalists, like journalists everywhere, wanted to make use of people. They probably couldn't have cared less whether she found her mother; they wanted her to interpret for them when they interviewed the refugees. Her goal was also clear: she wanted to find her mother. My goal was definitely clear: I wanted to find a way to her bed.

In musical theater, the most important characters are usually given an "I want" song to sing in which one way or another they convey their goal to the audience. So if this had been a musical we had an "I Want A Story" song, an "I Want Mommy" song, and my own "I Want You, Babe" song. And so, each in pursuit of his or her own goal, into the refugee camp we ventured.

My first impression was how dark the hundreds of Cambodians staring at us were. It reminded me of my travels in India. No, they were not that dark, but darker than the city Thais, certainly. And how they stared. Silently. Expectantly. And in the midst of them were those lying on the ground being treated by Thai and Cambodian nurses. Those with IV bottles dangling from the tamarind tree branches above; those too weak to brush away the flies from their eyes and mouths; those obviously more dead than alive. And as we walked toward those dying of malnutrition, disease and the wounds of battle, I noticed men throwing the bodies of men and women over a fence where they were rapidly piling up.

We stopped beside two young girls lying side by side. They were not emaciated or wounded but seemed to have been felled by a combination of hunger and disease and the madness of the Cambodian communist leaders. For these two teenagers were typical of the rank-and-file of the Khmer Rouge. Both were very pretty and both stared up at the Cambodian woman from Australia. Finally, one of them spoke to her. I asked her what the girl said. She said they wanted to know why she hadn't cut her hair short as Pol Pot had ordered. And that showed clearly the limited parameters of their world. Nothing existed outside of the framework of Pol Pot's bloodthirsty plan for Cambodia. And if Pol Pot told these and a million other teenagers to kill, then that is what they would do.

The woman began interpreting for the journalists. I had remembered to bring some candy for situations such as this. And I placed a pack of M&M's into the right hand of each girl. They looked over at the packet and then at me. It was then I realized they were too weak to open them. I stooped beside them, opened the packages and poured the candy into their palms. Slowly, with determined effort, they placed some into their mouths.

We moved on to a Thai nurse who was busy brushing a swarm of persistent flies out of the mouth of a woman in her thirties. The woman's eyes were open but she seemed near death. I asked the nurse if she thought the woman would be all right. She said, "I don't think so."

And it went on. At some point — the reason escapes me — I left the three of them and began walking. I assumed I was in

Thailand heading toward the Thai army. As I walked, I passed a line of Khmer Rouge fighters. I felt a brief frisson of fear course down my back. These were the real thing. Middle-aged men who did the fighting and the killing. Most wearing the *krama*, the red neckscarves. The cold smiles. I suddenly understood the phrase, "the smile on the face of the tiger." And I walked on. Still they streamed out of the jungle and toward the camp. Finally, at one point, one of the Khmer Rouge men turned to me as he walked by. He must have spoken in Thai because I don't speak Cambodian. He said, "*Antarai* (danger)."

I said something like, "What danger? The Thai army is up there at the treeline."

He spat as if in derision of the Thai army. "That is the *Vietnamese* army," he said.

After a few seconds of realizing how close I had come to capture or death, I turned and walked back in the direction of the camp. To this day, I wonder at the irony of being saved from the Vietnamese by a soldier of the bloodthirsty Khmer Rouge. I sometimes wonder if, whatever his crimes, he had gained Buddhist merit in saving me.

I walked past an area of Cambodian children, no doubt orphaned by the war, and in a bit of Thai and a lot of gestures, we talked. They produced some drawings they had done of Angkor Wat and village scenes and gave them to me. I had nothing left to give them. Then I remembered that a Cambodian go go dancer on Bangkok's Patpong Road had taught me to sing some lines of "Tell Laura I Love Her" in Cambodian. And so, much to the delight of the children, I serenaded them. Here, in the midst of poverty, disease, danger, the fighting and the dying, I sang of what would be young Laura's heartache of losing her beloved Tommy and of his eternal love for her — a ballad from the America of the late (and innocent) 50's. A time when no one knew where Cambodia was. A time when one death could still mean so much; in stark contrast to those millions of Cambodians dying of disease, hunger and methodical beatings — dying unknown and unserenaded.

Eventually, I moved on in search of the Cambodian lady and my newfound Norwegian friends. I found the two journalists standing in the center of dozens of refugees looking over their notes. I asked them where the Cambodian woman was.

"Oh, she's gone," one of them said. Without looking up from his notebook.

"Gone? What do you mean gone? Did she find her mother?"

Both of them began chuckling. "She's from Australia, all right. But she's a journalist who was sent up by a newspaper to get the refugee story. There was no mother. That was just her cover story she made up to get into the camp."

Needless to say, I was dumbfounded. Had this been an early silent Charlie Chaplin-type movie, the caption here would have read: "Sexist gets his Comeuppance." She had used my lust for her the way an experienced combatant uses an opponent's aggressiveness and strength to execute a judo throw. And Cambodians being the world's most innocent people, if *she* could trick me, *anybody* could.

From that moment on, until we got back to Bangkok, the journalists and I argued about whether or not her cover story was "very professionally done" as they said, or "a heinous lie," as I contended. We had about reached Bangkok when I finally became convinced they were correct. I suppose the only crime of a journalist is not to get the story. And she hadn't really harmed anything except my ego.

While I had been in the camp, the urge to do something had been overwhelming and I did manage to get an address from a Thai nurse where people could send money directly. This information I managed to get into a Bangkok hotel magazine. I can only hope it did some good.

Still, for years I felt pangs of guilt. While there had been the dead and dying all around me, I had been captivated by and interested in the charms of a beautiful Cambodian woman. How callous could I be? And then years later I read Kurt Vonnegut's novel, *Jailbird.* In it he posed this question: "And what is flirtatiousness but an argument that life must go on and on and on?" And I thought, Yes! That is exactly it. When helpless in the face of death and the dying, flirtatiousness is itself a denial against giving up. Against giving in. Against capitulation. A way of not allowing Death to have a final victory.

Still, even now, a few times a year, I wake in the early morning darkness and think, "She used me! That Cambodian chick *used* me!"

UPDATE 23 YEARS LATER

January, 2003: Living in Thailand again means traveling out every month or two to get yet another tourist visa so that I can legally return. Friends assured me it was not difficult to get a visa at the Thai-Cambodian border of Aranyaprathet where I had not been for nearly a quarter of a century. And so it was that I headed for Bangkok's Hualumpang Train Station to catch the 1 p.m. train to Aranyaprathet.

I ignored the touts outside the building and once inside headed for the information counter. Two young Thai women informed me that the train was only about US$1, but it took six hours, was third class and had no air-conditioning. They suggested that I go to the bus station and take an air-conditioned bus. Very seldom do the employees of one organization suggest to a potential customer that he would be better off going to another organization. This being Thailand where anything and everything is possible, it is possible the women are getting kickbacks from the bus company. But I don't think so. I think they sized me up as being a bit too long in the tooth for a rugged, non-air-conditioned, six-hour train ride and decided to be kind.

So I grabbed a taxi and headed off for the Morchit bus station. On the way there, the thought occurred to me that just maybe the young women working at the bus station might find me a bit too long in the tooth for a bus ride and suggest I take a plane out of the country to renew the visa. Fortunately, they did not.

The bus left at 12:40 and cost about US$3.50 for the four-and-one-half hour journey. A very pleasant trip in which although Thai love songs were played, thankfully, the TV was not turned on. Nor did the bus driver indulge in the much-loved Thai bus driver pastime of racing other buses. As we neared our destination, the land became flat and dusty and I was pleased not to be coming here in either the hot season or the rainy season.

We arrived at the bus station in Aranyaprathet and everyone piled out. A few *tuk tuks* and their drivers waited nearby. I wasn't certain how close the town was so I wasn't sure if I needed a *tuk tuk* (samlor) or not. A young, dark-complexioned Thai man with a saucer-shaped hat looked me over and asked me where I was going.

Me: I need a hotel.

Him: Which one?

Me: I don't know; I haven't been here for a long time.

Him (pointing): The one right back there is one thousand baht a night (about US$23).

Me: Is this the town beginning over there?

Him: No. Aranyaprathet is about two kilos away. How many nights you stay?

Me: One.

Him: So why not stay in the Inter Hotel inside the city, only 500 baht?

Me: Is it a good hotel?

Him: Sure. You stay only one night, you spend one thousand

baht on hotel, you stupid.

He started to walk off.

Me: Wait a minute. The driver wants 40 baht to get to the Inter hotel. Is that a good price?

Him: Good price.

(I would find out later it should have been 20 baht. But it *was* a good price: for the driver.)

Me: OK, thanks. You speak good English.

Him: Thanks.

The Inter Hotel is on a quiet street, a very quiet street. Almost like being in a Florida retirement community. I am quoted a price of 550 baht (US$13) which I accept. The room is clean enough and has air-conditioning. I see no other guests, Thai or foreign, until later that evening.

I decided to walk about the town. I remembered Aranyaprathet as a rather depressing little town, and it still is. However, just across the Cambodian border are seven casinos which Thais and others love to flock to, especially on weekends. As gambling is illegal in Thailand, the Cambodian and Thai owners are doing very well indeed.

After walking for a while, I hire a motorcycle taxi to take me around the town for about 20 minutes. The woman vendor of fruit next to him asks me how much I will pay. How about 100 baht, she says. For 100 baht I will go to Ayuthya, I say. She laughs and translates for the driver. He smiles. Slightly.

As I ride about on the back of his motorcycle he talks. As his Thai is not Bangkok Thai, and as my Thai is somewhat limited, our conversations are not always clear. But 45 minutes later he drops me off at the hotel and asks for 200 baht. I decide not to bother bargaining and pay him what he asks.

Inside the hotel restaurant, I am the only guest. I order Thai omelet with pork and a chicken dish. Within minutes a piece of chicken is stuck in my throat; it won't go in or out. I can still breathe but it is serious. I stand up and keep coughing and choking. Tears stream down my face. I wave the only other person in the room over: the waiter. He rushes out and calls the hotel manager just in the other room. He enters, sees me standing up by the table, and asks if I want the bill.

No, I don't want the bill; I am f**king dying here, got it?! But I have to try not to laugh while choking. I motion for the waiter to hit my back hard. Being a Thai, he is reluctant to hit a *farang* hard on the back but gives it a try. He does bring me water which seems to do the trick. I calm down but decide that I need no more food for the night. The night is pleasantly cool and I take a walk. The people of Aranyaprathet seem neither overly friendly nor unfriendly. They are no doubt used to foreigners arriving here for visa purposes; either to go on into Cambodia or to simply get the visa and reenter Thailand again.

The next morning I check out after breakfast. The woman at the front desk is dressed in long-sleeved shirt and jacket. She complains about how cold it is. When it is pleasantly cool for a foreigner, it is freezing weather for a Thai.

I walk through the town, look about the Market (Backpacker) Motel but spot no backpackers. Perhaps they are all out packing their backs or whatever backpackers do. I hire a *tuk tuk* for 50 baht to take me to the immigration station at the Thai-Cambodia border. We arrive at a dusty area with busses, vehicles, refugees, long lines of patient Thai vendors pushing their wooden two-wheeled wagons returning from Cambodia, beggars, child-beggars, immigration officials and a marketplace. The sun is beating down; dust rises from the dry ground; confusion is everywhere.

A young Cambodian man about 18 or so approaches me and begins speaking in English. He shows me a book of his foreign "friends" and how they paid him a few thousand baht for his assistance in getting a visa. I tell him thanks but no thanks.

However, I notice he has several immigration forms for both countries and seems to know how to save me quite a bit of time. I demure but he follows me as I walk. I continue to watch my shoulder bag carefully and politely ignore the entreaties of beggars. He also warns me to watch my shoulder bag.

The young man meets up with a man in a white uniform; a Cambodia policeman who looks over my passport and asks for the money. I know the correct amount is 1,000 baht and I know Cambodian immigration officials often like to charge more if they can, so I immediately give him the thousand baht so he will know that I know how much it is. The boy says it is 1200. I say no, it is 1,000. The boy says OK but give him 100 baht tip. Reasonable enough. And I made my point that I know how much it is and this is in fact a tip. So I give the tip as well as the 1,000 baht and the policeman walks off to his booth. While waiting in a bit of shade in the midst of the chaotic, confusing, cacophonous, sun-drenched scene on the bridge between the countries, the boy begins filling out my paperwork for me. He has definitely done this before.

I notice a sign on the Thai immigration building:

WARNING
Leaving the kingdom for gambling purposes may not be safe for personal life and property Thai authority cannot be responsible.

The "Eastern Border of Thailand" sign is in three languages. The line of Thai vendors returning from Cambodia stretches out a long way. I can only feel sorry for people having to make their living in such a manner.

The policeman returns and hands me my passport with its visa for Cambodia. The boy points out where else I have to go and even gives me a Thai immigration form for when I return.

Inside one building, there are three short lines: Those with Thai passports, those with foreign passports and those with "border passes." Those waiting in the "border passes" line are very dark-complexioned, poorly dressed, and one man holds a chicken in his much callused hand.

The boy walks with me right into Cambodia. The town of Poipet is just ahead and from what I can see of it, is dusty and less interesting than Aranyaprathet. We pass the seven gambling casinos that draw the Thai gamblers and he mentions that Cambodians are not allowed inside to gamble. I tell him a bit about how over twenty years before the Vietnamese army and Cambodian *Khmen Dang* ("Red" or communist Cambodians) were fighting very near here. He says they are not there any more but there are very young Vietnamese and Cambodian women if I want them. Over 20 years ago, Cambodian women were killing each other or else starving or dying of disease while fighting the Vietnamese. Now they are no longer starving or fighting; they are simply kept somewhere in brothels. Progress comes slow for women in poor areas of the earth.

Anyway, I give him my usual excuse whenever a Thai man asks if I want a woman. I tell him I am old now: *gae lao*. Unfortunately, he misunderstands it as *gin lao*, ("drink whiskey"), and he enthusiastically says, yes, sure, we can do that. Finally, I tell him I am heading for the Holiday Palace Casino, hand him 200 baht (US$4.65) and bid him goodbye. He seems satisfied, thanks me, and walks off.

Once out of the sun and inside the Holiday Palace, my bag is checked and I am allowed to enter. The area looks more like a shopping mall than a casino. I stroll around the huge space off of which are several shops. A pawn shop offers gold necklaces and a mobile phone shop offers the latest deals on mobile phones. In the center of it all are tables and a buffet lunch. There is also a luxurious Japanese and a luxurious Chinese restaurant. I decide to take a rest at what appears to be a Starbucks ripoff. The color of the logo is the same shade of green but the Palais Coffee design has an Asian face surrounded by stars. And so, not far from where Cambodians once lay dying, I sit back in air-conditioning and enjoy my cappuccino frappe and strawberry waffle.

I enter a doorway marked "casino," allow myself and my possessions to be cursorily checked, and enter. There are the usual sounds and lights of a casino and the usual games preferred by Asians: Fan tan, baccarat, horse racing machines, poker slot machines. And a poker table for Western tourists. I try my luck at the poker slot machine and win about 200 baht. I walk to a roulette table and place 500 baht on two numbers and one row. I lose it all in one spin of the wheel. The girl in charge says, "Sorry."

I walk out and cross to the nearby Holiday Poipet casino. Inside it is much the same but not so spacious. I check at the desk and learn that a single room ranges from 1,000 to 1,500 baht, depending on weekday or weekend. These casinos are nowhere on the level of Las Vegas but on the other hand they have more dignity and cleanliness than those of Macau. And the dealers sometimes apologize when a player loses. What more could a gambler ask?

After a while, I leave the casino, and, recrossing the small bridge, walk to the Thai immigration booth. There is no problem and I am soon in search of a *tuk tuk* to take me back to the Aranyaprathet bus station. But a crowd of children spot me and surround me holding out their dirty little hands for money. I give them change and when I have nothing left for the last of them, he points to my bottle of Sprite I have just opened. I gesture to ask if it is OK for me to take one drink. He gestures back that it is OK. I take a swig and hand it to him and he is happy.

A 50-baht *tuk tuk* ride gets me back to the bus station where I hand a woman 180 baht for a ticket to Bangkok. She also hands me a bottle of water and a small package labeled "layer cake." While I wait, memories flood in and I can't help but wonder what happened to the two teenage Khmer Rouge girls too famished and weak to open the bags of M&M candies I had given them. If alive, they would be in their thirties now. I silently wish them well and I board the bus to Bangkok.

Soon we are on our way. Along the way, I doze off into a kind of half sleep and images of both Aranyaprathet trips crowd in on me, including the bizarre image of young Cambodian refugees being tended to by Thai nurses on the floor of a casino. When I wake up we are in Bangkok.

By (the wrong) Train Through Southern Thailand

In his book, *The Great Railway Bazaar*, Paul Theroux described the State Railway of Thailand as "comfortable and expertly run." But what about the adventurous but simple-minded traveler who fails to notice what kind of train he's boarding or, worse yet, manages to board the wrong train. What happens to him? The article below reveals the brutal answers.

A s the Thai travel agent spoke into the phone, I couldn't help notice that she bore a slight resemblance to Monica Lewinsky. I wondered if anyone had ever told her that. Finally, she replaced the phone on the hook, looked up at me and smiled sympathetically, alerting me to the fact that the news would not be good. "I'm sorry. All flights to Phuket are full for four days."

What really galled me was that I wanted to travel to Nakorn Si Thammarat on the opposite coast from Phuket and, even were a flight available, I would still have a lot of land traveling to do. But the train from Bangkok meant a ride of over half a day.

It was Thailand's hot season and the sweat exuding from every pore seemed to carry off my patience with it. "But how can Thailand promote tourism to the South with so few flights added during a holiday?"

The patient tourist agent shrugged. Perhaps she was asked this question several times a day. "Maybe you go by train better; or fly north to Chiang Mai."

Her suggestion to travel north reminded me of my trip to Burma years before where in Rangoon a government official informed me that traveling to the south was forbidden but I could always go north to Mandalay and Pagan. But I had headed south by train then, and, if need be, I would go into southern Thailand the same way. It began to seem as if everywhere in Asia, only the north was on limits or convenient for travel, while the south was off limits or difficult for tourists to reach. Which meant that, like Burma, Thailand's south was probably lush, unspoiled country and all the more reason I refused to be talked into a northern journey.

An hour later I was at Bangkok's Hualampong Station in line for a ticket to Nakorn Si Thammarat. The ticket was for a "rapid train" which would leave at 5:30 in the afternoon and arrive at Nakorn Si Thammarat at 9:30 the following morning. A journey of 16 hours. But, never mind — it was the "rapid train" and I had a first class ticket.

I boarded the train and sat in the seat to which I was directed. As the time neared for the train to pull out, the car began to fill up, and several of the seats designed for two, were occupied by three persons (including my own). But if it was crowded and hot, with people sitting, standing and lying down, I was certain that at any minute, when the conductor came, he would stare at my ticket, laugh uproariously, and conduct me to my proper (reclining) leather seat in an air-conditioned car provided with all kinds of private facilities. It was not to be. He came, punched my ticket, and moved on.

The woman sitting opposite me began waving goodbye furiously to her husband and the small child outside the window. But as the train pulled out, neither the cries of the woman, nor the prompting of her husband could get the child to altar its gaze, which remained fixed on one spot before it like an Andy Warhol stationary camera, perhaps hypnotized by the movement of the train.

I now began to realize that the "rapid train" was not an express or *the* "international express" to Malaysia. Despite its name, it was obviously a "local" train, which might also help to explain the lack of other foreigners. My guidebooks all informed me that the train did not stop at Nakorn Si Thammarat and explained where to get off at a nearby station and how to proceed. However, I was assured by a fellow passenger that this train did indeed stop right at the city. Probably the writers of guidebooks never thought a foreign traveler would take a "rapid" train and were describing only the various expresses.

As I was unable to stretch out my legs while sitting, I decided to pass the time away in the dining car. At first, all was well. But, after about 15 minutes, a mosquito flew into the speeding car from a nearby window.

It was about the size of a tarantula and, as he strode across the table, he shoved my bottle of Singha beer out of his way and began helping himself to my *khow phat* (fried rice) with fried egg. I sat in fear and amazement as he went about his business giving me you'd-better-not-make-any-sudden-move glares. Suddenly the train lurched and he tumbled from the table onto the floor. He picked himself up and stalked off rubbing what must have been a bad pain in his lumbar region. But as he limped away, he turned to give me a you'll-be-hearing-from-me-about-this look. I knew that look well: it was the same ominous glance I was often given in a Bangkok bar by bargirls who believed (probably correctly) that I had done them wrong.

The day turned into night, and as the hours passed by so did the stations: Nakhon Pathom, Ratchaburi, Phetchaburi, Hua Hin, Chumphon, and, the last major station before Nakorn Si Thammarat, Surat Thani.

A very friendly young Thai student approached me on the train, asked me my destination, and then handed me the most incredible pamphlet I've ever seen. It's title was: *Keys to Solution of World Problems by Peace Envoy.* Its subtitle was: *Nations will prosper, When leaders are honest, But Doom will befall All countries and states, when those who act as intermediaries Are naught of ethics.*

There was also a photograph of the movement's "Prime Director," a young and bespectacled man in a white uniform with gold braid and several medals adorning his chest. His address was "Valley of Divine Paradise, Land of Religious Harmony." The group's more mundane goals were to end wars and conflict among men, but it was the "prophecy chart" which most demanded my attention.

It was a diagram of circles and dates connected by arrows. Events prophesied included:

A.D. 2007 Bourgeoisie/Aristocracy to be all destroyed by Communism & Democracy. A.D. 2957 Religious War. A.D. 4457 World Annihilation War (followed by) opening of New Era. Phra Shri Arayamettraya will proclaim a new religion.

I am happy that I did not ask the obvious question of who would be left to believe after a World Annihilation War, because the young student got off the station with me and kindly led me to my hotel where I managed after a hot bath to sleep for fourteen hours. I decided to plan my return train trip more carefully and avoid any mistakes. Little did I know then the exciting denouement was yet to come.

During my stay in southern Thailand, I noticed that whenever I mentioned I was returning by train, someone would suggest the "tour bus." But as I would leave from Surat Thani rather than Nakorn Si Thammarat, I knew the trip would be faster and this time I had paid just over US$10 for a *berth* of my own. And, besides, I now had a ticket on an *express* train.

When the time came to leave the loveliness of southern Thailand, I arrived at the Surat Thani railway station early. One or two trains pulled in and out and about an hour before my train was due to leave, I watched a Haad Yai–Bangkok train pull out. It was difficult to read the exact time of my train on the envelope I had been given, but when I had mentioned 'express' at the station, a man had said 6:47, which seemed right. Finally, people began boarding the train to Bangkok and I also boarded and headed for car number 5. I had a bit of a walk as it was the last car on the train. As I walked, the train began pulling out. Finally, I opened the door to what should have been a sleeping car lined with private and well-kept berths. It was, in fact, a dining car.

I checked my ticket carefully, checked the car's number, then, finally, determined not to panic, sought assistance. A man who seemed a cross between an official and a conductor studied my ticket and envelope carefully. Then he spoke with a chuckle in his voice. "You are on the wrong train. You should have been on the Haad Yai to Bangkok train. Too bad you missed it; it's a good train."

"But . . . but isn't this the *express?*"

"Sure, but so is that. During the summer we have two express trains."

This led to an incredible number of consultations and discussions between and among policemen, ticket conductors, train officials and interested passengers. *The foreigner is on the wrong train without a bed or even a seat. The train is full. The plot thickens.*

At last, a kindly policeman motioned for me to pick up my bags and follow him. As we walked the entire length of the train, causing all heads to turn our way, I began to feel like Poe's "*Masque of the Red Death*" entering one eerie room after the other. We passed through the air-conditioned, first-class car of reclining seats, the cars with berths — the softness of which I would never know — through the 2nd class cars, the 3rd class cars, the 10th class cars. As we continued, I noticed the lights seemed dimmer, there were more people per car, and their skin was darker.

A woman who spoke a bit of English assured me that they would try to help and that by the time the train reached Petchaburi there might be a seat available. I smiled and thanked her all the while knowing that if I couldn't get a seat before Petchaburi station (about seven hours away) I would be dead, anyway.

The policeman and I continued through yet another restaurant car and finally we arrived at our destination: the baggage car. Two boards were quickly fixed up and covered with a thin cloth. A pillow was added. This was to be my bed. I had heard of bed and board before, but never literally. It was in fact rather touching, because primitive and uncomfortable though the bed might have been, it was the only resemblance to a bed in the baggage car, and one of the workmen was giving it up so that I could use it. I lay down on it while policemen, officials and workmen stood around watching like interested but detached scientists observing the result of a somewhat precarious experiment.

The board was surprisingly comfortable, but, not surprisingly, about six inches too short. Nevertheless, I assured my audience that it was perfect, and, after a reasonable amount of time, announced that I was heading for the dining car. Unfortunately, as with the Bangkok to Nakorn Si Thammarat train, the dining car closed at 10:30, forcing passengers to return to their seats or beds or, in the case of anyone too stupid to get on the right train, the baggage car.

Fortunately, while I sought refuge in the dining car, the monster mosquito from the first train never caught up with me, and as I drank my Singha beer, hoping 10:30 would never come, I chatted in broken Thai with the diner opposite. I spoke as nonchalantly as possible as if asking about rice paddies or rubber trees: "I don't suppose there are any bandits in this area . . . ."

I waited for the expected roar of laughter and exasperated exclamation to the effect that "you idiot, there isn't a bandit a thousand miles of here." It never came. Instead, he nibbled on what appeared to be an incredibly spicy reddish-brown Thai dish laced with thousands of tiny chilies and remained thoughtful for several seconds. And then launched into incredibly precise directions as to how I could find bandits in the hills. The most unnerving thing was that he seemed simply to be giving directions to a zoo or botanical garden. *Excuse me, Mac, can you tell me how to get to the bandit insurgency cultural show and rodeo? Oh, sure, bud, just three blocks down the road, hang a right at the Safeway, make a left at Mcdonald's, and another left at the Howard Johnson's. You can't miss it. Thanks.*

When I returned to the baggage car, I was asked for my ticket. I explained that it was still with the policeman who had asked for it. Was I sure? Absolutely. After a thorough search of an official's desk and a search for the policeman, the ticket was found. In my pocket. Smiles all around. Profuse apologies from me.

I lay down to get what sleep I could. The only sounds being the clicking of the wheels on the rails, the muffled voices from the rear of the baggage car and the constant peeping of what sounded like birds. Birds? I lifted my head. Less than two feet from me were stacked 20 rectangular boxes, each with four holes in each end, and six holes along each side. From nearly half of these holes the heads of chicks poked out of the boxes, and their eyes looked up at me beseechingly. I knew exactly how they felt, but despite their constant sleep-preventing peeps, there was nothing I could do for them or for me.

During the few periods in which I nearly attained sleep, I would be suddenly awoken by the *whuuump* of a chick which had reared back and then, in a desperate charge, lunged its head and neck through a hole vainly hoping to force its body through. It was nearly dawn before sleep reluctantly took hold of me. The clicking of the wheels transformed into music and I started to dream of Monica Lewinsky gyrating on stage as a go-go dancer at the Suzie Wong bar on Soi Cowboy.

What might have been only minutes later, I awoke. I felt strange. As if I was being watched. I opened my eyes and looked around. The train was slowly passing through a village station and the side door to the baggage car had been opened. Several villagers were silently observing the foreigner lying on the boards with the concerned looks of men and women who have just bet their favorite chicken on whether or not it is a person or a corpse. Now I knew how Lenin felt in his mausoleum. I waved. Broad smiles. Exclamations of surprise (and in the case of those who had guessed wrong, possibly regret). The foreigner lives!

We pulled into Bangkok, an hour overdue. I headed for my hotel, and after a hot bath, broke my previous record for uninterrupted sleep.

MURDER AT THE HORNY TOAD BAR

&

OTHER OUTRAGEOUS TALES OF THAILAND

Harry Boroditsky, Private Eye

"He's not happy. He'll be better off — dead."
"Yeah?"
"That's not true is it?"
"Not from where he sits, I don't think."

— *Double Indemnity*, James M. Cain

Murder at the Horny Toad Bar
A Harry Boroditsky Mystery

Chapter 1

It all started with that phone call. I wish now I had never an swered it. But I did. And right away I could tell something was wrong from the tremor in the voice on the phone. "You're tremoring," I said.

I didn't mean to be unkind but even before I moved to Bangkok I never could stand it when women's voices tremor. Other, more intimate parts of their luscious anatomies can tremor all they like. They can twitch and flutter and shake and wobble and shimmy and shudder and quake and quaver. But not their voices. That pisses me off. And the girl was sniffing and snuffling and sobbing as well. That was too much. I let her go on a bit before screaming into the phone. "Stop tremoring!"

The girl quieted down. I could hear her breathing. "You're breathing," I said.

She spoke softly. "Harry, something very bad happen. Impact everybody. You better come right now."

Christ! If I had told Lek once I told her a thousand times: Never use 'impact' as a verb. 'Affect,' yes; 'impact,' no. Further proof that all the money I gave her for English classes she gam bled away on one of those goddamn loony-tune bargirl games. I'd have to get out the spanking brush again and she'd have to do her hair up in pigtails and bring her red heart-shaped lollipop and lacy Snow White panties and Baby Duck bonnet with pink ribbons and white cotton socks and black penny-loafers and "Daddy's Special Little Girl" brand schoolbook bag. Not that I'm kinky, understand. But there's only one way to deal with a Thai bargirl's lack of financial discipline. And that's with more discipline. Anyway, I figured I'd deal with that later. Something sounded seriously wrong. "Is Good Pork Betty all right?"

"She OK. But something very bad happen here, Harry. Hurry!"

Four h's in a row. Not bad. Lek was the most alliterative of all the go-go dancers of the Horny Toad. Of course, the Horny Toad wasn't what it once was. When the damnable night market impregnated Patpong Road with its foul stench-ridden seed, the Horny Toad moved once or twice and then finally ended up at a remote spot on the bank of the *klong* behind the Hilton. And if you don't know what a *klong* is, fuck you, because I'm not gonna explain every goddamn thing.

I looked at the 22-year-old girl on the bed. My bed. My girl. Well, at least for tonight. The naked Thai beauty who was even now smiling up at me in her gorgeous feminine languor. In her gorgeous languorous femininity. In her languorine, feminous gorginity. She was Thai through and through. Her eyes were the blackest I'd ever seen. Her body was the most curvaceous. Her smile was the loveliest. Her hair was the longest. Her cheekbones were the highest. Her skin was the smoothest. Her nipples were the nipplest. Her — well, you get the picture.

Her eyes widened and she looked at my naked body the way most bargirls look at my ATM card. She was a nymphomaniac. And she wanted me. Again. And again. And again. I wanted her again too. But I knew duty called. I saw the disappointment on her face as I spoke into the phone. "All right," I said, "put a Singha on ice. I'll be right there." I slammed the phone down.

The girl looked about to cry. "Jimmy, why you go? I love you."

"I'm Harry," I said, "and I love you too but something's not right at the Horny Toad. I gotta get down there." She crossed her lovely legs and stretched, no doubt a ploy to dissuade me from leaving. I could feel my Johnson spring into action. 'Magic Johnson,' some of the go-go dancers at the Nana Entertainment Plaza called it. I looked at the way her beautiful, silken stream of pubic hair dove down between her satin-smooth legs. I gotta get down *there*, too, I thought. But that would have to wait. I patted her lustrous wedge-shaped fur. "Keep it warm for me, baby."

I decided to forgo the shower. No time. Besides, it was the beginning of the cool season, only 97 degrees Fahrenheit out. I reached into the bottom drawer, shoved aside several dozen empty Mehkong and Viagra bottles and grabbed a-hold of my five-shot Smith & Wesson Police Special. I snapped it open and spun the chamber then blew into each hole to remove any leftover debris from my last shootout.

The girl on the bed hadn't moved. Except her eyes. "Oh, Harry, you good blow."

"You got ten seconds to get out of here, Dang, and nine of them are gone." I didn't mean to be unkind; it was nothing personal; but when a friend of Harry Boroditsky needs help, they get it. And nothing is gonna delay that.

Sure, I know, the name sucks. I had an Italian father half Polish on his Romanian mother's side and an Irish mother half Caucasian on her Eurasian brother's side. Anyway, friends just call me Boro. Enemies call me Ditsky. But not for long. If you get my drift.

I loaded each chamber with a special hollow-tipped round and spent a bit of time trying to fit my silencer onto the revolver before remembering that silencers aren't made for revolvers; they're for semi-automatics. So I threw the silencer to Dang who liked to do some very unusual things with it. Some very sensual things. If you get my drift. I didn't mind. Except for the muffled sighs and the escalating series of moans, the silencer kept her quiet. Like a pacifier for a baby. And, besides, whenever I used my semi to shoot some dickhead dead with a bullet through that silencer it eased my conscience to know that said dickhead died engulfed in the sweetest and most intimate female scent imaginable. There are worse ways to die.

Anyway, I strapped my revolver into my cross-draw leather-and-lace holster, and finished dressing. Dang finished dressing just before me. Of course, she didn't wear much underneath. Or overneath, for that matter. I cuddled her in my arms as we walked to the front door.

"When I see you again, Harry?"

Dang was one of the girls in the 10:00 show at the Devil Witch bar; and if you don't know where the Devil Witch bar is or what it is she straps on in the show, fuck you, because I'm not gonna explain every goddamn thing. "Don't you worry, darlin'," I said, "I'll be by real soon."

I thought I saw a shadowy figure duck into an alley just as I walked outside but I couldn't be sure. The moon had disappeared behind a dildo-shaped cloudbank and the darkness was too dark. The black was too pitched. Besides, it was about 3 in the morning and it might just have been a leftover drunk from the Thermae Coffee Shop several blocks down Sukhumvith Road. Coffee shop, my ass. If that's a coffee shop, I'm Janet Jackson's black leather bustier. Anyway, I was in a hurry.

I hailed a *tuk tuk* and Dang slithered into the back. She whispered her destination to the driver, then turned to smile at me. Just before she roared off, she blew me a kiss. She seemed happy. A little too happy. I checked my wallet. Sure enough, she'd taken the ATM card again. What the hell, there wasn't much in the account and she was worth it. Especially when she dressed up in her glow-in-the-dark, red-and-black lingerie with the mesh stockings and purple garter belt and frilly white gloves and stiletto-heeled, knee-high, black leather boots. Not that I'm kinky, understand.

What I didn't know then was that what waited for me at the Horny Toad would make me forget all about ATM cards, lingerie, garter belts and Siamese nymphomaniacs.

Chapter 2

I had never known Lek to be afraid of anything. Yet the fear in her voice over the phone had come across loud and clear. Whatever had happened at the Horny Toad had scared the bejesus out of her. Thanks to the skytrain it didn't take me long to arrive at the Horny Toad Station.

As I crossed the street, I barely avoided getting knocked down by a running man. I assumed it was yet another failed assassination attempt, wheeled about, and drew my revolver. I pumped a few shots into the darkness at his rapidly disappearing form but when I kicked the body over with my foot I realized it was just a bus driver fleeing the scene of an accident.

Damn! The fear in Lek's voice had spooked me. I had to calm down. Besides, if I sent a few rounds after every Thai bus driver fleeing the scene of an accident, I'd never have enough ammunition.

The winding dirt lane leading to the Horny Toad Bar was deserted. I took out my pack of Marlboros. The increasingly strong gusts of wind made it difficult to light up. It had already begun to sprinkle and I could feel it would start pouring in a minute or two.

I paused to look up at the two-story ramshackle wood-and-brick Horny Toad Bar. They didn't make them like that anymore. A lot of wonderful memories began flooding back. I loved the place but the brutal truth was it was a forlorn bar in a remote area of Bangkok which had obviously seen better days.

A blue-and-gold neon sign in the shape of a beer bottle flickered on and off above the wide wooden door like an indecisive whore. The few bug-stained neon beer signs in the windows lit up the surrounding darkness for several yards on either end of the bar. And in the darkness I could just make out still more darkness. I couldn't see the *klong* behind the bar but I could sure as hell smell it.

In the distance I could see boards being blown loose from half-completed buildings whose construction had halted when the economy collapsed. Huge white sheets covering a side of the nearest building had been loosened by the wind and they fluttered majestically in and out like panicky ghosts hanging on for dear life.

I thought for a moment about how different a man I had been when I first arrived in Bangkok, "still pissin' Stateside water." "Cherry boy," the bar girls called me. It was Good Pork Betty who made sure I didn't stay a cherry-boy for long. I had never told her I was cherry — she just knew. She and the girls looked me over with the same expression Michelangelo must have had on his face when he looked upon the blank ceiling of the Sistine Chapel for the first time. Because the bar girls in the Horny Toad were in their own way artists as well; and they knew that sooner or later one of them could and would use her talents to vastly and irrevocably alter what they saw before them. And what they saw before them had been my virginal Mr. Johnson.

I pushed open the wooden swinging doors and entered a dimly lit barroom filled with gloom so thick Lorena Bobbitt could have cut it with a knife. There were no customers. Only several dispirited and crestfallen bargirls. They still wore their bikinis but the music had been shut off and no one was up on stage.

Lek pointed toward the rear of the bar and told me Good

Pork Betty wanted to see me in the back room. "She want see you *leo leo*," she said.

Well, I didn't like the sound of that because I figured it might be concerning my unpaid bar bill so I tried to play it casual. I said, "Oh, yeah, what's up, Lek?"

She jumped up, threw her arms around me and began crying so hard she couldn't answer. I turned my head to avoid the smell of fish sauce and garlic and perfume and wondered what could have caused such unhappiness. Lek always wore Nevada Sunrise perfume. I knew that because that's the same perfume my minor wife wore the day I dropped the dime on her and they took her off to the Big House for Little Ladies in need of Discipline.

I pried her arms from my perfectly sculpted body and told her to hang loose. I crossed the bar area, pushed open an ancient teakwood swinging door which still had the initials "WHC" (Whore House Charlie) carved into it, and entered the back room. Water was pouring from the skies, monsoon winds blowing, banana fronds and palm leaves getting torn to shreds, and — there she was. In a kind of high chair, wearing her blouse over her Thai *phasin*, a kind of sarong. I knew the blouse was supposed to read "Good Pork Betty" across it but because her cheboobs were so humongus the "Pork" always got buried in the cleavage and it read, "Good Betty."

And because it was the rainy season that meant it was the edible patanga beetle season. And that's when millions of these rice beetles or crickets or wannabe cockroaches are caught in nets above village houses in places like Lopburi and Suphanburi and Farangmoneybuiltthisplaceburi and Igotchorwalletburi and sold to vendors in Bangkok who fry them in oil outside the bars; and the bar girls love them. *Farangs* (foreigners) brave enough to eat one fail to understand that the real danger is not *in* the beetle; but *on* it: the little buggers are often covered with DDT. And so the *farang* soon finds himself afflicted with swollen arms, diarrhea, itching, headaches, etc., and heads for the hospital where the nurses can't resist giggling over yet another *farang* idiot checking himself in with DDT-poisoning.

So, anyway, here's Good Pork Betty sitting by an open window, wind blowing her silver-streaked hair, popping these crickets into her mouth the way we eat popcorn. Of course, a lot of crickets don't make it into her mouth because of the raging wind but Betty didn't seem to notice.

She's busy biting the heads off the crickets and spitting them out before popping the rest into her mouth. So the floor was covered with cricket heads, wings, antennae, legs, all of which crackled, popped and snapped when I stepped on them. In fact, the whole fucking room sounded like it was crackling and popping and snapping. It was like being in the middle of a firefight in Flatbush at 3 a.m.

Here I was facing the woman that rumor-control said had done the nasty with every combatant in the Vietnam War on both sides! Including not just Green Berets and Montanard villagers and Army Rangers and Viet Cong satchel carriers and Navy fucking Seals, but even the mysterious LRRPs — the wigged-out phantoms on Long Range Reconnaissance patrols.

I could tell she'd been crying. In a selfish way, I was pleased by that. Because whatever she wanted to see me about at least it couldn't be my long overdue barbill. I checked the well worn rattan chair beside her for water snakes and poisonous spiders and sat down. A 'fuck-you!' lizard on the wall made his usual utterance which sounded exactly like "fuck you!"

"What is it, Good Pork? Has something terrible happened?"

She began sobbing quietly. Her breasts shook and bobbled in different directions at the same time — like a bar girl's loyalty. Bobble. Bobble. Bobble. In the old days she spoke no known language; today, she could speak a bit of Thai and English. She handed me a small 'made in Nakorn Phanom' flashlight. "Harry

. . . out there. You go look-see."

I turned to look where she was pointing just in time to have a detached beetle wing fly into my eye. Now we were both crying. Anyway, she had been pointing to the dank, dark, deserted *klong.* Wiping my eye, I got up and headed out the back door. The unrelenting wind and rain practically knocked me over. I leaned forward into it and struggled as best I could. Above me, the "Happiness is a Red Cock (whiskey)" neon sign was squeaking loudly and swinging wildly. I hoped it wouldn't come down and crush me. God knows how Bernard Trink would have written that one up in his website column: "Harry Boroditsky dies of red cock during fierce blow! But I don't give a hoot!"

Lightning flashed. I was certain I spotted an eerie figure darting behind some bushes across the *klong.* It looked similar to the one I had spotted outside my apartment. Lightning flashed again but across the *klong* all was dark and still.

I moved to the edge of the canal and looked down. It was then that I saw the body. He was lying face down, his head away from the bar. Like an incensed, inebriated bargirl who felt she had been shortchanged, the wind pummeled me every step of the way. With great effort I managed to reach him. I stooped beside the body, the soles of my shoes completely flat, and maintained my balance. It had taken me years to balance that Southeast Asian way and I was damn proud of myself for having learned it.

I brushed away wet leaves and banana fronds and bits of coconuts from the back of his head and examined him with the flashlight. Someone had clubbed him more than once, crushing the skull. Someone who had been enraged beyond reason.

I brushed away more leaves and canal-side debris that clung to the body and gently turned it over. I wiped mud from the face of what had until recently been a clean-shaven man about thirty-five. His sightless eyes wore the expression of a tourist whose wallet has just been stolen in a short time hotel by a Thermae girl while he was in the shower: surprise, disbelief, horror. I closed his eyes just like they do in the movies and let out a long sigh. It was worse than I had thought. A lot worse. No wonder Good Pork Betty and the girls were sobbing their eyes out.

Despite the damage to the back of the skull and the mud-covered face, there was no doubt who it was. It was Brothel Billy. Lek's lover. More importantly, the adopted son of Whore House Charlie. Whore House Charlie had disappeared about the time Jim Thompson did, and if you don't know who Jim Thompson was, fuck you, because I'm not gonna explain every goddamn thing. And here I was stooping beside a clammy *klong* face to face with Brothel Billy, a man who, had he lived, might have become almost as great a legend as Whore House Charlie. I looked up through the storm and swirling debris toward the faint neon lights of the Horny Toad.

There were only two things I knew for sure: I knew this would be the greatest case of my career. And I also knew if I wasn't careful it would be my last.

Chapter 3

I struggled against the gusting wind and driving rain to reenter the back room of the bar. I sat back down in my chair and wiped water from my face with what I hoped was a clean towel Good Pork Betty had placed out for me. The 'Fuck You' lizard on the wall said, "Fuck You!" Betty was still quietly sobbing, her purplish red beetle-nut lips quivering.

"Betty, I'm sorry. I truly am. I know how much Brothel Billy meant to you."

She stopped sobbing and looked at me. "You find the man who killed him, Harry! You find that man." She picked up a

mangda beetle and crushed it in her hand. "And then you bring
that man to me." She popped the beetle into her mouth and
began chewing.

I nodded. "Betty, I'm going to have to question you and the
girls."

Her eyes widened the way a bargirl's eyes widen when she's
sitting with her local lover and she spots her overseas money-
sending lover unexpectedly coming in the door. "You don't
suspect one of *us*, do you, Harry?"

"God, no, Betty. I mean I've got to learn all you know about
when and how it might have happened. You know the drill:
Who might have had motive, opportunity. When did you find
the body? Who found the body? Have you noticed any strangers
around lately? Anything out of the ordinary? Anything at all?"

In her Thai and broken English, Betty assured me that there
had been only the usual assortment of jaded, cheap Charlie local
customers and free-spending oil riggers from Saudi Arabia. And,
except for a recent party, not many of those anymore. No new
bargirls. And no bargirls left suddenly. Lek loved Billy and all
the girls liked him. After the party, during the cleanup, Betty
herself had gone to throw some trash into the Thai-style recycle
bin (*klong*) and stumbled across the body. I realized this would
not be an easy case to solve.

In between her sobs and beetle-crunching, I managed to learn
that last night had been an especially happy time at the Horny
Toad. The show was better than ever. That's why so many
customers came. Lek, Oy and Noy had even practiced their
acts for a week on their own time during the day. I could just
picture Thai bargirls needing practice to perfect their unusual
and unorthodox methods of opening beer bottles, propelling
balloon-popping darts and writing letters. They'd even painted
the walls of the bar with cartoon characters to add life to the
place. And Lek had worked hard to make everything perfect

even though she'd developed stomach cramps.

I stood up, shielding my face from flying beetle parts with one hand and shielding Mr. Johnson with the other. "Betty, I promise you, whatever it takes, I Harry Boroditsky will solve this case."

"You good man, Harry. You be careful."

The first order of business was to head for the men's room. One of the good things about the Horny Toad was that nothing ever changed. In the men's rooms of the new bars, above the urinal there was often some announcement for a book or a pub or something; a man could hardly unravel his Johnson and take a piss anymore without splashing an ad. Not in the Horny Toad. Here there was the usual graffiti from days of yesteryear: A faded "Trink the Dink" in black ink, and in blue ink someone had scribbled: "Flush hard, it's a long way to Nick's Number One." And if you don't know what Nick's Number One was, fuck you, because I'm not going to explain every goddamn thing.

On the wall was a small condom dispenser. Someone had drawn an arrow pointing to it and written: "This gum tastes terrible." The wind outside screamed like a Thai transvestite whose operation had gone horribly wrong. I glanced out the tiny window only to get a brief glimpse of a figure on the other side of the *klong* darting off into the darkness. It was the same figure I had seen before. Maybe he was just some kind of pervert but I didn't think so. I figured the figure might figure into this case. Go figure.

I packed up Mr. Johnson and exited the men's room into the bar. It certainly was more colorful. The girls had indeed painted the walls with cartoon figures and each window now served as the mouth for a kind of dirty old man figure whose black goatee was painted beneath. His bright red tongue lashed out toward paintings of scampering bargirls the way a wall lizard catches flies.

I gathered the dozen or so girls around me. Some were still sobbing. Cat was sobbing on Oy's shoulder. The two were lesbian lovers. Not that that mattered much as Good Pork Betty had a 'Don't ask, Don't tell' policy but they loved the pun on their names: Cat-Oy (kateoy — the word for Thai transvestite). Ha, ha.

I tried to speak with an equal amount of sympathy and authority. "Girls, I need your help in solving this case. Think now: Did Brothel Billy have any enemies? Have any of you seen suspicious strangers around lately?"

Either they were too shaken up to speak or else too frightened to speak in front of the others. I realized I would have to deal with them in a way I seldom dealt with bargirls: one on one. I decided to interrogate them in the storeroom behind the bar. I also decided to talk to them in ascending order of importance. I would interview those who knew Charlie least first and those who knew Charlie most last. I swiped several strangely scented paint brushes, strangely scented empty beer bottles and a strangely scented dildo off my chair, sat down, and called in the first girl.

It was soon clear that most of the girls were too new to have any information and none of them could think of anything that happened out of the ordinary. The party had been planned to honor Brothel Billy as he reached 35 years of age. Lots of locals showed up who hadn't been there for many months, if not years. It had been loud, rowdy, fun. No fights, no brawls.

Oy and Noy also seemed genuinely upset but completely at a loss. Finally, I called in Lek. I thought she might have heard or seen something even if she didn't know it was significant. It was difficult for her to talk without crying.

But even with her swollen eyes and stomach cramps, Lek was stunning. I mean, we are talking long black hair, high cheekbones, incredibly smooth skin, the voice of an angel and eyes so dark and huge they could melt the heart of Utah's Senator Orrin fucking Hatch. And her gorgeous legs were so long when she walked down Sukhumvit, they stretched from *soi* 4 to *soi* 11. They appeared to be longer than the two poles of Bangkok's famous Giant Swing but that may have been illusion because of the skimpy outfits she often wore. Lek also wore Turquoise Entrapment lipstick. I knew that because my ex-secretary had been wearing it the day the cops found her in that seedy, end-of-the-line, motel room off Santa Monica's Black Dahlia Boulevard.

She blew her nose and looked up at me. "My man's gone now."

Right. One of the songs from *Porgy and Bess*, 1935. Maybe it was a coincidence. Maybe it was Lek's subtle way of sending me a clue. Brothel Billy had once mentioned Lek was from a village in the northeast said to be so fucked up even the buffaloes were dysfunctional. Who knew what Lek was up to? I decided to follow her lead and stick with musical theater. "The Sun will Come Out Tomorrow," I said.

"Why they kill Billy, Harry? Why?! You no can get something that way!"

Right. Translated into English, from *Annie Get your Gun*: "You Can't Get A Man with A Gun." Was I on to something here or was I reading into it? After all, Hard Hearted Hannah, the Vamp of Savannah 1924 had no relation to Hard Hearted Noy, the Vamp of Klongtoey 2004. I decided to go for broke: "OK, Miss Saigon, Meet Me in St. Louis."

She stopped crying. "What you talking about, Harry? I no Vietnamese girl!"

I realized then I had been barking up the wrong mango tree. It happens sometimes with the best detectives. I tried to avoid staring at those smooth, silky, curvaceous legs. After all, she was practically a widow. But I could feel Mr. Johnson struggling for space; like a spastic whore caught in a mosquito net. As usual, Mr. Johnson's interest in a maiden's marital status was negligible. "You know, Lek, I mean, Brothel Billy was sometimes said to, well, to fool around." Such as dressing up nurses in stewardess uniforms and stewardesses in nurse uniforms, but I wasn't about to rub chilies in the wound.

She looked up and narrowed her lovely eyes. "Brothel Billy love me! He never Butterfly me! Never!"

I knew I had to calm her down. "All right, dollface, all right. But are you sure you didn't hear or see anything suspicious at the party?"

She grew thoughtful during which time she crossed and uncrossed her gorgeous, succulent legs. Like the Energizer Bunny, Mr. Johnson renewed his efforts to make his presence known. "Billy he talk with one man at the bar. Maybe two, three minutes. I think the man no like Billy. I see he talk soft but he not good man."

"You know his name?"

She shook her head. "But Betty she know him, I think."

I stood up. "OK, Lek, many thanks. I'll check with Betty."

I had foolishly stood up too quickly and Mr. Johnson, reveling in his new-found freedom, pushed unashamedly outward, bulging the crotch of my trousers out like a signal at a railroad crossing. Lek stood up, took a step toward me and, through the hard-pressed khaki, patted Mr. Johnson on the head. "Better him sleep now."

She turned and left the storeroom before I could point out that being patted on the head by a beautiful woman is not exactly an inducement for Mr. Johnson to retire from the field.

I sat on the chair facing Betty. The 'Fuck you' lizard started to say something but I drew my revolver and blew him away. Sure, maybe it was behavior displacement because of Mr. Johnson's frustrating day but I was in no mood for nonsense from a fucking *chingchok*. I turned to Betty and explained about the man at the bar. She knew him all right. An English property developer who had been trying to get Brothel Billy to sell his shares of the Horny Toad Bar so he could tear it down and build a condominium.

Betty would never sell but Brothel Billy had the majority of shares. I knew now I was onto something. I thanked Betty and told her now she could call the police and tell them about the body. As for me, it was time to pay a call on a certain real estate developer. It would be an awkward visit because I had once been intimate with the New Orleans woman the real estate mogul married. She was a redhead. He was a dickhead. They both hated me. He had once threatened to kill me on sight. The redhead both hated and loved me; the way all women feel about men. Especially those who jilted them. But I was determined to track down Brothel Billy's murderer wherever the trail led. Regardless of danger. I had built a reputation. People in Bangkok who knew what they wanted didn't just call on a P.I. — they asked for the best: Harry Boroditsky. But even I failed to realize I would meet my match with the evil genius I was soon to face.

Chapter 4

- The next day dawned bright and sunny. Except for the thick clouds and persistent rain. I stopped the *tuk tuk* on the half-shabby, half-upmarket Sukhumvit Road *soi*, ignored the come-hither looks of the male and female rambutan sellers, waded through puddles of dark, smelly water and entered the gleaming office tower.

I stepped around the sleeping guard and entered the lift. I pressed number six. The doors opened on the fourth floor. TIT. This is Thailand. The offices of *Bangkok-Bali-Bangladesh-Brooklyn* Real Estate Developers had taken up the entire building. Whatever they had paid for the smoked glass cubicles and Cubist paintings and perfectly placed clumps of bamboo could have paid my Bangkok living expenses for the next several years.

A beautiful Thai secretary with bright black eyes and shoulder-length, raven-black hair looked up at me and smiled in delight. I recognized her as one of the girls I had saved from the clutches of the slave trade when I solved one of the most dangerous cases of my career: the Brothel of the Seven Gables.

She jumped up and threw her arms around me. I liked her warmth and the touch of her silken smooth skin; unfortunately, she wore a kind of perfume which smelled like a cross between a rotten durian and a squished Laotian water snake. It took all I had, but I finally managed to pry her hungry, aching-for-love arms from around my muscular, well-tanned body.

"Happy, I am so hairy to see you!"

Sure, her English wasn't perfect, but whose is? "I'm Harry to see you too, Angelpuss, but I've got to see your boss."

She spoke quickly into an office intercom and then said, "She be right out, Harry."

I looked at the color computer printouts on the wall. The first showed her in a bikini on a beach somewhere. The rest seemed to be of a party in a bar that looked like the Horny Toad. "Nice," I said. "Very nice."

"Yes. My boss get new color printer, Harry."

"I meant *you* look nice, Angelbreasts, but the pictures are nice two."

"Only 2,300 baht."

"Thanks, sweetheart, but I'm not in the mood for a short-time at the moment."

"No, Harry, I mean the new color printer cost only two thousand three hundred baht."

"Oh. Sorry, doll-lips." I thought about a recent short time I had had on Soi Cowboy. Drinks with bargirl, 270 baht, plus 30 baht tip, 500 baht bar fine, 1500 baht for the girl. So color printers were now exactly the same price as a short time on Soi Cowboy. There was a message there but I wasn't sure what it was.

Suddenly, a wave of *Hungry-Tigress-on-the-Prowl* perfume hit my nostrils. It made me more than a bit dizzy. Never-to-be-repeated bedroom scenes with a gorgeous southern belle over-flowed my memory banks like a rapidly rising *klong* during the rainy season. Without turning around, I said: "Hello, dollface." Her deep, southern, sensual voice was as raspy as ever. "Mah husband is out of town, Harry. And whatevah made yiu think he would want to see the lykes of yiu?"

I turned to face her. Betty-lou was as gorgeous as ever. She wore a simple, short emerald green dress with a very low, feast-your-horny-eyes-on-this neckline, an expensive pearl necklace and very black, very high-heeled shoes. Curls of auburn hair cascaded down to her narrow waist. I couldn't stop thinking of how I had once wallowed in those gorgeous soft strands of red hair as they fanned out across my fluffy white pillow.

One of the things Betty-lou wasn't wearing was a bra. And I remembered the tips of her beautiful nipples were so long they stretched into another time zone. By day those lovely nipples tended to lighten and resembled the apricot shade of slightly over-ripe plum mangos; by night they darkened into the purplish brown tint of a badly bruised mangosteen. I stared into her gorgeous Viagra-blue eyes. "Brothel Billy's been murdered," I said. I wanted to see how she would react to the news. Her beautiful face revealed nothing. She could be cold as a Hoboken hooker's heart when she wanted to be.

Without a word she turned and walked toward her office. I blew a kiss to the secretary and followed Betty-lou. As she walked, her high heels did the job they were supposed to do and her figure swayed back and forth like a snake charmer's flute. And, sure enough, Mr. Johnson awoke from his nap. My shoes squeaked from the water I had waded through and my squeaks seemed timed to alternate with the clicks of Betty-lou's high heels. We could have played a duet for wide-eyed tourists in the Oriental Lobby.

Betty-lou sat herself down on a corner of her desk, causing her flimsy green dress to rise. She pointed to a chair. At the sight of her gorgeous white gams, Mr Johnson pointed to Betty-lou. Mr. Johnson had a photographic memory and he was remembering it wasn't only Betty-lou's voice that dripped corn-pone and honey. I took a seat and crossed my legs to discourage any further amorous adventures on the part of Mr. Johnson.

Without offering me one, she slipped a cigarette from a silver cigarette case and lit up a cigarette, formed her mouth into an "O" not unlike Lauren Bacall in a movie I had seen, and blew out the smoke. Her voice was steeped in sweet hominy and mint julips. I half expected Robert E. Lee to walk in the door, hand me his sword and surrender. "So y'all think mah husband killed Brothel Billy, is that ryght?"

"Well, I wouldn't go that far. But — "

The bitterness began to enter her voice. "How farh would you go, Harry? Y'all used to go pretty farh. Every week! Remembah? And then you disappee-ah for over a yee-ah and then just becauze some low-life gets himself killed, you dare show up hee-ah as if nothin' happened!? As if you hadn't jilted little ole me!? Or is that jist how y'all go 'bout your bizness?"

Well, technically speaking, I'm not certain the word "jilt" would apply to a married woman getting it on the side but I knew better than to quibble over semantics with an angry southern lady. I did what any man would do in a similar situation. I lied. "I was looking for something more serious than a fling, dollface. I was just your flavor-of-the-week and in time you would have replaced me."

"What did y'all expect little ole me to do, Harry?" She leaned forward in anger, inadvertently revealing her luscious breasts. Mr. Johnson reacted like a champion racehorse just out of the gate:

'And it's Mr. Johnson by a length moving up fast on the inside!' Her
blue eyes narrowed and her breasts heaved. "Did y'all expect
little ole me to dump mah multi-millionaire husband for some
sleezebag, disreputable, luv-em-and-leave-em, private eyeahh who
didn't have two satang to rub togethah?"

At least now I had the high moral ground. I was leading her
to believe she had dumped me instead of the other way around. I
glanced out the window. Just as I did, a stealthy figure, the same
one I'd noticed skulking about since this case began, raced across
a roof and disappeared. Whoever was following me certainly
didn't want me out of his sight. This case was beginning to stink.
In fact, I hadn't smelled such a stench since Whore House Charlie
fell (or was pushed) from the roof of a Thonburi brothel into a
bin full of durian.

"A man was killed, Betty-lou. A man who was almost as great
a legend as Whore House Charlie. And your husband was seen
arguing with him."

She knit her perfectly plucked brows. "Brothel Billy was
tryin' to git more money for his shares in the Horny Toad and
that is no doubt the cause for any unpleasantness between them.
Mah husband and ah could tear the Horny Toad down and
build a 34-story skahscraper."

"And Brothel Billy wouldn't sell?"

"Sure he would sell. But he wanted too much. You should
leave my husband out of this and chase aftah whoever inherited
Brothel Billy's shares."

"His shares?"

"Yes, his shares. That person would have the motive for killing
him. You're a detective. Y'all must know who that is by now."

"Uh, oh, yeah, sure. But that's confidential." She had me there.
This opened up a whole new line of investigation. "Those pictures
on the wall out there — that the party at the Horny Toad?"

Dollface scooted off the desk, walked behind a partition to

another desk, fiddled in a drawer and returned. She handed me a package of prints. "Mah husband's assistant took them. Maybe a trained detective lyke yiu can fahnd somethin' that others couldn't."

Her voice reeked with sarcasm so I decided any comment would be superfluous.

She ran her fingers along the bulges of my perfectly sculpted chest. "I'll go powder mah nose," she said. Her lips formed a lascivious smile. "Then we'll go to mah place," she purred. "Y'all deserve a reward. Ah've still got the Real Estate Special, yah know."

Ah, yes, the glow-in-the-dark, red-and-black lingerie with the mesh stockings and purple garter belt and frilly white gloves and stiletto-heeled, knee-high, black leather boots. Not that I'm kinky, understand. But Mr. Johnson definitely deserved a treat. And after that I would make a surprise early morning visit to the Horny Toad. That way everyone above the bar would be asleep, allowing me to search for clues.

It didn't take long for Mr. Johnson to satisfy Betty-lou, he'd had experience. 'Nuff said? After I saw her fall asleep with that special thank-God-for-real-men smile on her face, I killed a few hours downing Singhas and fending off hookers in the Thermae. It was nearly three in the morning by the time I reached the Horny Toad. The yellow moon was full but parallel rows of clouds streaked across it making it look like a set of brass knuckles about to come crashing down on me.

I pried open a small window of a short hallway that led to the storeroom. Once inside, I snapped on my flashlight and began prowling about all the rooms. I wasn't certain what it was I was looking for. I just had that gut feeling that something wasn't right. Like when I barfined that girl from Patpong with a prominent Adam's apple and deep voice and she refused to take off her shorts in bed but was anxious to please in less orthodox ways.

But after searching for hours, I had come up empty. There

seemed to be nothing out of the ordinary. In fact, before the Horny Toad was a bar it had been an upscale brothel and before that the home of a Thai-Chinese importer. It still bore traces of its elegant past: At the center of the ceiling was a vault-shaped skylight; above the baseboard the walls had raised paneling, and the elaborate molding that ran along the walls just below the ceiling was the popular type known as egg-and-dart motif which, considering what went on during the sex shows, was highly appropriate.

I was about to call it a night when something glittered in the light of my beam. I moved closer and saw that it was a bullet in the wall, just beneath a window facing the *klong*. I shined my flashlight directly onto it. It was the bullet I had used to send the 'fuck you' lizard into eternity. It had gone right through Betty's office wall and lodged into the bar's wall. I felt about the area where it had entered, then noticed how rough the wood was in that section. It was then I realized my gut instinct was correct: I was onto something. Finally, after an hour or so of brilliant induction which would have astounded Sherlock Holmes himself, I made myself some coffee and woke up the girls. I told them to get dressed and come down to the bar area.

They arrived in various stages of dress and undress, a barefoot and braless Lek in a short skirt and T-shirt. Good Pork Betty yawned just as a passing mangda beetle headed her way. I waited for her to stop coughing and swearing and then I announced that I had discovered the identity of the murderer of Brothel Billy. A frisson of shock passed through the room like an electric current. The only sounds were the rhythm of the light rain on the roof, the sound of bugs tapping against the light bulb, and the wall lizards scampering about trying to do the nasty with one another. The room stank of stale beer, garlic, beetle nut and chilies.

And guilt.

Tears spilled from Lek's beautiful dark brown eyes as she stared at me. "Who, Harry? Who killed Brothel Billy?"

I pulled up a chair and straddled it. I stared back at her. "You did, Lek."

Chapter 5

For several seconds after I had accused her of killing Brothel Billy, Lek was stunned into silence. The room was so quiet you could hear a dildo drop. Then Lek exploded. "What you talk?! You crazy! I love Billy!"

"Yes, and I'm sure he loved you. In his own way. But Brothel Billy liked women. A lot. There was no way he could ever have been faithful to one woman. Just like the man who adopted him: Whore House Charlie. The durian never falls far from the tree. The bargirl never falls far from the bed. The dildo never — well, anyway, I think finally you couldn't take it anymore. So you killed him."

"You crazy! How I could kill Brothel Billy? I just a girl."

"That's right, Lek. You're a girl. And girls have weapons. Trollops pack wallops. I thought it was a bit strange that someone as experienced as you would want to practice her act for a week. At no pay! What bargirl does anything for no money, Lek? But you were really only practicing one technique. Perfecting it, in fact! Projecting darts accurately to pop balloons."

"You crazy! *Bah bah bow bow!*"

"It had to be a perfect shot. And it was. You killed Billy by shooting him with a deadly dart from your venomous vagina!" Her beautiful eyes got real large. She started for me but Good Pork Betty pushed her back into her chair. "I gotta hand it to you. You were able to pull off the perfect murder. In front of a room full of people. And nobody noticed." I turned to Good

Pork Betty. "Betty, where exactly was Lek when she shot off the darts in the show?"

Betty walked to the stage and positioned herself by lying back. I walked to her and gestured from her legs to the closed window across the room. The one on the *klong* side. "You see, Lek? You had a direct line of fire."

"You crazy! That window always closed!"

"Sure it is. But not for that shot. For that one shot the window was open." I removed the photographs of the party from my pocket and showed her one. Above several drunken *farangs* and several happy bargirls sitting at tables covered with beers and ladies drinks was an open window.

I turned to Oy. I could see the fear in her eyes. "And you, Oy, were in on it. Someone had to open that window. That was your job." Oy started to protest but I held up another picture to her and then to Good Pork Betty. In the photograph, Oy was almost an unrecognizable blur as she reached up to shut the window.

Lek was almost beside herself now. "You crazy! How I know when Billy he walk by outside?"

"You didn't. But that's where Noy came in." Noy jerked upward in her chair like a Levitra-enhanced erection. "She must have told Billy she had to talk with him about something very important. So she positioned him perfectly; just like you'd all practiced for a week. She knew exactly where to stand to make certain he would be in the line of fire facing toward the canal. Just like actors marking their spots on stage before a performance. But an audience was the last thing you wanted. And then you covered it all up by bashing his head in to conceal the dart wound. Very clever, girls."

I walked around the room, touching the painting below the window. "I've seen how accurately you pop balloons with darts, Lek, you're a natural shot. Even the girls at the Long Gun can't hold a candle to you. Inner thigh ordnance and love button bazookas are your specialty. But for this shot it took a while even for you to get the range. You needed time to perfectly hone your magic muscles of murder. Hundreds of misses nicked the wall around the window. And those nicks had to be covered up. You girls didn't paint the room to make it brighter; but to conceal a murder. And, to avoid suspicion, you had to paint faces around *all* the windows. And you don't have stomach cramps, Lek. That was a clever cover story. I'll bet dollars to donuts, baht to bagels, mangoes to murder, durians to dildoes, your honeypot is sore from all the practice."

I let that sink in before continuing. "You had it all figured, didn't you? A great shot, Lek. You even compensated correctly for windage. No LRPP sniper in Nam stalking a VC in the triple-canopy jungle ever made a better shot. You developed the perfect passion pit of punishment. And if it hadn't been for a 'fuck you' lizard making too much noise and a spaced-out secretary proud of her new Canon color S200SPx printer you might have got away with it. And if I check the Bar Girl Inheritance Records Bureau on *soi* Jaidee, I'll bet I'll find that you were in line to inherit Brothel Billy's shares in the Horny Toad."

I saw the look in Lek's eyes. She knew the jig was up. As those lovely brown almond eyes flooded with tears and anger, I knew there would be no more denials. I only hoped she wouldn't use Perry Mason TV cliches like, 'Yes, all right, I killed him. And you know what, I'm *glad!*'

"OK, I kill Billy. And you know what?"

I groaned.

"I be happy I kill him. He say he love me but he butterfly with every girl he see! I glad he dead!"

It was all too much for Good Pork Betty. The adopted son of Whore House Charlie murdered by someone she had trusted. She fainted, collapsing in a disheveled heap.

"I'm ashamed of you, Lek. You should know vaginas are to

give life, not take life." I turned to Noy and Oy. "I'm surprised at you two, too. I would have thought ladies of your caliber would never get involved in something like hairy pie homicide. A woman's tunnel of love was meant for lust, not liquidation. But let this be a lesson for you: there's a very thin line between love and hate. Human passions can — "

I had foolishly taken my eye off Lek, and the sound of Lek's silk panties sliding down her smooth legs registered just a second too late. Lek had darted (no pun intended) into a corner, lifted up her flimsy skirt and placed a tube inside what literary Chinese in Bangkok's Chinatown might refer to as her Cave of the White Tiger. She faced me with her lovely lethal legs apart. The dart inserted firmly in the tube between them was aimed straight at my heart.

"Get your hands up, Harry."

I could tell from the hatred in her eyes that she meant business. If she ever released that Death Dart from the silky silo of destruction between her gorgeous legs, I was finished. There was little any man could do against a miniature Cape Canaveral run amuck. I raised my hands.

"Noy, get his gun."

Noy hesitated but started walking toward me. I knew if I let them have my gun, it was all over. Even if I lived I would be the laughing stock of the Bangkok bar scene. How would I face the crowd at Nana Plaza? Or the Nanapong boys? Or at Jool's? Or at Washington Square's Texas Lone Staar Saloon? Who would ever buy me a beer again? And, it went without saying, I'd never have another case.

It was suicidal but I had to act. I reached for my revolver. Too late. I heard the whoosh of the dart as it left its lunchbox launchpad and headed directly for me. By the time my hand touched the butt of the gun, the pointed object of my destruction was already flying across the room heading straight for me like a heat-seeking missile. There wasn't time to run or to duck. I knew I was finished. Slings and arrows and darts of outrageous fortune sooner or later find every man in Bangkok. In one form or another. I barely had time to wonder how the headline would read in the *Bangkok Post*. 'Farang Murdered; Dartist Flees the Scene.' I wondered if Trink would mention it in his website column: 'Punters should bend an elbow over at the Horny Toad run by publican Good Pork Betty; a watering hole with cold beer, beautiful hoofers and they've got a great darts team. Nuff said?'

I had solved the Case of the Honey Pot Projectiles, but it looked like it would be my last.

Chapter 6
The Stunning Conclusion

The tip of the Death Dart was but a few inches from my throat when, suddenly, an elderly but incredibly spry Caucasian leapt from the doorway, and flung himself right in front of me. With the speed of lightning, he thrust out his hand and the dart lodged deeply into his palm. An inch from my throat.

Blood began dripping down his fingers. He pulled out the dart, snapped it in two, and threw it to the floor. Then he unhurriedly licked up the blood on his palm. I knew I had seen him before. Then it hit me: He was the man who'd been following me since this case began! The shadowy figure!

I could tell he was packing a gun. In fact he was concealing several. I could detect a belt holster, an inside-the-pants holster at his crotch, a shoulder holster, an ankle holster and a small-of-the-back holster. At least I hoped it was an inside-the-pants holster, otherwise he was a little too happy to see me. His belt was lined with several speedloader pouches, a Rambo knife, a Roy Rogers secret decoder ring and a beer bottle opener.

"You're the shadowy figure who's been following me," I said. "Who the hell are you?"

He gave me what I can only describe as a rueful smile. "You were only a pissant kid last time I saw you, Boro."

"Only my friends call me — " I stared at him. The freckles. The blue eyes. The Huck Finn grin. "Oh, my God, it can't be! Whore House Charlie!"

"The very same."

Whore House Charlie had been a legend long before he disappeared in the late 60's, about the time of Jim Thompson's disappearance. Charlie had had the brilliance to buy up broken-down, mosquito-infested, rat-infested, ant-infested, wooden brothels with holes in the roofs and to combine them with solariums in which the beneficial rays of the sun warmed and caressed the two (and often more) bodies writhing in ecstasy on the luxurious beds below. His redecorated and refurbished solarium-and-brothel houses were converted into a string of modern and healthful brothelariums which became an instant success.

"What the hell you doing here, Charlie?"

"I'm takin' over this case."

"On whose authority?"

"I'm a private detective and I been on this case since I first learned of the murder."

"A detective! But what about your string of brothelariums?"

"Sold those off long ago to a guy who wanted to disappear, kid."

"Oh my, God. You don't mean — "

"I don't mean nothin', kid. When a man wants to disappear, what he does is his business."

"But where have you been all these decades?"

"Undercover. You got a problem with that?"

I thought about how the Thai police always make the perpetrator reenact the crime. And how it might actually be dangerous to be around Lek when she shot yet another dart during the re-enactment. After all, she was goin' down for Murder One and she had nothing to lose if she took me out as well. That's when I remembered the wisdom of my old granddad. Just before they hanged him, he turned to me and said, 'Boy, always beware of whores with sores and tarts with darts.' I realized I had nothing to gain from personally bringing these debauched dancers with vindictive vaginas downtown to the Big House. If this shamus with a Huck Finn grin wanted to claim credit for solving the Case of the Homicidal Harlets, what the hell.

"All right, Charlie," I said, "it's your case; take 'em away. I'll wake up Good Pork Betty. She'll be mighty happy to see you again."

"No. Let her sleep." His eyes seem to mist over as he stared at the heap on the floor. "I still love her but it's better she doesn't know I was here. I'm shacked up with 22-year-old twins from Nakorn Pathom and they're jealous as hell." He blew Betty a kiss and then pointed to the door. "All right, girls, let's go. No sudden moves."

The three girls headed out the door followed by Charlie. I called out to him. "Hey, Charlie."

He turned and looked at me.

"Thanks for saving my life."

"Don't mention it," he said. "This is nothing compared to my cases in Bangkok during the war."

As he stepped into the next room, out of my line of vision, I heard the girls' voices. "Oh, Charlie, you so stlong!" "Charlie, this your gun?" "Charlie, you so BIIIGGG!"

And I heard Charlie's voice: "Hey! Knock it off! Stop that! Oh! Oh! Oooohhhhhh!"

And I figured, despite what they had done, there was no way those girls would end up behind bars. But whatever their fate, I knew the Horny Toad was finished. I looked about the room that had served generations of horny men so well, and then walked over to Good Pork Betty. I kicked her awake. I helped her up and she placed my hand on her shoulder. I knew I would have to lie so I crossed my fingers behind my back. "The authorities have taken Lek away, Betty."

"But the bar will be closed now, Harry. What I do?"

"You'll find another job," I said. "A woman with your skills can get hired anywhere."

She looked up at me with mournful eyes. "I think you know before who kill Brothel Billy. How you know, Harry?"

"I wasn't sure, Good Pork. But I worked a similar case down in Manila. You remember Virgin Valdez and the Case of the Murderous Muff Maidens?"

Her eyes widened. Sure, she remembered Virgin Valdez, all right. They had been hot competitors for the affections of Whore House Charlie at one time. "I remember."

"Well, she killed a man at the Spider's Web Bar in Manila the same way. I figured this might be a similar case of a catapulting cunt."

"She dead now?"

"No, Good Pork, but don't worry, she'll be behind bars for a long time to come."

Well, strictly speaking that was true. Nobody in Manila would let her work *inside* bars anymore, so now she performed her special services behind them. I figured it wouldn't hurt to let Good Pork think her old adversary was in prison.

I went to the window and looked out at the stagnant *klong*. The stench hit me in the nostrils like a physical blow. I always wondered why they called this city "The Big Mango." It should be something like, "The Big Rambutan" or "The Big Jackfruit" or "The Big Durian." Yeah, that was it: The Big Durian. It stinks to high heaven, and some love it, some hate it. Just like the fruit. Me, I love it. And the more rotten it is, the more I feel at home: huMAn NatURE.

I suddenly felt more weary than ever. I had solved the Case of the Blow-dart Beavers but that wouldn't bring Brothel Billy back to life. Whore House Charlie had disappeared decades ago, suddenly reappeared, and now I had no doubt he was about to disappear again. By brilliant inductive reasoning and the playing of hunches, I had put Lek's lethal love pouch out of business for good. But I felt sad. As if a part of me was missing. And that reminded me of my missing ATM card. I'd have to find Dang and then it would be time to hit Soi Cowboy again. Or, better yet, the Darling Massage parlor. Maybe two for one in a sandwich with lots of slide-and-glide. And if you don't know what slide-and-glide is, fuck you, because I'm not gonna explain every goddamn thing.

This concludes *Murder at the Horny Toad Bar* — A Harry Boroditsky Mystery. We hope you enjoyed it. If you did, please tell your friends; if you didn't, *please notify your local private eye immediately.*

The Case of the Uneven Playing Field

When the school librarian led me into the rare book room, locked the door, threw her arms around me and passionately kissed me, I suspected she wanted something. We had been lovers in college but ever since I'd moved to Bangkok I hadn't seen much of her. In a desperate attempt to forget about me, she'd become a mystery writer and librarian and joined Suspects in Custody (SinC). But I could see the look of hunger in her eyes. I couldn't help but wonder why she'd sent that urgent e-mail begging me to visit her in California. A matter, she said, of life and death.

She was dressed in the usual style of the modern librarian: fuschia-streaked hair, nose ring, lip ring, studded leather neck collar, studded velvet-trimmed black leather blouse, short black skirt, plaid socks, sling-back sandals trimmed with fur. Each of her fingernails had been painted a different color.

I pried her hungry, tattooed arms from around my muscular, well-tanned body. "Take it easy," I said, "I've still got jetlag." Truth to tell I had had quite a night at Bangkok's Patpong Road before just making the flight but I had long ago learned that truth is just one of many things that seemed to upset women, so, for their sake, I usually avoided it.

"You don't like me anymore, Harry?" she asked.

"Sure, sweetheart," I said, "I like you just fine. In fact, if I could relive my life, I'd marry a librarian."

"That sounds like a great title for an autobiography, Harry," she said.

"Or a song."

She patted me on the behind. "Or a bumper sticker." She grew suddenly still.

"Something wrong?" I asked.

"No. Just listen."

I listened. I didn't hear much of anything.

"Can't you hear it?" She asked. "The sound of pages being turned, books being checked out, people *reading*. Have you ever heard a more beautiful sound than that, Harry?"

Actually, I had. In a Thai canal-side brothel lying in bed with two beautiful and kinky sisters from Buriram while the wind blew and sheets of rain slammed into the tin-and-thatch roof. But my finely honed detective instincts told me this was not the time to mention it. "Never, I said."

I glanced at the books lining the wall behind her desk. It was either the mystery section or a recipe section; these days it was hard to tell. "So what was it you wanted to see me about, doll?"

She looked out the window. "The playing field."

"What about it?"

"It's not level."

I stared at the playing field. "It looks level to me," I said.

She sat down on the near corner of the table, a move which did nothing to conceal her gorgeous gams. "Oh, well, that's because you're a white heterosexual male who's been suppressing women for thousands of years and you can't see it . . . Nothing personal."

It was talk like that that made me remember why I loved Bangkok. But I gave her my best Boroditsky smile. "I never take nothing personally, kid. Any suspects?"

"We suspect that the invisible conspiracy of white heterosexual males which has been suppressing women for thousands of years has been favoring men over women when it comes to being pub-

lished in the mystery field. That's why the field's not level."
I chuckled.

She cracked her knuckles and knit her perfectly plucked brows.
"Something funny?"

"Sweetheart, the publishing business has become even more
dirty and callous and bottom line than the private eye business.
It's *all* bottom line, sweetheart. Look what happened to Parnell
Hall. If publishers drop guys like him, how can you say the dice
are loaded in men's favor? And do you really think Robert Parker
wanted to start a series with a female detective, Sunny Randall,
no less? He knew which side of his bread was — "

She looked through me as if I'd made a non-sequiturial remark about the weather. Her flimsy skirt offered little resistance
as she crossed her not unattractive legs, reminding me of the days
when she dressed up for me as a slatternly airline hostess. Not
that I'm kinky, understand.

There was a husky determination in her voice. A determined
huskiness, you might say. A sensual hoarseness like the D.A.
dame on *Law and Order*. "So, will you take the case?"

Truth is, I needed the money. And this wouldn't be the first
client who didn't let facts stand in the way of their theories. If I
only took cases from well adjusted clients, I wouldn't have any
cases at all. Besides, the sooner I wrapped this case up, the sooner
I could get back to Land of Smiles.

"All right, doll, you got yourself a detective."

She jumped up and started to wrap her arms around me again.
Truth to tell, she was a good looking Sheila. But the
Death-by-Taco-Bell-Twilight perfume she wore was the same my
ex-wife used to wear just before she went to the Big House and
that gave me the strength to resist.

I pried her aching arms from my perfectly sculpted, masculine
torso. "I got work to do, doll. And you know what they say
about relationships that begin in the rare book room. They rarely

work out."

She pouted. "As a comedian you're a bust, Harry. I glanced down at her Wonderbra. "As a bust, you're a comedian."

"Get out of here and start working the case before I cancel your subscription to *Library Journal*, you animal!"

I left the library while wiping Nevada Sunrise lipstick off my lips and chin. This was one of the strangest cases that had ever come my way and I had a feeling that if I couldn't break it, it would break me.

Sure, I know, my name sucks: I had an Italian father half Polish on his Romanian mother's side and an Irish mother half Caucasian on her Eurasian brother's side. Friends just call me Boro. Enemies call me Ditsky. But not for long. If you get my drift. And I was determined to get to the bottom of this case. If it was the last thing I did.

The next day dawned bright and sunny. Condom-grey clouds scudded across a Viagra-blue sky. I made my way across town to the Association of Literary Agents. I figured maybe here I could discover the male conspiracy that operated undetected inside the publishing industry.

At first, the secretary with the green hair and military camouflage makeup didn't want to open up their books but when I mentioned I was working on behalf of women mystery writers, she got friendly. A little too friendly, if you catch my drift. A gentleman doesn't kiss and tell, but let's just say from the taste, I'd say her lipstick was Turquoise Entrapment. I knew that because my last secretary had been wearing exactly that when the cops found her in that sleazy, end-of-the-line, hotel room in Pattaya Beach. But, no, it seemed that the majority of literary agents, especially those handling fiction, were women.

So I made my way over to the Publishers Association. I figured this might well be the place. But I found that the vast majority of editorial assistants — those people who decide if a manuscript will be sent up the chain of command — were young women from Smith and Vassar and places like that. And they loved women writers. And the majority of associate editors and editors who worked in the mystery field were also women.

One of them eyed me suspiciously. She was a real tomato: a tall brunette wearing a skirt about the size of Long John Silver's eye patch. "Aren't you Harry Boroditsky?" she asked.

"Sure," I said.

"I knew your first wife."

I tried not to stare in the direction of her gorgeous gams. "Oh, yeah?"

"She said you never put the toilet seat down during the entire marriage."

"My first wife was an Akha hilltribe woman and we lived in the Golden Triangle where there were only squat toilets," I said. "Nobody had toilet seats."

"That's the dumbest story I've ever heard."

"Yeah, but you'll have to admit it's a story with legs." Whoops. "I mean, a-legedly. I mean allegedly."

"Get out of here, Harry."

I knew when to take a hint. Every great P.I. does. Anyway, I still had to check the statistics on active buyers of mysteries. But again the news was bad: More women than men.

This wasn't going well. Not well at all. If I didn't find something to confirm my client's theory, I might not receive my paycheck, not to mention other less conventional forms of remuneration. If you get my drift. But I had one card left to play.

I headed back to the library. It was lunchtime and nobody was at the desk. Dollface and I were supposed to meet for lunch but she had called and postponed our meeting because she was having lunch with the Women Oppressed by White Heterosexual Ignoble Males Support Group. (WowHim). The Ladies Who

Lunch, as Sondheim might say.

I quickly checked through back issues of *Publishers Weekly*, the special mystery sections. I hoped to discover that macho Mike Hammer-type detectives were all the rage, but there it was: "Well, now that the white heterosexual male detective in an urban environment has gone the way of the dinosaur . . ."

Of all the lousy luck. The mystery field was completely open to any talented woman or man provided New York publishers thought they could sell at least thirty thousand copies of a hard-cover novel. And since most novels didn't sell that many, most manuscripts of either sex were rejected. But from what I had uncovered, there had never been a better time to be a female mystery author with a female protagonist. In fact, contrary to what it had been like when Ray and Dash and Mac were alive, women writers and/or women detectives almost seemed to be preferred. But I knew I couldn't sell that to my client. I had to come up with something. And fast!

I knew I needed help with this one and made some quick phonecalls. But Matt Scudder had left to attend a meeting for people addicted to AA meetings; Meyer said Travis McGee was off on his boat doing the nasty with some young chick who would eventually be killed but whose demise Travis would avenge; his third wife said that Judge Dee was practicing his calligraphy with his fourth wife and couldn't be disturbed; and I knew if I involved Coffin Ed and Grave Digger Jones, they might just start shooting everybody in the library to insure they got whoever was guilty.

So I decided to drop in on an old friend living in retirement at the edge of town. It was dark by the time I got there. The Cialis-yellow quarter-moon curved bosom-like against the night sky. The stars twinkled as brightly as the glitter on a go go dancers face. I knocked on his door. A raspy voice from inside said: "Velma?"

"No, Moose," I said. "It's Harry. I got a job for you." Moose Malloy wasn't exactly what you would call the intellectual giant of our age; he would never be invited to host a Nanapong Dance Contest; but I knew he was the one man who could help me. And if I told him it was something Velma wanted, he'd do it.

We worked all night. He at his assigned task, me at mine. It was rough, but by morning we were both finished. Just in time. I headed for the library.

Dollface was sitting at her desk when I walked in. She wore a bright red dress with a pearl and jade necklace. A colorful parrot was perched on her shoulder. I dropped the large grey envelope in front of her. She gave me a strange look, the kind she used to give me when I would buy interesting but skimpy outfits for her to wear, then she opened it. "These look like . . . birth certificates."

"They are," I said.

"They are!" the parrot said.

"But, what — "

"Take a good look at them." I pointed to the one on top.

"Parnell Hall? But, what — "

"Look more closely at the name."

Her eyes widened. "Parnella?"

"Parnella?" the parrot said, spreading its wings in shock.

"That's right, Angel Eyes. Parnella Hall. And this one."

"Roberta Parker!"

"Right. And look at all the rest. Male mystery writers who have been dropped by their publishers. Only they weren't born male. Every single one was born a woman. And every single one underwent GRS — Gender Reassignment Surgery! When their publishers found out their little secret, they were dropped. Only those making too much dough were kept on."

"This is incredible! I knew at mystery conferences something was strange about Parnell Hall's singing! And what about male mystery writers who have had their novels rejected?"

"You were right all along, glamour puss. The fix is in. They get paid money under the table to get 'rejected' so as to make it look as if its not fixed in favor of men. The truth is, the mystery publishing field is as phony as a Jesse Ventura wrestling match."

"I knew it! You see? Harry, you're wonderful!" She jumped up and kissed me hard on the lips. I recognized the brand of lipstick by taste: Heat Wave a la Mode. The same kind my ex-Thai girlfriend had on the day I dropped the dime on her and the Thai cops took her off to the Big House by the *Klong*. "I can't wait to tell WowHim!"

This is where I knew it could get a bit tricky. "That might not be smart, sweetheart."

"Not smart," the parrot said.

She eyed me suspiciously. "Why?"

"You wouldn't 'out' a gay person who didn't want to be outed, would you? For whatever reason, these women carry them-selves off as men. They deserve their privacy. But at least you'll have the satisfaction of knowing that you were right. Of know-ing that you're not in reality a self-indulgent whiner, a self-centered, strident, puritanical, humorless fanatic wallowing in self-pity; a constant complainer with the IQ of a dying Breadfruit tree in northeast Thailand during a particularly severe drought, blaming your problems on a non-existent uneven playing field controlled by men. You'll know that you were right all along. Isn't that satisfaction enough?"

She thought for a long moment. "You're right, Harry. But I am going to tell everyone about how male authors who are rejected are paid off under the table."

"Sure, doll, you do that."

"Do you think people will believe me?"

"Why not?" I said. 'Send in the Clowns,' I thought. I turned to the window. "And take a look outside," I said. "The playing field."

"Oh my God, it's uneven!"

"Uneven!" the parrot said.

"It sure is."

"I knew scheming men were behind an uneven playing field!"

"You got that right, sweetcheeks."

"I'll go powder my nose," she said. Her lips formed a lascivious smile. A wave of her Hungry-Tigress-on-the-Prowl perfume hit my nostrils. "Then we'll go to my place," she purred. "You deserve a reward. I've still got the Librarian Special, you know."

As she walked off, the parrot shifted its weight on her shoulder and glared back at me, as if he was privy to my dirty little secret. That's when I realized it wasn't a parrot at all. It was a falcon. Which was fine with me because falcons don't squawk. Maltese or otherwise.

But I had done my job well and now I would have my reward. I smiled, remembering the last time she dressed up in her 'librarian special': the glow-in-the-dark, red-and-black lingerie with the mesh "overdue-brand" stockings and purple "check-me-out-brand" librarian garter belt and frilly white gloves and stiletto-heeled, knee-high, black leather boots. Not that I'm kinky, understand.

I glanced out the window. Men sure were behind the uneven playing field. At least one man. Moose Malloy. While I had been doctoring documents, he had worked all night to transfer earth from one side to the other. I had told him his Velma would be proud. And, sure enough, what Moose didn't know, was that before she disguised herself as a librarian my sweetheart had been his Velma. She didn't get that necklace on her librarian's salary.

In fact, dollface had entered the Witness Protection Program. A little known fact is that most librarians are actually people who dropped the dime on some badass hoodlums somewhere and were trained as librarians and placed in the Witness Protection Program.

Librarians: you can't live with them; you can't live without them. Sure, she was a little ditsky. They all were. But I'm Harry Boroditsky and this is one librarian who fits me like a glove. If you get my drift.

And, yeah, I cooked the books a bit about my findings. But hey, the client was happy; and she was about to make me happy. Isn't that the way all cases should end?

This concludes *The Case of the Uneven Playing Field*, a Harry Boroditsky Mystery. We hope you enjoyed it; if so, please tell your friends; if not, *kindly inform your local librarian immediately*.

MURDER AT THE HORNY TOAD BAR & OTHER OUTRAGEOUS TALES OF THAILAND

Memoirs of An Oversexed *Farang*

"This need. This derangement. Will it never stop? I don't even know after a while what I'm desperate for. Her tits? Her soul? Her youth? Her simple mind? Maybe it's worse than that — maybe now that I'm nearing death, I also long secretly not to be free."

— *The Dying Animal,* Philip Roth

"When I first began writing, I knew that my female characters were very, very weak and unconvincing, and I thought, what's the best way to really improve that? The best way is to have relationships with a lot of different women. The best way to do that is to pick up whores."

— William Vollman, author, *New York Times* interview

The Art of Closing the Deal

"Hello."

"Oh. Hello."

"Can I sit here?"

"Um, yeah, sure."

"You come this bar before?"

"Um, maybe once."

"What your name?"

"Harry. Harry Boroditsky."

"My name Nong."

"Hi, Nong."

"Where you come from?"

"America."

"OK. I happy America."

"You happy America?"

"Yes."

"OK. I happy Thailand."

"What hotel you stay, Ailley?"

"I live in Bangkok now."

"You have apartment?"

"Yeah."

"How long you live Bangkok?"

"This time? Three years."

"You have wife?"

"No."

"What you do?"

"I'm Bangkok's greatest but least principled detective."

"OK. You want Nong go with you?"

"I'm sorry, Nong, you are very pretty and your curves are in all the right places and I appreciate your lifting your bikini top to demonstrate your remarkable assets, but unless it's absolutely necessary as a way to solve a client's case, professional detectives do not indulge in the sensistic impressions of the phenomenal world nor would we ever — "

"I can give you special."

"Oh. Why didn't you say so? Let's get the hell out of here."

Why We Love Them

Richard, a *farang* friend of mine, passed away recently but for many years he was happily married to a lovely Thai lady. I mention him because a year or so before he died, he told me that his Thai wife was so upset with my photobook *Thailand: Land of Beautiful Women* that she couldn't stop badmouthing it. Well, I thought, the late writer, Kingsley Amis, said something like: If your writing hasn't pissed anybody off it probably isn't any damn good. So I didn't mind. Besides, as all writers eventually learn: controversy sells books; silence sells nothing.

But then he told me something incredible: There was a discussion group formed at Thammasat University especially to condemn my book! And he knew this because his wife, a magazine editor, had taken part.

A discussion group held by professional, young Thai women just to denounce me! I couldn't believe it — my ego soared! In fact, I found it to be a very definite turn-on, and it wasn't only my ego that soared. But then I thought — why didn't they invite me? My God, can you imagine the scene?

Beautiful, curvaceous, succulent middle-and upper-middle class Thai women on a university campus sitting around a table in their middle-and upper-middle class outfits and perfumes and hairdos and high-heeled shoes and they are ALL GATHERED TO CENSURE ME ME ME ME!

Can you just imagine their well-scrubbed, perfectly perfumed, lovely jade-white, Thai-Chinese, flawless, goddess-like, complexions ? Their perfectly pressed Gucci business suits, Racket Club slacks, Salvatore Ferrugamo dresses, Yves St. Laurent skirts, Versace blouses, Charles Jourdan matching handbag and shoes, Prada purses, and *maybe* even a few *school uniforms*! Their pleated navy blue office skirts rising up their long, lovely jade-white, Thai-Chinese legs as they cross them; all the while, fervently, passionately, fervidly denouncing ME! The mind boggles! *And nobody invited me!!* Why? What did I do wrong? Please, lovely ladies, if in the future you want to hold a DENUNCIATION SESSION OF DEAN BARRETT, please, *please*, *please* invite me as guest of dishonor.

I mean I would have been the first one to suggest I needed to be punished for what I did. Yep. No question about it. Just be kinky and creative in your punishment is all I would have asked. You would have found me repentant and willing to take my medicine. We could have adjourned the meeting and reassembled at the Cave bar on *soi 33*. But, hell, not inviting me to an all-Thai-female discussion group denouncing my book is cruel and unusual punishment.

So these gorgeous creatures are sitting about drinking coffee and tea out of, well, out of what? Fine china, maybe? Styrofoam cups? Dunno. But I bet they had a small dish of some kind of refreshments. Some Thai desert, maybe: coconut pudding in banana leaf cups or maybe Thai cookies. Or maybe they just grabbed a few bags of shrimp-flavored potato chips from the 7-Eleven. Shrimp-flavored potato chips always go good with denunciation sessions of Dean Barrett.

OK, so there they are around the table: now picture those perfect, dazzling bright, sparkling white teeth sinking into the smooth, creamy white coconut pudding enclosed within the tiny forest green banana leaf cups, a bit of white rice flour stuck to their full, warm, lustrous, perfectly formed red lips; lips expertly coated with lip gloss — a watermelon shade, maybe, or perhaps orange toffee or honey rose; and they naturally brush the bit of white rice flour away with their soft, tender pink tongues or deftly dislodge it with one long, delicate, professionally manicured, perfectly varnished, fingernail — their healthy, glowing, blush-hued, cheeks made smooth with Revlon New Complexion Skin Defense Softener, and their female deity bodies glowing with vitamin-enriched moisturizing gels, soft-texture cleansing foams, anti-dehydration toners, and various skin-whitening emulsions.

The room replete with earthy and warm and sensual feminine scents mingling with the seductive flowery fragrances of the most mysterious of perfumes and cologne sprays — pink peony, amber, mango musk, sandalwood, lily of the valley, rose, orange, peach, orchid, honey, and, of course, night jasmine. The mind boggles! And the lovely feminine scents a bit more evident than normal perhaps because of their impassioned umbrage and righteous anger at none other than yours truly!

All the while the light-complexioned, perfectly groomed, provocatively scented, Thai women — the reddish pink of indignation just visible beneath the soft beige Revlon Love Pat moisturizing powder covering their cute-as-a-button cheeks — are furrowing their lovely brows and, in distaste, pursing their smooth, full Maybelline wet-shined lips, and beneath soft, supple, lashes made longer with L'Oreal Longitude Lash Out Mascara and above Revlon's "brazen berry" eyeshadow, looking down at (and down on) the women pictured in my book: equally beautiful dark-complexioned *Essarn* women — ricefield workers, construction workers, highway sweepers, beach sweepers, fishermen's daughters, farmer's daughters, hill tribe women, classical dancers and go go dancers. If *that* scene isn't an incredible turn-on, if *that* portrait isn't the gateway to Erection City, I don't know what the hell is.

Oh, sure, Hemingway, Henry Miller, Bukowski, they all had their fan clubs but *me* — I get my very own Denunciation Discussion Group! Wherever they are, I'll bet those other writer guys are eating their hearts out.

But the best part is yet to come. Because Richard told me he had bought my first photo book decades ago, *The Girls of Thailand*. And his wife was aware of the fact that, despite her denunciation of *Thailand: Land of Beautiful Women*, Richard had always liked *The Girls of Thailand* book.

And his birthday was coming up. So guess what his wife bought him for his birthday? You guessed it: a copy of *Thailand: Land of Beautiful Women*. "Go figure," said Richard.

I ask you: Is it any wonder why we love these women?

They're Everywhere!

She is lovely. Pure Thai. Beautiful chocolate brown skin, light blue top, black trousers, white shoes, long black hair pulled back by a ribbon. She stares at me and smiles, then whispers something to the one standing next to her. The attractive one dressed all in white. I think she has chosen a kind of dress to resemble a nurse, no doubt figuring her customers will go for it.

They both turn to me and smile shyly. Then she approaches me and flashes me a big Thai smile. Her cheekbones are so high aircraft probably have to be warned away when she is in the area. I have not seen her in here before. Perhaps she hasn't worked here long. "Excuse me," she says.

Of course I will excuse you, my succulent lovely. You can have any drink you like. I will barfine you in a New York minute. Despite our age difference you and I will have the greatest love affair since Humbert Humbert and Lolita. Since Abselom and whatshername. Since — "

"When did you have your last urination?"

Say what? Oh! Right! I forgot. I'm not in a bar. While waiting for an ultrasound of the abdomen at Bumrungrad Hospital, I forgot that not all Thai girls (especially nurses) ask foreign men for a lady's drink. Sorry about that: force of habit. As Kurt Vonnegut would say, "so it goes . . . ."

A few days later at the same hospital, my doctor asks me if I would chat for a few minutes with a young doctor about to go to the States who needs to practice her English. Sweetheart of a guy that I am, I agree.

I enter a small room and there is a cute 22-year-old who says she is going to do her residency in Washington or somewhere. I mean, she is *really* cute! She in her white coat, me in my blue shorts and plaid T-shirt. We chat a bit, maybe for five minutes when she motions toward one of those small bed/gurneys and asks "May I examine you?"

WHAT! Say what! The most beautiful four words I had ever heard. Apparently, she needs to make sure her English is good enough when examining patients. She's not sure of herself. A lady in distress needs help. What could I do?

I lie on my back and she starts unbuttoning my shirt asking me to correct her as she speaks to me about where the pain might be, etc. She begins to press on my chest, then stomach, then asks me to loosen my belt, then finally she says, "Now I will palpate your abdomen." Oh, yes, there is a God. This gorgeous creature is now going to PALPATE MY ABDOMEN. All in the name of medical science! And, sure enough, she begins her palpitations.

Up to this point, all had gone pretty well. But not long after she started palpating my abdomen, Johnny-among-the-maids (AKA Little Brain) woke up. He most likely assumed he was back at the Darling Massage Parlor or perhaps he thought he was back in the glory days of the late, much-lamented La Cherie Massage Parlor off Patpong. Whatever, he began to stir. I did my best to will him to be still. But Johnny-among-the-maids was up and about and determined to make his presence known. Coincidence or whatever, the doctor stopped palpating my abdomen, smiled and thanked me for helping her.

One day I will figure out if she was a good girl, too innocent to know what she was doing, or if she was a shameless flirt who just wanted to see if she could DT a *farang*.

Five minutes later, a female assistant taking my blood pressure pointed to the hair on my arm, smiled and said, "beautiful." Jesus Christ!

Bumrungrad is the most erotic hospital I have ever experienced. Once you've tired of Bangkok bars, try to get sick or get into some kind of accident so you can go to a Thai hospital. It's a great adventure.

Cambodian Women

According to my Thai visa, I have to leave Thailand every three months. I often go to Cambodia. I like to go to Cambodia because that is where I can still beat the bargirls in pool. Thai bargirls are damn good at this game. They play it every day and more often than not they whup my behind on the pool table. Especially the lesbian type — the undersized, thick-set, roly-poly ones with hair cut short. Cut-rate jeans and no-nonsense top. Tough to win a game against them.

They easily sink ball after ball while their Significant Other — usually a gorgeous doll with long black hair and a perfect feminine figure I would crawl on shards of Singha Gold for — sits nearby and watches, occasionally favoring me with a lovely Thai smile. So the lesbian ("tom" in Thai) gets both the victory *and* the girl.

So it is that if I want to win a game of pool I have to fly to Cambodia. Sometimes, life is like that.

Cambodian bargirls are a lot easier to beat; maybe because they're starting from scratch, so to speak, no pun intended. Pol Pot and the other nutcase, murderous Khmer Rouge probably included pool players in the category of being "educated" and had them executed along with anyone wearing glasses or speaking English — hence the shortage in Cambodia of good pool players. So, anyway, I head for Cambodia in good spirits knowing that I might at last be able to beat somebody on the pool table.

I also like Cambodia because if it is possible that there are wackier women in the world than Thai women, it is here in Cambodia. Wackiness in a woman attracts me. And Cambodian women have it in spades.

So after I win five out of six games from a Cambodian girl working behind the bar of a kind of pub, she returns behind the bar and I sit at the bar nursing my Tiger beer while chatting her up. Her English is slow and broken but not bad. Which is good because my Cambodian is non-existent. I look her over and smile at her.

"You are very pretty, you know. You must have many boy-friends."

"No. No boyfriends."

"None at all?"

She shakes her head.

"But haven't you ever been with a man?"

She thinks that over for a minute. "Yes. I go with men. But they customers. Not boyfriend."

"Oh, I see. But you never had a boyfriend?"

"Never." She thinks again. "But I had husband."

"Oh. I see. You never had a boyfriend but you had a husband."

"Yes. But he no good. Hit me. I get police. We finish."

"OK." I pause to think that out and to take a hit on my beer. "But isn't it possible that sometime before you got married, your husband was your boyfriend?"

She shakes her head emphatically. "No! I *know* him. But he not boyfriend."

"Oh, I see. You knew him and then married him. Just kind of skipped the boyfriend step, right?"

"Yes."

Like I said, I've always been attracted to wacky women. Especially those I can beat on the pool table.

And now in Cambodia the North Koreans have opened up a

restaurant called Pyongyang. The other day I was walking past when two lovely North Korean waitresses were waving goodbye to a busload of Koreans.

As even my South Korean friends in America tell me, North Korean women are extremely innocent. There also seems to be something almost excessively wholesome about them. God knows, as an American GI stationed in Southeast Asia during the Vietnam War, I did my best to rid Asian women of excessive wholesomeness, and to prune it immediately whenever and wherever it cropped up, but, not unlike pestiferous crabgrass in a garden, it still appears.

I smiled and waved to the waitresses wondering if they would scowl at this green-eyed, long-nosed, foreign barbarian, moribund, decadent, bourgeois, imperialist, warmonger from across the Western Ocean. But they smiled back and gestured for me to enter the restaurant.

I thought of unleashing on them my entire three-sentence Korean vocabulary: "How's it going?" and "You are very beautiful" and "Eat two meals a day," (as opposed to three, a North Korean government admonition to its starving people). But I simply smiled and gestured to show I was too full already and waved goodbye.

Besides, mucking about with lovely North Korean women in a Cambodia full of lovely Cambodian and Vietnamese women might be like eating Death by Chocolate: too rich for a man my age. I mean, I have to draw the line somewhere.

Anyway, I figure I can always check out the Korean waitresses on my next trip. In fact, my goal is to get them to a bar with pool tables so I can see if I can whup them or not. Pool table diplomacy. If I can, I might fly to North Korea next trip and try my luck on the pool tables there.

Nana Plaza

The older I get the more I tend to sit *outside* go go bars and watch the action rather than inside and watch the girls dance. Because over the decades I have seen go go dancing until it has come out of my ears; and I often find it is outside the bars on places like *Soi* Cowboy and Nana Plaza where the show is at its best.

One night not long ago I was sitting at Lucky Lukes, along the rail of one of the open-air beer bars at Nana Plaza; the one not far from the shrines. It was about 6:30 at night and already Nana was coming to life. The bars' neon signs were lit up, the sequence of their lights timed to flicker or rotate or gyrate or whirl or twirl or spin or do whatever they could to attract attention. The huge red lips of the Red Lips bar pulsated away. The mirrors of several parked motorcycles reflected these lights in all directions.

Go go dancers in street clothes and street makeup walked by, eyeing the potential customers (and being eyed by them) and heading for their respective bars. Many stopped to *wai* the Buddhist and Brahman shrines, some lit incense or bought garlands or fruit from nearby vendors to place on the shrines. Others stood about deeply engrossed in cellphone conversations, no doubt assuring men overseas that, no, they definitely were not working in the bars anymore so please keep those checks and wire transfers coming.

Men of all shapes and sizes and ethnic backgrounds were walking in or sitting about the beer bars drinking beer and sharing laughs with the girls serving them, killing time while waiting for the dancing to start. Children chased one another around the bars, a bar girl holding a gigantic stuffed snake chased screaming bargirls about. A black cat sat on the roof of the Lollipop Bar silhouetted by the light of the second floor Hog's Breath Saloon. Several cats stalked and chased one another about the various wooden and tin roofs, delivery vans delivering bags of ice and crates of beer and soft drinks had somehow managed to squeeze past an elephant standing with its mahout near the entrance to the Plaza beside a stand selling snacks of beetles, crickets, scorpions, worms and other Thai delicacies.

The sounds of bargirls speaking English, Thai, Laotian and Cambodian mingled with those of the Germans, Americans, Koreans, Japanese and others speaking their languages. The TV's were loud (Yes, both kinds — televisions and transvestites) as were a few already inebriated foreign men with their shirts off.

A dwarf stood in front of one bar trying hard to guide locals and tourists inside, a one-armed Thai boy was saluting people with his stub, well made-up little girls were selling garlands, and shabby little boys offered to shine shoes. Hill tribe women in hill tribe costumes hawked hill tribe purses and clothing. There was the usual abundance of flowers sellers, peanut vendors, watch sellers, map-of-Thailand sellers, sexy-shaped-cigarette lighter sellers, wicker basket sellers, puppies-with-nodding-heads sellers, clothes sellers, stuffed toy sellers, loud sounds of the latest music, drunken laughter and motorcycle engines piercing an air tinged with humidity and reeking with eroticism.

I was simply sitting on my stool at the rail watching the action and drinking my Singha Gold when a well dressed Thai woman walked up to the rail and said, "Dean, hi, do you remember me?"

I have a terrible memory and try as I might I couldn't place her. I didn't think she was a dancer I had barfined recently because I hadn't done that for a long time, well, at least not for three or four nights.

It turned out she was the wife of an American fellow selling man-sized condoms in Thailand and I had met them both at a party. Nice people. She was here now (with her bodyguard) to sell condom machines to the bars. After we chatted a bit, she reached into a large box, scooped out a huge handful of condoms and gave them to me, then went off to do business.

I wasn't sure what I was supposed to do with that many condoms and had no place to put them so I simply kept them in my right hand while drinking beer with my left. Then a Thai woman holding a *luk-krung* baby walked up to the rail and handed the baby to the bargirl sitting next to me, no doubt a close friend.

The bargirl was wearing a back-revealing top which clearly revealed a scorpion tattoo on her right shoulder. She had been munching fried grasshoppers with *nam prik* and sauce and discarding only bits of legs before placing the entire grasshoppers in her mouth. Mmmmmm-good! They chatted for a minute while I made faces at the baby who stared at me as if I were from another planet.

The girl noticed me playing with the baby and without asking handed it to me. The baby sat in my lap, its shoulder supported by my left hand, my right hand still clutching the condoms. The baby was I think about seven months old and suddenly it leaned its head over and the bargirl started berating me about didn't I know how to hold a baby and didn't I know I was supposed to support the neck of a baby?

Well, no, actually, I didn't know how to hold a baby as I never had one and nobody told me little kids don't have enough common sense to hold their heads up without assistance. So I moved the baby a bit so my torso could support its neck and I held it from falling with my left hand but my right hand still had the condoms so there was no way I could take a swig of my beer and

— worse — meanwhile the ladyboys stopping to buy garlands observed me doing this and started giving me the eye because apparently they figured anybody kinky enough to hold a baby in one hand and a stack of condoms in the other would be up for anything.

I looked around Nana Plaza trying to see the ladyboys, vendors, bargirls, hill tribe women, tourists, drunkards, locals, elephant, cats, dwarf, one-armed boy, flashing go go signs, exotic shrines, etc., etc., through the eyes of someone who had never been here before; someone, say, who had just arrived from Kansas. I think there is no doubt he would feel he had suddenly been dropped into the Twilight Zone. One Step Beyond.

But it sure beats Kansas.

No Question about it

"Come inside, hansum man."

Here we go again. One of the hazards of living near Bangkok's *soi* 33 off of Sukhumvit Road is having to walk home past the beautiful women in beautiful gowns standing out in front of upper class bars including those known as "art bars."

These bars have names such as Dali, Monet, Renoir, Gaugain and Van Gogh. How much the beautiful, perfectly made up women in and outside these bars know about these painters is unclear. What is clear is that suckers for a pretty Asian face such as myself would do well to avoid walking down *soi* 33 if we hope to make it home at a reasonable hour.

Which is why despite the short ten or fifteen minute walk I often prefer to take a motorcycle taxi so that I can whiz past the beautiful women without being enticed inside. And sometimes I carry a shopping bag to make it clear that I am on my way home and cannot stop for a drink. I do think it says a lot for Thailand that it is a country in which a man has to resort to tricks and tactics in order to avoid the company of beautiful women.

If Ejaculation City had a Main Street, *soi* 33 would be it. I smile to the lady who has just called me "hansum man," and I point to the Villa Supermarket bag I'm carrying. "I can't come in, you beautiful woman. I've got to get this ice cream home."

She switches to Thai: *Bai dui, dai mai*? (We go together?)

I do my best to gently discourage her: *Khatort, khab, phom gae laeo.* (I'm sorry, I'm old now).

She switches back to English. "No problem, I do for you!" She's persistent enough and gorgeous enough to persuade me to take her home (what woman isn't) but I want to try to get some writing done, so I decide to give her my ultimate escape line: *Khatort, khab, phom puchai burisut.* (I'm sorry, but I'm a virgin.)

But this only excites her. It must be the challenge. "No problem, I teach you! *I teach you!*"

"Another time, gorgeous." I wave goodbye and continue walking. In front of another bar the girls are dressed as flesh-revealing cowgirls: cowgirl hats, skimpy tops, short shorts, boots, etc. As I walk by it happens. The epiphany. The illuminating moment. That instant when I know. The one nearest to me smiles and says, "Papa, where you go, Papa?"

I think, that's strange, I didn't see any old guy walking behind me. I turn around and look. Nobody. No question about it. She's talking about me! *Me* she called papa! I wag my finger at her: "You call me papa one more time and I'll give you a spanking."

She turns and sticks out her shapely rear. "OK, I like."

I forgot — with Thai girls you can't win.

I reach my apartment, pour out a generous splash of Wild Turkey on the rocks and sit in the dark on my balcony overlooking an intersection. Papa. She called me Papa.

Hemingway Wrestled the Wrong Bull

"What you do?"
"A ballad. I'm writing a ballad."
I knew she didn't know what that was but I also knew it would buy me a bit of time to write. I figured she would get bored watching me and walk away. But she stood by the desk staring at the notebook like it might be some kind of magic formula for making men buy bargirls drinks.

"What ballad mean?"
"A kind of poem." I knew she didn't know what that was either but I thought she might go back to watching the ghost story soap opera in the other room. She didn't. I took another hit on my Singha beer, drained the bottle and set it down. She padded over to the fridge on bare brown feet and got me another one and then stood exactly where she had been standing.

It wasn't until I came to Bangkok that I had the experience of trying to write with a beautiful, sensual, not to mention almost naked, 26-year-old woman standing by my desk. Hemingway described inserting a blank sheet of paper into the typewriter and trying to create as "wrestling with the white bull." Me, I had to wrestle with the white bull and the naked brown woman.

I looked up at her. Her fine black waist-length hair spilled over her soft brown shoulders. She was at least wearing panties and slippers. But her breasts were bare, brown and more than ample and her nipples were so long I could have hung half the clothes in my closet on them. Worse yet, the light behind her cast elongated shadows of her breasts onto the open pages of my notebook. I don't know about other writers but I find it hard to write in a notebook which has nipple-shadows streaking across it. I could feel my desire to write being replaced with other more prurient desires.

"Lek horny." She placed her hands on her breasts, gyrated in place and laughed.

I felt a stirring in my lap. I knew I had to act fast or it would be too late. "Hey! Our deal is, you stay here tonight but I have to work for awhile. Right?"

"You no like Lek?"

"I like Lek too much. But there is a time and place for everything. You understand?

She giggled and pointed to the bedroom. "Bed here. Lek here. Lek have time. Have place."

"Lek, why can't you have a headache sometimes like an American woman would?"

Her dark eyes blazed and widened. "You want Lek have headache!"

"Well, I just mean-"

I saw once again the familiar pout. "You no like Lek. I know. Lek go back to bar now."

She turned and walked off into the other room, leaving the door ajar. The TV went off. I could hear her getting dressed. Then it was quiet and I knew she would be sitting in front of the dresser mirror combing her hair.

I was determined not to give in to her. I knew it would set a bad precedent. I held onto my determination as a drowning man would cling to a piece of wood and stared at my notebook. Five seconds. Ten seconds. It seemed as if her nipple-shadows had become embedded in my notebook.

I got up from the desk and walked into the bedroom. I stood behind her and placed my hands on her shoulders.

"Stay here, OK?"

She expressed her displeasure with me by combing her hair more furiously. "Why? You no love Lek. You love play with pen and paper. You want Lek have headache."

"No, I don't want you to have a headache. But you know when I write I think with my big brain and when I see Lek my little brain takes over. Then I cannot write anymore."

She stopped combing and stared at me in the mirror. "Little brain? You have two brain?"

"Of course. Every man does. This one here is big brain; the one down here is little brain. When I see you big brain goes to sleep, little brain wakes up. Big brain says go work at desk. Little brain says take Lek go bed and play. So I put big brain in this drawer here whenever I go to the bar to see Lek and only listen to little brain. But when I write I need big brain, not little brain."

She smiled with delight. "I think I like little brain. I know he like me too much."

She got up, backed me up and pushed me down on the bed. In seconds she had stripped to her underwear then sat on my legs and began unbuttoning my shirt. "Maybe tonight I do something nice for little brain."

Poor Hemingway. All his life he had been using the wrong brain to wrestle with the wrong bull.

You Remember Me?

I was sitting at the desk in my Bangkok apartment working on a novel, trying not to remember that just minutes away *in any direction* were beautiful, available Thai women. But whenever I feel tempted (every night) I always try to keep in mind the apt warning Bukowski had given writers:

WHEN YOU LEAVE YOUR TYPEWRITER YOU LEAVE YOUR MACHINE GUN AND THE RATS COME POURING THROUGH

Bukowski knew exactly what he was talking about. And so I was determined to work, not to play.

It was after 11 p.m. Outside was pretty quiet: a dog barked, motorcycles roared past, the bell of some vendor sounded as he pushed his cart under my window. Probably the squid seller. Or is that the one with the Clarabelle the Clown horn? Anyway, by Bangkok standards it was a quiet night. I had downed a couple of Wild Turkey on the rocks and was writing pretty well.

My cell phone rang. I don't get many calls which is why I leave it open even when I write. That and the fact that aging parents in the States have the number in case of emergency. I didn't recognize the number.

"Yeah."

"Hi. You remember me?"

A girl's voice. Sounds of music and laughter somewhere in

the background. I didn't recognize the voice either.

"You didn't tell me your name yet."

"You want me to come up now?"

"Come *here*?"

"Yes, my girlfriend want to meet you."

"Hey, sweetie, I don't even know who you are. How did you get this number?"

"You joking right?"

"Look, I'm kind of busy right now. I'll call you back when I can, OK?"

"My friend have big breasts. I think for sure you like her."

"Actually, I'm a cute face man, and then a leg man. Not a breast man. So I think you may have the wrong number. So like two ships passing in the night, we'll just have to-"

"OK, never mind. But I think maybe my husband he find out where you live."

I took a looong hit on my Wild Turkey. "Your husband?"

"Yes, he police colonel, remember?"

"What did you say your name was?"

"Dao."

"Dao — star?"

"Yes. Now you remember?"

"Oh, sure. Let me guess: You've got black hair and dark eyes and brown skin, right?"

"Yes!"

"And we met where?"

"You know. After disco close we go get *somtam*. You eat *somtam* get sick. I take you home in taxi. "

"Oh! We met in that Siam Square place, right?"

"Yes!"

"OK, I remember you. But what's this about your husband?"

"He think maybe you do something with me."

"Why he think that?"

"He find your card."

"My namecard?"

"Yes."

"How did he get that?"

"He find in my purse."

"How did my namecard get in your purse?"

"When you throw up in bathroom, I take one."

"Why?"

"Silly. How I can call you if no have your number. Have to make sure you OK."

"Great. But now he has the card."

"Yes. But I tell him you too sick. We do nothing. No make love. I tell him you no can get it up."

"Great. Does he believe you?"

"Not sure. But you sound OK now."

Sure. Real Okey Dokey. I love to try to write wondering if at any moment some well-armed and pissed-off Thai police-man will be pounding at the door. "I'm OK now, Dao. Thanks for everything."

"So you want me to come up now?"

Baby Care Hostess

I haven't flown Thai International for years so I don't know about now, but once upon a time each flight I was on had a young stewardess with a big button pinned to the front of her uniform — BABY CARE HOSTESS.

And for whatever reason, these were invariably the cutest girls on the plane. And so of course I planned my strategy carefully. I always sat in an aisle seat and pretended to be working on the blueprint of the next issue of *Sawasdee* inflight magazine, of which I was then editor. In fact, the blueprint had already been corrected by the head office in Bangkok and I was now flying to Hong Kong to have it printed. But you have to remember that although most Thais are not an *intellectually* curious people, they are nonetheless a very *curious* people, and so I would throw out my net and wait for the fish to swim into it.

"All right, men, don't shoot until you can see the whites of their BABY CARE HOSTESS buttons!"

And would you believe, faster than you can say "Dirty, reprehensible, unredeemable, sex-crazed, old man" five times fast, she would stop by my seat, lean close to me, and say, "Excuse me, sir, are you the editor of *Sawasdee* magazine?" (Her "Excuse me" always came out like "Accuse me" but that of course simply made her more adorable.)

And, sho nuff, as I live and breathe, that there sweetie-pie fly with the big BABY CARE HOSTESS button had done fallen into the spider's web. The fish was thrashing and the net was full.

The battle was over before it had hardly begun.

Although, after a while, these particular hostesses being so innocent, there was little challenge in the game. And so I moved on or I should say reverted back to my normal activity on a plane: mentally undressing the hostesses. But that too, remember, is something of an art form.

For example, I love women in crinolines. Especially those sexy, swaying Victorian cage crinolines that revealed just enough of a woman's ankle to make men faint dead away. But cage crinolines became extremely wide, ridiculously so, in fact, and there is no way a BABY CARE HOSTESS could wear one on an airplane and still maneuver efficiently down the aisle. So crinolines are out.

And so I would go on mentally dressing and undressing the BABY CARE HOSTESS, testing, testing, testing: *pasin*, *longyi*, kimono, cheongsam, *sarong*, mumu, *lava lava*, gown, robe, kilt, jumper, pinafore, frock, tight skirt, short shorts, bikini, studded leather, creamy lace, velvet with fur trimmings, fur with velvet trimmings, studded leather cheongsam with lace trimmings, kimono with thigh-high cheongsam slit, and, finally: nothing at all.

I tried as many creative combinations as my wine-drenched mind could conceive, but by the time I finished, I would almost invariably conclude that the outfit that would best suit the BABY CARE HOSTESS was the one she was wearing: the Thai International uniform.

Still, such exercises do keep the mind sharp. Especially at 30,000 feet up.

That was many years ago. Still, I have kept my promise. The one I always silently made as I smiled to one of them and left the plane: BABY CARE HOSTESS, I'll have you in mah mind.

Why I can't get any writing done in Thailand

It was going to be a good writing day. I had that feeling. Some times you just know. Some days you struggle, curse, drink and swear; other days it all comes out as if your fictional characters are writing the book for you and you're just taking dictation. I knew this day would be a good one, the type every writer loves.

So I was at the computer, cold beer beside it, more in the fridge where that came from, studying the work I'd done the day before, ready to rock and roll. Then my cellphone rang. Not being in business, I get few calls so I usually leave it open even when writing.

It was an SMS message from somebody. It was from Dave, my scuba diving buddy, who had just married a lovely lady from Buriram. It said, "I am looking at Nong in her school uniform." I should explain.

Three weeks earlier I had gone with them to attend their wedding in Buriram. One of the bride's friends was a lovely 21-year-old college student in her third year. And was said to be a virgin. Virgins being rarer than unicorns in modern Thailand, that fact kind of floored me.

Anyway, during the outside reception in front of the tiny house in the tiny village in the middle of pea green rice fields, one of the elderly farmers got enough rice liquor in him to get up from his table of elderly rice farmers and wander over to ours to talk with the *farangs*. I hadn't known this area had once been a Communist training ground but now it was all safe and sound. I wondered what he had done during that period.

The farmer gave me a missing-tooth grin and started grilling me on whether I was married, why not, and when would I, and all that sort of gobbledygook. I told him that I had been divorced from a Hong Kong Chinese woman for many years but was in fact marrying again very soon. When he asked when and where I answered next week right there. Of course I did this because I was aware that our conversation had the attention of the women at the next table including Nong. So when the old man asked who I was marrying I gestured and said "Khun Nong."

The women laughed a great deal but I did hear Nong's friend ask her if she wanted that and I heard her say emphatically "yes." Still, I thought no more of it and after a few days returned to Bangkok.

But it was now three weeks after the wedding and Dave and his wife had returned to Buriram to see her parents. And they saw Nong. Hence, Dave was so considerate as to send me that message from Buriram.

So I stared at the message for a few minutes determined to ignore it and keep writing. I went through the motions for nearly ten minutes, but then of course as all weak-willed people do, I gave in, and sent a message back: "What color is the uniform?"

I did manage to start writing again in the few minutes before his reply came but his reply was: "White blouse, long black skirt."

Great. I could see the once promising writing day evaporating before my eyes. Now, I would sit and stare at the computer screen and think of Nong with her beautiful face, her long, lustrous, black hair and chocolate brown complexion and willowy figure in her white and black school uniform — or I could try to write. So I struggled with that dilemma for a bit before getting off the next message: "Is the skirt pleated?"

The message came back almost immediately: "Yes."

I sent the message back immediately: "I want!"

Then, blissfully, all was quiet for nearly an hour and I thought well, that was that. And I was actually getting some writing done. Characterization, plot, pace, it was going the way it should be going. Then the phone rang again. Someone was sending me a message. I said to myself: Jesus Christ, you're an adult! Act like one! If you have any strength of character at all, you'll wait until tonight to look at that message. Of course, while I was thinking that, I was opening the message.

It was from Dave: "Nong has school holidays soon and may be in Bangkok for ten days. Can she stay with you?"

OK, now this was getting serious. Now I had to think carefully and sensibly and with the wisdom of an older man. I mean, I do have *some* sense of perspective on life and have gained *some* maturity over the years.

I looked at it this way: I am a writer. I have a lot of projects I need to get done. I am much, much older than this young woman, and nothing of lasting value could possibly come out of her staying with me for ten days. *It would be the wrong thing to do!* Nong, on the other hand, was a beautiful 21-year-old Thai virgin college student with long black hair, a great smile, a great figure, and the exact shade of dark brown complexion that drives me nuts.

I continued to lecture myself: "Look, you long-in-the-tooth, oversexed, immature, satyr, she is *21 years old*, speaks very little English, and you don't have ten days to waste. You would end up getting very little work done. Not to mention the expense of all the Viagra you'd have to buy. And what if she falls in love with you or you with her or even if you both fall for each other? It would be a disaster. Besides, you cherish your *freedom*, remember? You're an aging, cynical, intellectual who loves to read and write books; she's a college student at the age where she probably loves discos and karaoke. <u>IT WOULD BE THE WRONG THING TO DO!</u>

I reflected on this for quite some time, maybe all of ten seconds, then grabbed the cellphone. I wrote: "Many thanks, but I don't think so." And then I pushed the send button.

Then I checked the message I just sent. It read: "If she brings her school uniform."

Jesus Christ, my little brain had taken over from my big brain automatically! Some kind of automatic pilot was in control of my actions! Like Donald Sutherland being taken over in that movie about the body snatchers but in my case it's my *own* body!

Alas, as it turned out, I had to be in the States while Nong was having her vacation and so the tryst was not to be. Not yet, at least.

But that is one example of why I can't get any writing done in Thailand. Why can't Western women who detest men like me realize *I'm* the victim here?

Happy New Year! (but where am I?)

God, that must have been some party. Happy New Year! But, wow, my head is splitting and my stomach doesn't feel any too stable. But this clock says it's 6:16 p.m. and I *gotta* get out of this bed. I mean, after all, I am Harry Boroditsky, Bangkok's sexiest, bravest and least principled detective; and my reputation is always on the line. It wouldn't do for —

Oh, shit. I'm not in a bed. It feels more like . . . a floor. And what the hell are all these empty wine and whisky and beer bottles doing scattered all over like ten pins? Mekhong and Singha. Well, then, at least I must still be in Thailand. And that smell! Pungent, spicy, peppery. Oh, yeah, there it is: spilled *somtam*; maybe I'm in Northeastern Thailand. Stupid dog, licking up all the . . . wait a minute, I don't think I have a dog.

And where's my dresser that is supposed to be right here? And the vanity mirror my Thai girlfriend is always preening in front of? And the table she does her homework on? And the chest with the special school uniforms and Betty Boop garter belts and Daisy Duck black mesh stockings? (Not that I'm kinky, understand.) Somebody has rearranged my bedroom. Shit, wait a minute, this doesn't look at all like my bedroom. I gotta get — Oh! My head.

Well, at least I can stand up straight. Oh, Jesus, I don't think this is my apartment. And there's a strange woman in the bed. Long black hair, well proportioned brown face, large eyes, full lips. A lovely Thai woman, all right, but I'm sure I never saw her before. Wait a minute, she's smiling at me. God, I hope I'm not married because now my little brain is —

Oh, wow, I just noticed something important: except for my massive hangover I've got nothing on. But hold on here: The woman is smiling at me in that special satisfied way. Great, except it's been a few years since I could put *that* kind of smile on a woman's face. Was I better than I knew? *That* kind of smile appears on a young Thai woman's face only when she's talking with her friends on her cell phone or heading to the Emporium to do some shopping. But who the hell is this woman, anyway?

Wait a minute, what was that noise? Somebody just slammed the front door of the apartment!

"Honey, I'm home!"

Jesus Christ! It's a man's voice. OK, don't panic, think! It's New Year's Day, I don't have a clue as to where I am but as Bangkok's most remarkable detective, I have to apply logic to this situation. My detective-trained mind immediately hones in on the only two possibilities:

A. I'm gay, but don't remember being gay; and the guy is addressing me. Or —

B. I'm straight, was messing with his woman, probably his wife, and the guy is addressing her.

Either way, it is not likely to be a happy ending for the home team. I snatch up the sheet from the bed, leaving the woman naked, race toward the window, almost make it but trip over the damn dog, and land hard on the floor just as a shadow (no, Old Time radio fans, not the Shadow) falls across the bedroom doorway.

So here I am, Bangkok's most seductive detective, wrapped in a sheet, moaning in pain on the floor because the &#@%* dog tripped me, the woman in the bed still smiling at me mysteriously. In a bedroom I don't recognize.

A guy enters the bedroom. A big Thai guy. *Luk krung*, maybe.

An extremely well built probably disgustingly virile guy. In a trench coat. Dark hair, swarthy, boxer's flattened nose, thick neck. This looks like trouble. He glances at the woman in the bed, then at me. My life passes before my eyes. Bargirls I've known. Bargirls I've done the Deed with. Bargirls I wish I had done the Deed with. Barbills unpaid. I start to mouth some kind of excuse/apology but before I can say anything, he says: "Jesus, man, I'm sorry. We thought you'd be away."

I'm relieved in a way because this means that his "Honey, I'm home" line had been directed toward the woman, not me, but the plot definitely seemed to be thickening. I say, "Say what?"

He says, "Yeah, she said you'd still be in Chiang Mai."

So that was it. Here I was thinking I was cheating on this guy with the woman in the bed and now it turns out this guy is cheating with her on *me*. But who the hell is she? I don't remember this woman!

Suddenly, I notice the guy stare anxiously past me toward the woman. He kicks several Essarn Beaujolais Nouveau wine bottles out of the way and walks over to the bed. I follow. We look down at the woman and I see what I probably would have noticed when I snatched the sheet off her except for the excitement of the moment and my urgent need to escape the premises. There are four or five bullet holes in her chest. The smile on her face isn't one of sexual contentment after all; she's been dead awhile and *rigor mortis* has set in. This is not good. This is bad. Worse is to come.

The big man reaches into his trench coat and pulls out an FBI shield. Under his thick eyebrows, his dark eyes cloud over like those of a go go dancer who has just seen her free-spending steady customer leave with another dancer. "You bastard! You killed Gretchel!"

Gretchel? I've known a lot of Thai women in my time but I don't recall knowing any Gretchel. I knew a Noy or two back in

'68 and a Dang back in '76 and a Lek back in '89 and a Nok back in '93 and a Moo back in '02. I did know a Som back in '03 but she turned out to be a ladyboy so I don't think she counts. But, anyway, Gretchel? I don't recall knowing her. I can't recall how I got into this house or who this woman is or —

Suddenly, the big guy punches me hard in the stomach and throws me down on the bed. He grips my shoulders in a vise-like grip and starts shaking me violently. Back and forth. All the while screaming. "You wanted Gretchel? You see now? You wanted Gretchel?"

The voice very gradually transforms from male into female and I suddenly realize I'm being shaken awake by a pretty young Thai woman. "Gretchel" becomes "special" and "see now" becomes *keemao*. "I ask if you want special but you *keemao* I think. You drink too much! You fall asleep!"

And then I realize I am lying under a sheet in my bedroom. One of my girlfriend-temporarily-up-country regulars is shaking me. The dream nothing but a nightmare caused by too much beer at the Texas Lone Staar Saloon. She says, "Harry, you too much drink, I think; today Happy New Year day! I go back Lone Staar now!"

She quickly dresses and gives me a sniff-kiss on the cheek. Much relieved to have escaped from the nightmare, I give her a big tip.

I plump up the pillow, turn out the light and roll over, happy to be safe and sound in the familiar reality of my own bedroom.

Wait a minute, what was that noise? Somebody just slammed the front door of the apartment!

"Honey, I'm home!"

The Great China Scholar

As a young man I grew up in Groton, Connecticut, known then as "Home of the Nautilus, Submarine Capital of the World." Now it is known more for the malodorous Pfizer Chemical plant which, to the gratitude of millions, created and churns out Viagra. So the town might be said to have gradually but surely followed the advice of the love children of the late '60's: "Make Love, not War."

I have never been quite sure why but even when very young I knew exactly what I wanted to be in life. I wanted to be a Great China Scholar. I was fascinated by Asia, especially anything Chinese. And in those days in Groton, Connecticut, we didn't know much about things Chinese.

So I began my quest for knowledge by going to yard sales and buying anything I thought might be from China and later to estate auctions still looking for items from the mysterious Middle Kingdom. While others had heroes ranging from Elvis to Wyatt Earp, I wanted to be a scholar of things Chinese like John King Fairbank or A. Doak Barnett. The example today would be Yale's Jonathan Spence. And I bought books on China, books on Mao Tze-tung, books on American Far Eastern Policy, and learned what I could of China's history and culture.

I had no doubt I would one day become the head of the East Asian Studies Department at a prestigious American university or, failing that, might accept the head of Chinese Affairs at the State Department, or, failing that, would end up in charge of the

American Secret Agent fighting the Chinese Commies while Saving the Beautiful and Grateful Chinese Girl Section at the CIA.

I was of course very young when China went communist, but I still remember the radio announcers speaking hysterically of a "bamboo curtain" descending around China like the "iron curtain" which had descended around the Soviet Union. For better or worse, I had a writer's imagination even then, and when I heard the term "bamboo curtain" it conjured up the image of a lovely and mysterious Chinese woman with dark almond eyes peering out at me from behind the bamboo strands of a curtain in the back room of Rick's Café where I was supposed to meet an important Chinese defector and escort him to freedom.

Then, when the Vietnam War was getting underway, the announcers all described Southeast Asia as part of "China's soft underbelly." I mean, Jesus Christ, was it just *me* and my oversexed imagination or was everybody describing Asia in sexual terms? "Bamboo curtain?" "Soft underbelly of China?" How could I *not* want to go there?

So I crossed the Thames River to New London, marched into the Army Recruiter's Center and announced that I would like to join if I could get to learn the Chinese language at the Defense Language Institute in Monterey, California. He gave me the language proficiency test and I passed. I then had to list three languages in case I didn't get my first choice. I desperately wanted Chinese so I listed Chinese mandarin, Chinese cantonese, Chinese Hokkien dialect.

He was not pleased with that and had me list again. So I put down Chinese, Japanese, Vietnamese. (I had no fear of being sent to Vietnam because I was in my early 20's and, being young and indestructible, no harm could come to me.)

It was only after I had left his office that I realized I had nothing in writing. Duh. But, as it turned out, the Army was as good as its word. I got my year of Chinese mandarin at DLI, got a bit more training at Petaluma, and, in its wisdom, the Army then sent me off to — you guessed it — Bangkok.

Where for the first time in my life I came face to face with Thai women. In the flesh. And that was the end of my plan to be a Great China Scholar. In fact, that was the end of any sensible plan I have had for several decades.

Not that I'm complaining, understand. Because the way things are in America today, had I actually become a university professor of pimply faced, beer-guzzling, politically correct, health-nazi, non-smoking, college kids, I might not have lasted too long. I would have made some jocular remark about a co-ed's curvaceous legs or some co-ed in search of better grades would have come to my office and seduced me (not difficult to do) and I would have faced scandal, dishonor, disrepute and possibly legal charges.

So it is just as well that I washed up on Thailand's humid shores that happy and sweltering day in March of 1966. And in any case I am happy to report that I have continued my China studies even while in Thailand. Because over the years, I have noticed more and more Thai go go dancers with the tattoo of a Chinese character on their shoulders or backs or elsewhere.

And whenever I see one, I always invite her over for a drink immediately so I can try to make out what the character is. Because the Chinese language does not have an alphabet so it is easy to forget characters if one doesn't use them often or gets drunk too often or both.

Usually, the character on the girl's arm or shoulder or back will be a common one and after a drink or two, I thank the lady and leave. Sometimes, I will spot an accursed simplified Chinese character and, needless to say, do not associate with any woman who would put such an unsightly Chinese scratch on her shoulder.

However, occasionally, I come across a dancer with a complicated Chinese character tattoo, the meaning of which I am not sure of. In that case, it becomes necessary to barfine her and take her back to my apartment because that is where I keep my Mathew's Chinese-English Dictionary.

This is a very special dictionary listing Chinese characters by number of strokes in the character as well as by 214 "radicals," for example, the "fire" radical or "water" radical or "bamboo" radical. The radicals give clues to the meaning and/or sound of the character. So, unless the character is one of the communist simplified characters (which may have eliminated the radical), it is possible, with patience, to track down even complicated characters.

The problem comes about because Thai go go dancers have very little in the way of patience. While she lies naked on the bed nibbling on some shrimp chips or beetles fried in oil and watches some goddawful Thai soap opera, I prop the dictionary against her breasts and, carefully checking the character on her shoulder (or wherever), attempt my scholarly research. Always a firm believer in combining scholarly research with sensual pleasure, I happily go about my business occasionally having to ask the girl to HOLD STILL, DAMN IT!

So, although living now in Thailand, I am pleased to report that I am still taking time out to study Chinese characters. Once a scholar always a scholar.

Whether I would have been happier as a respected professor of Chinese Studies on the green and spacious campus of a prestigious university doing my research in a musty library or am happier doing my research with a naked Thai go go dancer on my bed in a Bangkok apartment, who can say? But a local newspaper has just described the troubled Muslim southern part of Thailand as "Thailand's soft underbelly." Ye gads, here we go again.

Bored with the Rings

I admit it. I only suggested to the coffee shop waitress that we see *Lord of the Rings* because I wanted to nail her and I figured she might want to see that. Sure enough, it worked. So here we are waiting to go inside. Some Thai women still show up with a friend on the first date to assist in sizing up the *farang* male and to show that they are respectable. Or they don't show up at all.

But in Thailand the times they are a-changin'. This one not only showed up and showed up on time, she looks great. Lustrous, jet-black hair way, way down her back, off-the-shoulder, blue-and-white frilly dress revealing her jade-white shoulders which with any luck I will at some point in the future sink my teeth into and lick like there is no tomorrow, and a hemline just about at her knees which, with any luck will at some point rise higher when she sits down, and shoes high enough to almost be called platform shoes which make her look even more adorable.

Over her shoulder she has a cute yellow and white purse shaped like a fish complete with big black eyes, fins and tail. I must be hungrier or hornier than I thought because I wouldn't mind taking a bite out of that either.

We chat a bit and it is clear she is the intelligent type. She has had some higher education at some sort of university and some English training at AUA. She says she saw the first in this *Ring* trilogy and thought it was kind of repetitive. Good girl. It *was* repetitive. One danger facing the main characters after another going nowhere. No dramatic arc under which the main characters travel, etc. Neither of us bothered to see the second one. I begin to suspect she only agreed to see this last one in the trilogy to date me. If so, we are of like minds and — there being any justice in the world — should be on our way to bedside bliss soon after the show.

She sits down and sure enough her dress rises. She has what must be a perfect figure. Now we sit through one thousand ads. At last the movie starts.

I miss lots of the beginning because my writer's imagination is focused on various bedroom scenarios with her and in trying to achieve the best sitting position so that I can glance at her curvaceous legs without it being too obvious. And, in any case, this *Lord of the Rings* promises to be worse than the first two.

Somebody has found a ring in the water and two guys are fighting over it. It is a plain gold ring, nothing special. Hell, Thai bargirls would take one look at that and throw it back at anybody who offered it.

Some king has just said: "I take my leave." What is this, second rate, hand-me-down, Shakespeare? And this little disgusting creature hopping about on the rocks with his wrinkled face and oversized blue eyes and babbling to himself — the one in desperate need of a hair transplant — isn't his character kind of pinched from that little guy in *Star Wars*?

Yawn. Woken up by somebody's cellphone going off. The waitress and I exchange smiles. Jesus, her legs are beautiful. And the light from the screen is illuminating her shoulders in the dark. They are so smooth and feminine and sexy. I really feel an urge to bite them. Maybe I was a vampire in a past life.

Somebody in the movie just pointed to a pass in a mountain and said those who went in there never returned. Yeah, reminds me of Patpong in the old days. But how many more banal, hackneyed, cliched lines like that do I have to sit through while trying to hold down my lunch?

And this feeble, fainthearted, hobbit with the ring is such a wimp. He keeps fainting and needing assistance from the fat little hobbit with the pseudo-Irish accent. It seems to me the one with the ring is a main character and the thing about main characters in fiction is that they must always be the engine of the piece. Things must not simply happen to them; *they must make things happen.* But this pathetic, wimpy kid isn't making anything happen. And he who violates a rule in fiction always pays a price. In this case the price is *boredom* because we lose interest in the character. Writing 101. So how did this inane rubbish win so many Academy awards?

Giant spiders, volcanoes, Weird enemy soldiers riding huge, semi-elephants into battle. Spectacle after spectacle. Big deal. If I had wanted to see a video game I would have bought one. And aren't some of these characters stolen from *Star Wars*? Oh, Jesus, she crossed her legs and the dress has risen waaay up! She is really beautiful. Her upper lip is perfectly heart-shaped and her lower lip is full, full, full. Why do we have to stay here when I'll bet both of us have better things to do (together) than watch this stereotyped inanity.

I feel like I've been sitting here for three days. Doesn't this silly garbage ever end? Now what? We've got to be coming close to the end of the movie and all of a sudden we seem to be in some idealized version of Olde Ireland. Hobbitville, I suppose. There's Irish cottages and Irish lilts and Irish type music. No wonder they've been babbling about "heather" and all that romanticizing of the rustics. Maybe we'll meet up with Paddy in the pub. People who romanticize tiny villages and rustic village people never lived or worked in one.

Jesus, I suppose next we'll see children and dogs. Where is W. C. Fields when we need him? Sure enough, a little girl just ran out of a cottage and into the fat hobbit's arms. She's made up like the flower sellers at Nana Plaza. Cutsie, cutsie. These film folks don't miss a trick do they? Layer after layer of emotional overload piled on at sloooow pace in an attempt to make us feel something. Who wrote this crap? The movie version, I mean. I say again: *emotion has to be earned!*

Now she's shifted position and she's leaning back displaying her lovely neck in all its glory. The nape of her neck is almost as inviting a meal as the nape of a Japanese woman's neck. The kind I love to bite into. God, how I would love to kiss all the way from the tip of her cute chin right on down to her well endowed breasts.

I restrain myself and look back at the screen. All these meaningful glances and insipid smiles between and among the actors and the hobbits and grown-ups with normal ears and the guy with pointed ears and the pale, white women with large nostrils and the oh-so-handsome fellah in need of a haircut might just make me throw up.

At least if the bad guys had won, there would be some interesting scenes of revenge or pillage or plunder or torture or *something.*

Ah, she has just stifled a yawn. We smile at one another. She's as bored as I am. I love this woman. Her eyes are beautiful, her lips are perfectly curved, she has a cute little nose and a chin like the prow of a custom-built yacht. Come to think of it, I'd like to bite her chin as well.

Now these hobbit guys walking toward the junk; are they supposed to be going on new adventures or is this symbolic of their deaths? In any case, would they pleeaaase just get on the damn boat and sail off into the phony sunset and *end this damn movie?*

I can't believe it, the credits! it's over! Thank you, God. I will burn joss sticks and say three Hail Malee's to some Desperate-to-be-worshipped Being-in-the-Sky sometime in the near future.

Oh my God! They're applauding! Several of the Thais in the

audience are applauding the movie! I look over at the waitress. She gives me a look which says, "These people are nutty." God, I love her already. But my body is so cramped from sitting for so long it aches all over and even if I can get her up to my apartment there is no way I can get *it* up. This stupid, boring, self-indulgent, video-game movie may have killed off Mr. Happy for good. I need a massage. A *real* one, I mean.

I wonder if it's possible to sue a movie studio for robbing a guy of getting laid.

An Expert on Thai Rice

Strange as it seems, I have become something of an expert on rice cultivation in Thailand. I have learned about the various methods, such as dry land rice, wet land rice, broadcasting and transplanting; I've learned about the different rice-growing seasons in different parts of the country; the festivals, the fun and the many hardships farmers face. The drought, flooding, snakes, beetles, weeds, plant eating crabs, worms, field rats, birds, heat, pain in the thumbs, pain in the lower back, etc. The sowing, the planting, the harrowing, the threshing, the plight of today's buffaloes, etc. I even figured out that any rice growing on Patpong Road was most likely what they call "miracle rice." And yet I have never once planted any rice nor did I gain most of my knowledge from books.

I learned about rice cultivation in two ways. First, by spending a great deal of time traveling through Thailand photographing the farmers at work and secondly by talking to the experts: the farmers' daughters. Those who now permanently or temporarily work as go go dancers in Bangkok and other places. Because it is my long-held belief that, whenever possible, scholarly research and intellectual inquiry should always be combined with sensual pleasure.

After all, if I can learn about rice cultivation from farmers' daughters in the comfort of an air-conditioned Bangkok go go bar why should I try to engage them in conversation in the violent heat and muddy fields of upcountry Thailand? For that matter, why sit in a dull classroom at Harvard University studying something like "Rice Cultivation in Southeast Asia" when I can go to the source, so to speak?

And some of the bar owners still complain that when the girls are needed back home for planting or harvesting they don't have enough girls in the bar. And when the crops are in and the girls aren't needed on the farms for a few months, then they have too many dancers. Well, we all have our problems.

Nevertheless, researching rice cultivation in this way is not quite as easy as one might think. First there is the noise and distractions. Remember also that the interviewee is an attractive young woman dressed in nothing but a bikini and boots, sometimes causing a less-disciplined interviewer's attention to wander. Then there is the serious problem of holding a go go dancer's interest in any one subject for more than thirty seconds.

In my usual technique I would of course ask the girl where she is from and what her father does. If she replies that he is a farmer I then ask if she has ever planted rice. Almost invariably, the answer is yes, and then I touch my thumb and lower back, complaining of the pain, then complain about the heat of the sun.

They usually laugh and ask if I have planted rice. I explain that I simply traveled a lot and photographed farmers at work. So the conversation usually goes something like this:

"So, Dang, in your part of the country, the rice season begins in April, right?"

"Yes."

"Does your village still use buffaloes or do you have the iron buf — "

"You buy me drink?"

"Uh, oh, yeah, sure." (I try to employ the method known to pompous academics as a "cross-cultural sensitive treatment.")

Her drink arrives. We toast good luck to one another.

"So the buffalo tramps back and forth over the harvested rice to remove the rice grains from the stalks. The Thai phrase for that is 'massaging the rice,' is that — "

Dang grips my leg and begins a rhythmic squeezing. "You want massage?"

"Well, maybe later. OK, now in transplanting the seedbeds — "

"You want barfine Dang?"

(Possibly it was the word "beds" which put that notion into her head.) "Well, that is certainly a possibility down the road, if not tonight, another time for sure. But I was wondering how old are the seedlings when you transplant them into the flooded fields and-"

Dang's hand strays to my crotch. "You pay mamasan five hundred baht and we go."

"Well, maybe we could just finish up here a bit. When you bend over and pull the roots of the rice seedlings from the seed plot, how many — "

One of the dancers yells something to her. She sniff-kisses my cheek and gets up. "Dang turn to dance now."

So, as you can see, this particular research method has its hazards as well as any other. This is not a job for timorous, ivory tower academics afraid to get their, um, hands dirty. It does take perseverance, discipline, and long hours of practice. Certainly I have had the long hours of practice.

I wonder though if I could apply to Harvard for a grant in agricultural studies. I will try to give it an interesting enough title full of fancy academic bullshit words to attract university interest. Something like, *A Semidialogical Exchange into the Nature of Sexual Cartographies in Agricultural Societies of Southeast Asia.* Except I don't know what a cartography is.

Fortunately, I haven't far to go for assistance in such bullshit because I own a copy of a feminazi book denouncing guys like me in Thailand called *Night Market*. The only reason they didn't denounce me by name was because their book was published before *Thailand: Land of Beautiful Women* came out and they obviously didn't know about the out of print *Girls of Thailand* book. They did denounce every other male who has ever set foot in Thailand, however, from Jack Reynolds to Christopher Moore. I was somewhat humiliated not to have been included in their angry invective, but you can be sure I will be next time.

One of their sentences reads (and it is typical of their gobbledy-gook): "The legitimizing trope of reciprocity cannot conceal the fear that in any given exchange of cash for material goods or labor one of the parties will be taken advantage of, thus rendering the falsity of the trope explicit."

Hmmm. If they mean that when I bought this book I got cheated, then they got that right. But have you ever noticed that humorless, man-hating, feminazis unintentionally write in the same hilarious way as Lewis Carroll did in his classic of nonsense rhyme, "Jabberwocky"?

But in Thailand nothing is explicit, certainly not the falsity of *tropes* (I'm guessing here but I'm assuming a trope is one of the creatures in *Lord of the Rings* like the hobbits, maybe?) In any case, most of the tropes running around Thailand are of the completely unlegitimized variety and it is best to give them a wide berth. And as for the legitimized types, the last time I ran into a legitimized trope it bit me in the ass just outside the Carnival Bar on the upper level of Nana Plaza.

Beware the Femiwocky, my son
For the trope doth falsify outgrabe

The Eternal Search

Once a man has lived in Thailand for a long period of time it is not so easy to live or even to travel abroad. Compared with Thailand, most other countries are kind of like their cuisine: bland and boring.

So within days of wandering about in other lands, I usually find myself keeping an eye out for Thai women and, failing that, for Asian women in general. It isn't that I have a desperate need to take someone to bed; it's just that the humor-loving, wacky mindset of a Thai woman makes good company.

Las Vegas is a perfect example. The kind of town you either love or hate. I didn't love it. I found the gambling casinos boring, the hotel themes too glitzy for my taste and the blatant hype off-putting. I mean a town that has to flaunt the late alcoholics of the rat pack and dredge up poor Elvis lookalikes and aging singers and billboards of Marilyn Monroe to attract people has got a problem. At least for me.

Vastly overweight women sitting at slot machines pushing buttons or pulling handles, constant noise, cigarette smoke, blinking lights and mechanical machines spouting out the words "Wheel of Fortune" may have an attraction for some; not for me. So I was quite pleased when my mystery writers convention was drawing to a close and I could get out of there.

But then I noticed something. Some of the female blackjack dealers looked, yes, indeed, *Asian*. Southeast Asian, in fact. And so I approached one of them standing behind a table with no customers and spoke in Thai. As it turned out, she was from Laos. But she pointed to several other dealers who were Thai or Chinese and to the pit boss, a Thai woman.

So I spent quite a bit of time chatting with these women and just having fun with them in general. My chats often got interrupted by people who were apparently there to gamble and who didn't seem to realize that gambling casinos exist for Western men to pick up Asian women not for people with too much money and too much time on their hands to indulge in boring games of chance. There seemed to be a difference of opinion about this but meeting Asian women made the town come alive for me.

When I lived in New York, it was much the same. There were not that many Thai women in my area of the East Village but there were a lot of Japanese. Almost every day I would see often stunning young Japanese women walking with somewhat shabbily dressed, even disheveled, African-American men.

Finally, I dated one of the women and she explained that many of them were from very good families in Japan and took one year off and went to New York to do what they could never do in Japan: date black men. Why sneak off to America to date black men? Well, something to do with the reputed size of their, um, willys. And to date a black man in Japan would have meant instant ostracism.

I thought about that for awhile and remembered reading a book about some white guy who had wanted to help with integration in the American South. He had actually taken pills to darken his skin and, until he finally talked about it years later, he had passed as a black man. As I recall, the blacks were not particularly pleased with what he had done.

Nonetheless, I wondered if I should do the same. The darker I got the more the Japanese girls might check me out. I did look for pills in drugstores but never asked any doctors for any prescriptions and, in any case, I was leaving for Asia. But sometimes I wonder about America. I mean if they have reached the point where a white guy who wants to make it with a Japanese girl has to take a pill to look like a black guy, what pills would a Japanese guy have to take to make it with a black woman?

Sometimes America makes my head ache.

My Kind of Woman

Over the years, my girlfriends have ranged the gamut from countryside girls who speak little English to intellectual writers who write beautiful fiction. And I am sometimes asked exactly what type of woman I prefer. It is difficult to answer the question intelligently because, for one thing, it is fairly easy to specify a type and then list characteristics of such a type; but equally possible to then meet someone with all the characteristics and have the meeting prove disastrous.

So I tend to answer that question in literary terms, with examples of spine tingling women found in literature. First, I like to quote Wilkie Collins. He wrote the more famous novel, *Moonstone*, but this quote is from his lesser known *Basil*: "Abroad, he had lived as exclusively as he possibly could, among women whose characters ranged downwards by infinitesimal degrees, from the mysteriously doubtful to the notoriously bad."

Indeed, mysteriously doubtful and notoriously bad women can be found in abundance in the area of Bangkok where I live, hence, I tend to linger in the areas of Bangkok where they congregate.

Next, I always wished I could have met the woman Bret Harte described in *The Luck of Roaring Camp*: "Cherokee Sal . . . perhaps the less said of her the better. She was a coarse and, it is to be feared, a very sinful woman."

And then of course there is my favorite description of the perfect woman from Raymond Chandler in *Farewell My Lovely*:

"I like smooth, shiny girls, hardboiled and loaded with sin."

Now we come to Henry Miller. And I must warn the reader that Henry doesn't pull any punches when describing his perfect dream date: "What I particularly wanted was to meet some low-down filthy cunt who hadn't a spark of decency in her. Where to meet one like that . . . Just like that?"

Well, Henry, pop back to life and pop over to Bangkok some night and we'll see what we can do for you.

But, I must be honest, there is one above all I wish I had been able to go out on a few dates with. Her name was Chamadevi, a 7th century Siamese queen, reportedly one of the most beautiful women in Thai history. She is said to have upset some higher power by flouting some religious custom and therefore had a singular curse placed upon her in the form of a horrible body odor. It is said this odor could be detected at a distance comparable to that measuring the sound of three trumpets of an elephant and seven beatings of a gong. One Thai scholar has calculated that distance to be a total of sixteen miles!

But think of the fun of arriving at some pompous fool's dinner party with Chamadevi as your date. Or even with Cherokee Sal. Because the one thing these women have in common is that they are never boring. Alas, as one grows older, one comes to find goodness and beauty still desirable but a trifle boring combination. After all, the heart of drama is conflict so if your woman is forever beautiful and good, where's the fun in making up after the quarrels?

And, of course, I mustn't forget to mention Mickey Spillane's Mike Hammer. In his novel, *The Twisted Thing*, Mickey described a woman all men would find irresistible: "I let my eyes follow the contours of her shoulders and down her body. Impertinent breasts that mocked my former hesitance, a flat stomach waiting for the touch to set off the fuse, thighs that wanted no part of shielding cloth."

Well, actually, there are some bar hostesses on *Soi* Cowboy and around Washington Square whose thighs also want no part of shielding cloth. But those very same thighs also want no part of men without money. As with snow removal in New York, shielding-cloth removal in Bangkok can be expensive.

But I cannot leave this subject without quoting from *A Woman of Bangkok* written 50 years ago by the late Jack Reynolds. His main character was a hapless *farang* being taken for a fool by the White Leopard, a diabolically clever Thai bargirl, and yet he could not resist her. (Sound familiar? And you thought you were the only one, didn't you?) Here it is:

> "For I was all the time romantically dreaming of lifting her up to my level through the power of my love, but at such moments I realized how foolish the dream was: She had already pulled *me* down a long way and there was still further to go."

So there they are: The White Leopard, Cherokee Sal, Chamadevi, and all the wonderful ladies just like them in literature and in real life who keep our lives from ever being boring. May the woman of your dreams be endowed with beauty, blessed with loins that want no part of shielding cloth and may she be "loaded with sin."

Thai Girlfriends

One of the things I like most about Thai women is their wackiness, their unpredictability, their lack of Western logic. Having a Thai girlfriend assures any man that his life will be full of surprises.

For example, there was the time I finally convinced a lovely Thai woman from Surin that it was time for her to take some birth control measures. She was in her late 20's and had never been on the pill. So the two of us headed for the Emporium on Bangkok's Sukhumvit Road and up to the third floor to Boot's Pharmacy.

We were at the doorway of the pharmacy when she turned to me and announced that she was too shy to ask for the pill and that I should do it. I assured her it was a job for a woman, not a man, especially this being Thailand, it made a lot more sense for her to ask the Thai clerk for it than me. Nope. She couldn't do it.

Finally, I gave in. "All right. What is the name of the pill?"

She said something in Thai. I practiced saying it a few times. She corrected my tones. Finally, I got it. "OK. So that is the name of the pill, right?"

"No. That is the name of the movie star."

It was at that point that I realized I was about to once again enter the twilight world of Thai logic. I tried to keep my quavering voice under control.

"What movie star?"

"The TV star. She has a series on TV."

"So what does she have to do with this?"

"She is taking the same pill. Everybody in Thailand watches this series, so just say her name and they know you want the pill she takes."

Needless to say, this led to more discussion and, in the end, she bought the pill.

All seemed well until a few days later. I was leaving on a trip for Europe and would be gone for a few weeks. When I told her that, her face brightened and she said, "Oh, OK, so I don't have to take the pill while you're away, right?"

Hmmm. What exactly do they teach them in the Thai educational system?

And then there was the pretty lady from Chiang Mai who worked in a specialty cosmetics store. She had a lovely face and customers would take a look at her wonderful, smooth, unblemished complexion and feel confident in her recommendations. There were several "cosmetic specialists" in the store and even a lady doctor. One day, the Chiang Mai beauty came to my apartment and handed me a piece of paper. In fact it was a piece of brown paper obviously cut from a brown paper bag. And on one side, the doctor had dictated a message to my girlfriend. It read:

I have a pimple because you kiss me alot. Doctor she said you juskiss me only one time aday it's enough.

And so there it was: A grown man, a writer, being told by a doctor in a message cut from a brown paper bag how many times a day he should kiss his girlfriend.

Hello. This must be Thailand.

When I was photographing the book, *Thailand: Land of Beautiful Women*, I decided the best way to puncture the stereotype of Thai women as subservient and obedient would be to include a few Thai dominatrixes in the photographs. I knew there were one or two houses of domination about and I wrote to one of them. The owner there agreed to my request.

As I was about to leave for the photography session, I looked about to see if I had anything the women might wear besides their own leather outfits. Just for variety. I noticed a bright yellow sarong on a shelf in the closet and decided to grab that and bring it along.

Out at Chateau Jade House of Domination all went well; I photographed three of the dominatrixes, and one of them agreed to wear the sarong.

As it turned out, the photographs came out as I wanted them to and I decided to use one in which one of the dom's was wearing the sarong. The book was nearly finished and ready for a blueprint when my girlfriend came out of the bathroom wearing the very same sarong. And that's when I remembered I had given it to her as a birthday gift. And she would of course be looking through the book when it appeared.

Now, she might say, "Oh, look, you used my sarong in the photography. Well, I'm glad it came in handy for you." Well, men who think women might react that way haven't been around women much. She would more likely have said: "How *could* you! How could you take my sarong, my *birthday* gift, and let another woman wear it?"

I felt the perspiration break out on my forehead. I called the designer and told him we had to meet for an emergency session. We huddled together in front of his computer and went into Photoshop. And then, painstakingly, the designer transformed first the color of the sarong and bit by bit the design as well. Swirls became lines, flowers became stars, patterns were eliminated altogether. By the time he had finished, it was a completely different sarong. Photoshop and the skill of my designer had saved my bacon.

Sarong experts, however, can usually tell a great deal about the origin of a sarong by looking at its pattern. And I sometimes wonder if some expert on Thai arts and crafts has looked at page 92 of *Thailand: Land of Beautiful Women* and scratched his head, trying to figure out what part of Thailand produced that strange design.

Present Perfect

The first English class I taught in Thailand was in 1966. There used to be an English school at Wangsalalom near Sanam Luang, the Parade Ground. Dr. Chalao's English Institute. Dr. Chalao died of cancer but she was a fine lady as were the Thai ladies on the administration staff.

There were also classes for those who wanted to learn Thai and I bought one of the books, *Let's Speak Thai*. Eventually, years later, while I was living in Hong Kong, somebody's Thai maid sat with me and we put the whole book of lessons on tape. I can't remember if I nailed the maid or not but that was a long time ago.

Anyway, the school is long gone now but I have many fond memories of teaching Thai students. And, of course, as every *farang* teacher in Thailand has, some very erotic memories as well. We always remember our first day.

I walked into the class and it seemed like I had died and gone to heaven. There were acres and acres of young Thai women, many in body-hugging school uniforms from nearby Thammasat University and many in normal dress. Gorgeous, stunning, ravishing, well groomed women in just about every direction. For several seconds I probably simply stood in the doorway, mouth agape.

There are certain experiences in Thailand many of us go through, experiences pleasant enough but shocking to the point of mind-numbing. For example, I enjoy sitting near the unisex bathrooms of certain go go bars such as the Long Gun on *Soi* Cowboy. It's fun to watch the tourists go into the "restroom" because inside that room on the right are skimpily clad go go dancers at sinks in front of mirrors, some topless, applying makeup or brushing their hair. While on the other side of the room is a communal urinal for the guys.

Watching the expressions on tourist faces as they stumble out is great fun. It's kind of a mix of bewilderment, astonishment, pleasure, and more than a tiny trace of a schoolboy's smirk when he has just seen dirty pictures out behind the school at recess. Of course, you might say that by sitting outside unisex bathrooms in go go bars to watch tourist reactions it's possible I have too much time on my hands to which I might say fuck you.

Anyway, getting back to the English school, somebody should have warned me about what I was going to face because I felt a decided stirring in my loins almost immediately and felt obliged to quickly sit behind the desk at the front of the room.

I hated to introduce myself while sitting down but what could I do? If I had known what it would be like I could have taken precautions. I would have strapped it down with cord or cable or bamboo or duct tape or piano wire or something but nothing and no one had prepared me for looking out upon enchanting female Siamese faces, perfect figures and lovely, curvaceous legs.

I placed my left hand in my lap as nonchalantly as I could, hoping that the principle of out of sight out of mind might work, but that only made it worse. Nevertheless, once pleasantries were over, I made a stab at teaching. I finished the first lesson with about ten minutes still to go so to fill in the time I asked if anyone had any questions about English.

A beauty in a school uniform raised her hand. Long black hair, beautiful smile, perfectly ironed white blouse, long black skirt, white socks, black shoes. She said she didn't understand the present perfect tense.

And I thought: present perfect? What the hell do I know about present perfect tense? I knew something about that stuff in college maybe but that was another time another place. What I wanted to say to her was: This is the present and you're perfect. But I wracked my brain and did my best to unclog my neurons, wiped the cobwebs off and kicked the neurons in the ass so they would once again start jumping the synapses like they used to do before I began indulging in too much of this and too much of that.

Finally, I felt confident enough to stand up and walked to the front of the desk. I mumbled something about present perfect referring to a completed action some time in the past. But to an indefinite time. She smiled and shyly asked if I could give an example. Jesus.

I gave her my best, most confident, smile. "All right. Certainly. Um, um, OK: the teacher *has given* a great deal of thought to what your succulent, curvaceous, young body looks like without your school uniform on."

Oh, Jesus Christ, did I *say* that or did I just *think* it? No, everybody is still smiling, nobody is nervously fidgeting, so I must have just thought it. Thank God for tender mercies. I try again. "OK, well, for example: The teacher *has spent* many hours wondering if he could be your personal, on-call, copulation tool."

Oh, Jesus, I knew this wasn't going to work. Why did I have to be born oversexed? And end up *here* of all places! The stress will kill me. I mumbled some insipid example that would be acceptable to *normal* people, grinning inanely all the while. And then she asked something about how present perfect differed from *past* perfect. Jesus H. Christ.

I stuttered and stalled for more time hoping the bell would ring. It didn't. "OK," I said. "Past perfect also refers to completed action in the past. But, unlike present perfect, completed action at a definite point. Of course, she ever-so-shyly needed an example.

"OK. Um, before I started teaching English to Thai women, I *had never seen* legs as perfect as yours." Oh, shit. "Um, I mean, OK, if I *had remained* behind the desk, the bulge in my trousers might have gone unnoticed." Oh, no.

I can't remember what I finally came out with, but she smiled and thanked me, her glittering white teeth contrasting with her lovely honey-brown complexion. She leaned back slightly and crossed her legs. I went back behind the desk and sat down. I covered my lap as best I could and wondered if I was really cut out to be an English teacher in Thailand.

A Test of True Love

Many years ago there was a bar on Patpong Road, Patpong II, to be exact. It was a go go bar and its name was Mike's Place. I don't remember Mike but I do remember Siriwan. She was a go-go dancer there. It would be hard to forget her. She was something out of a Playboy fantasy. A gorgeous face and perfect body formed by one succulent curve after another, the type of impossibly beautiful woman you see in America only on racy calendars on the walls of garages while mechanics in grease-stained overalls fix parts of your car which don't really need fixing.

Siriwan and I had spent many happy hours together in Bangkok and other than the usual barfine and normal expenses for a shor- uh, I mean, a casual stay, she had never asked for anything. And then one evening, while we were in bed watching television, she suddenly sat up and said she wanted to write and she needed a typewriter. She looked down at me with those big, beautiful dark eyes. Not to mention that she had nothing covering her big, beautiful dark breasts. Something about the way they hung down reminded me of the sad fate of Tom Dooley but never mind that.

I wasn't quite sure if she meant she wanted to learn to write English or to be a writer or what. But she asked in such a way that it would have been impossible to refuse. Besides, I was living in Hong Kong at the time and knew where I could get portable typewriters cheaply, so I thought, why not.

On my next trip to Bangkok, about one month later, I

approached the bar, carrying the slim typewriter in its case by its plastic handle. But just before I went inside I handed the typewriter to a young bar employee who sat in a chair by the door and I asked him to hold it for me for just a minute.

There had been lots of discussion lately as to whether or not Thai bargirls loved us for ourselves or merely for what they could get out of us. So I decided I would settle the question once and for all.

So I walked into the bar *sans* typewriter. I couldn't spot her dancing on stage but as my eyes adjusted to the light I saw her beautiful face and voluptuous body come toward me. Her face was lit up like a Christmas tree. No question about it — she was genuinely happy to see me.

Then suddenly she stopped as if she had been slapped across the cheek and her eyebrows knitted. The lovely smile disappeared replaced by a cross between disappointment and anguish. I expected her to ask something like "Hi, Dean, how you?" or maybe "Hi, Dean, how your trip?" or something like that. But as I was to learn over the years, Thai bargirls generally cut to the chase. She said: WHERE MY TYPEWRITEEEEEERRRRRRR?!!

I said: "Well, if I brought you a typewriter, do you love me?"

She said: "YEEEEEEESSSSSSS!"

I said: "Well, if I didn't bring you a typewriter, do you still love me?"

She said: "NOOOOOOOOOOOOOOOOO!"

I felt that was enough of a lesson for one day. So, I turned, opened the door, picked up the typewriter and handed it to her. Her face lit up again, brighter than ever. Still holding the typewriter, she flung her arms around me and kissed me. "I love you too much!" She said.

And that pretty much settled the argument right then and there. But it was also clear that what Thai bargirls might lack in love and loyalty they made up for in brutal honesty.

Later that night she showed her appreciation for my gift. So I have decided that the question as to whether or not Thai bargirls love us for ourselves has pretty much been answered. But, somehow, whatever the answer is, it's all right with me.

Brothel Visits

There has been a lot of publicity about how Bangkok police went into massage parlors and actually had sex with the women (without paying, of course) supposedly in order to have "proof" when they arrested them. But anyone who thinks Bangkok's Finest is alone in this sort of thing might enjoy this true tale of New York's Finest.

I was on my annual visit to the Big Apple and digging into a plate of *pad thai kai* (three times what it would cost me in Bangkok) when I spotted this jewel in the *New York Times*: "Officer Accused of Visiting Brothel During Bike Patrol."

It seems the young man was frequenting a Queens brothel while in uniform on bicycle patrol. The paper says "Officer Colon was scurrying off to a bordello at 147-16 Archer Avenue in Jamaica." Well, leaving aside for the moment the question of whether a "brothel" is synonymous with a "bordello" I mention this because we are all perhaps guilty of this sort of behavior at one time or another, because it might prove inspirational to Bangkok police, and because I think the article is an example of fine writing.

In the old days, the staid *NY Times* would have said something to the effect that Officer Colon "made his way" to said brothel. But the words "scurrying off to" conjure up a vivid image of one of New York's Finest in khaki shorts and oval-shaped bike helmet pedaling like mad, no doubt with head down to avoid recognition, but with a sly smile on his face knowing what wonders lay (no pun intended) in store for him at 147-16 Archer Avenue.

Not only that, Officer Colon, while pedaling along the hot, humid streets of Jamaica, hell bent for leather (figuratively speaking, as I have no personal knowledge of whether or not leather was in vogue at that particular establishment) was on a mountain bike. The paper says he "would ride his mountain bike from the 103rd Precinct station house and lock it in a nearby garage before going to the brothel." Which sounds reasonable enough to me but, after living in Thailand for years, pretty much anything sounds reasonable enough to me. Although in most Asian countries the police own the brothels so this kind of conflict does not arise.

Anyway, I know nothing about bikes but apparently mountain bikes are handy things to have. And something tells me the 103rd might be having a sale soon.

Bra Alarms:
for the Thai Girlfriend who has Everything

It's her birthday. Your lovely lady from Korat or Udon Thani or Sisaket is now having a birthday and you need to buy her a really nice gift. Problem is, you've already bought her lots of nice gifts. She already has gold bracelets and a gold necklace from that gold shop she took you to, bottles of Chanel perfume, jars of skin whitening cream and eye resuscitating cream and wrinkle-eliminating lotion and the latest cellphone from the Emporium, and a wardrobe full of clothes from Chaps.

Her upcountry dad still has that pickup truck you bought for him (although you haven't seen it lately) and you bought her family an iron buffalo to replace the real buffalo that had been struck by lightning. She sends (your) money back home every month so her younger brother can go to school and that way, as she explained, you gain Buddhist merit so you are lucky to have that opportunity. Not to mention the bride's milk money and gold you paid to get married to her. Although if you understood correctly that was supposed to come back to you at some point and still might but it sounds complicated and each time you bring up the subject she seems more and more distracted.

Anyway, it's her birthday. She's beautiful and loving, takes good care of you and is about the age of your daughter (or less) if you had one so you do in fact want to keep her happy; and you want to give her something different. Not the Patek Philippe watch she's been drooling over nor the BMW M3 she keeps pointing out to you when you go by the showroom. Something a bit less expensive but different. Well, thanks to American paranoia, there is now the perfect present. This from the pages of a New York City tabloid:

> A brand-new bra designed by an art-school student provides the ultimate in support — with a built-in alarm designed to protect women from rapists and muggers.
>
> An electronic sensor in the bra's under-wiring detects a racing heartbeat if the wearer feels threatened — triggering a high-pitched noise to scare off attackers.
>
> If it turns out to be a false alarm, she can disarm the alarm by pressing a tiny button on the front of the bra . . . .

And there it is: the perfect, totally unexpected gift for your Thai girlfriend. Although it is getting more and more difficult to keep abreast (no pun intended) of the idiocy of American society. But wasn't there a Sherlock Holmes novel is which the murderer was caught precisely because the dog *didn't* bark, meaning the dog recognized the murderer? As a writer of murder mysteries I am always on the lookout for a good plot. So what about a mystery novel in which a dead woman's bra *didn't* go off, which, to a clever detective, would mean her heart didn't speed up precisely because she knew the murderer? Maybe call it something like, *The Case of the Quiet Bra,* or *The Multiple Mammary Murders,* or *Trouble at Twin Peaks,* or *The Battered Bosom from Burriram.* Or maybe as a sequel to my own *Skytrain to Murder* I could call it *Bra Alarm to Murder.*

And I suppose soon we will be hearing this Captain's announcement: ". . . and at takeoff kindly turn off all cell phones, calculators, computers, and, er, ah, bras . . . No, no, madam I said 'turn' off, not 'take' off."

Anyway, there it is: the perfect surprise birthday gift for your very special lovely lady which her friends won't have. And, don't forget, you know how to turn off the alarm.

The Tourist

She showed up at the open-air Thai restaurant with a backpack larger than most suitcases. Her stringy auburn hair was pulled back into an untidy pony tail, her birdlike nose was sunburned, her pasty white skin was freckled, her skimpy tank top displayed enough armpit hair to choke a *klong*, her burgundy slacks were too tight and her open-toed sandals revealed bony toes.

As soon as she caught the eye of the hostess she put her palms together and gave her a big *wai* and then when her waiter came over, she *waiied* him. It was the tourist *wai*: overdone and stereotyped and delivered with a *huge* smile. She looked over the menu, still smiling.

There was something about this woman that irritated me. It might have been the superficial nature of her friendliness. It might have been that she reminded me of how I had acted in a similar manner so many years ago when I first washed up on Siam's shores. It might have been that I had been hustling the waitress for weeks but not much had come out of it. It might have been I was just in a foul mood because number 22 at the Magic Fingers Massage Parlor had been taken the night before and I had ended up with number 36. A bad choice.

She sat facing away from me, and as she leaned forward to order, I could see her canary yellow bra straps through the back of her white tank top which for whatever reason turned me off. She looked around the restaurant but before she could catch my eye to give me one of those infuriatingly insipid smiles I looked

away and busied myself with my Carlsberg and *pad Thai kung*.
When I again looked up — ye gads — she was walking over
to me. Smiling. She probably wanted directions about how to
get to a backpacker-friendly temple or how to get to some cheap
cockroach-infested flophouse on Khao San Road.

Every movement a kind of pose
If she *wais* me, I'm going to punch her in the nose

I had no choice so I looked up at her as she approached. I
tried my best to return her smile but it probably came out as a
pain-filled grimace. "Excuse me," she said.

I think: "How much horror can one day bring?"
She asks: "Didn't you write *Peach Blossom Spring*?"

I stared at her, taken aback. "Yes, I did."
"You're Dean Barrett."
"I am."
"I read your book *Don Quixote in China*. I thought it was
fantastic. You're a wonderful writer!"
I suddenly realized this woman was discerning, intelligent,
sagacious and perspicacious. I stood up and gestured for her to
sit down. What a wonderful person. Obviously perceptive and
discriminating.
What! So? You thought only *politicians* could be hypocrites?

223

Too Good to be True

It was one of the best go go bars I had ever been in. I was sitting at the bar surrounded by absolutely gorgeous Thai dancers in the usual skimpy bikinis and knee-high black boots and they weren't pushing me for drinks. Up on the stage I saw June and Joy, the famous twin dancers from the Mississippi Queen Bar on Patpong Road just as they looked in the late 70's. Energetic and full of vigor. Glasses and bottles along the bar shook from the vibrations of their booted steps as they danced to "Brown Girl in the Ring."

The girls surrounding me acted as if I was the only man in the world, the best thing they'd seen since the invention of sticky rice. They couldn't get enough of me. And they wouldn't let me buy them any drinks. They said writers don't make enough money for that; they would get what they need from their businessmen clients.

They wanted to know if there was anything they could do for me. One of the best looking said, "Ask not what your customer can do for you, but what you can do for your customer." These women were great! Sure, I knew it was a dream but what the hell I planned to enjoy it to the max.

"You can have anything you want," one of them said.

"That's right, I can, can't I? OK, watch this." I made a few Mandrake the Magician hand gestures and voila! Who should appear at the doorway but a genuine hard-featured, glaring-with-indignant-anger, humorless, strident, puritanical, Western *feminazi.*

The lovely go go dancers were astounded. *"She* is what you want?"

"Keep watching," I said.

The feminazi walked toward me but the closer she got, the more her attitude and facial expression changed. She crouched low so as to keep herself below me, placed her palms together to *wai* me, and a humble, apologetic look came into her eyes. She knelt before me.

"What is it you want?" I asked.

I saw her eyes well up with tears. *"Khun* Dean, I come to ask for forgiveness," she said. "All these years, women like me have been saying bad things about men like you. Men who come to Thailand and find happiness with wonderful Thai girlfriends."

"Really? And what are some of those things?"

She looked even more embarrassed. "We have been saying that men like you are socially inept; that you're afraid of 'smart' women; that you're exploiting women; that men with much younger women are intimidated by women their own age."

"I see. And now?"

"Now I have come to realize the error of my ways. The truth is Western feminazis like me are simply jealous. We know we can't possibly compete with the beauty and grace and charm and femininity of Thai women. We realize that although we've feminized America and turned American men into domesticated wimps, Thailand represents a threat; because it gives men a choice. And the easier it is for men to have sex, the less power we have. So we have reacted in this horribly childish way."

Her body language had become even more contrite, her voice more repentant. "And we have belittled the young Thai women attracted to *farang* men like you as well as men like you attracted to Thai women. It is not Western *men* who have created the myth of Asian female subservience; it is the Western *feminazi* who did this for our own selfish purposes. Because we know if enough men realize they have a choice, they will no longer be in our control. They will realize all our propaganda about men dating younger women being intimidated by older women is just superficial, American pop psychology bullshit."

I took a swig of my Singha and looked down at her with an expression just short of a glare. "And what of those so-called intelligent, independent women on *Sex and the City* and women like them?"

I watched tears of remorse and contrition course down her cheeks. "*Khun* Dean, the truth is, those four bimbos couldn't find Afghanistan on the map if their lives depended on it. All they know how to do is sit around babbling about commitment and empowerment and other stupid cliches. The truth is women like them have the best deal on the planet but they complain the most. They're whining, self-indulgent, self-absorbed, self-pitying, spoiled brats." She hung her head. "Just as I have been."

I nodded thoughtfully. "Very well," I said, "I believe you are sincere, but your sins are great, and if I am to give you absolution, you must promise a few things."

"Yes, of course," she said, "anything."

"You must say three Hail Malee's."

"Of course."

"You must say ten Hail Trink's."

"Of course, *Khun* Dean."

"And you must return to America to open up a Hugh Hefner fan club. And recruit as many misguided feminazis to your new cause as possible."

"Yes, of course. Whatever you say."

I allowed her to kiss the Lone Ranger and Tonto secret decoder ring on my finger. "Now be a good girl and repent."

"Yes, of course, *Khun* Dean, but, um, I have been a very *bad* girl." She placed her hands on her buttocks. "Shouldn't I have a spanking?"

"Well, I will monitor your behavior closely; then act appropriately. Now go forth and sin no more."

She kissed my ring again. "Yes, Khun Dean, thank you so much. I will repent from this time forth." And she crouched her way out of the room, backward, *waï*ing me all the way.

The girls laughed and applauded at the way I had handled the ex-feminazi, she-who-had-seen-the-light.

Then I heard a deep, masculine voice say, "What'll it be?"

I turned to face the bartender. He was a white guy in his 40's, thinning hair, flat, ex-boxer's nose, Brooklyn accent. His attitude unfriendly, or at least nonchalant. When I had lived in New York City I had seen bartenders exactly like him.

I smiled. "Nothing just now," I said.

He scowled. "Yah gotta order."

"Not right now, OK?"

He gritted his teeth and scowled. "Hey, bud, this is a bar. Yah gotta order."

He was beginning to piss me off. "Yeah, I know this is a bar, but it's *my fucking dream*! So I don' gotta order."

"I don't give a fuck whose fucking dream it is, it's *my* fucking bar, and I fucking say you gotta order."

"Well, I'm not gonna order and in *my* dream nobody tells me what to do. Right, girls?"

"That's right, honey."

I didn't like the sound of that. The voice was a little too deep and resonant. I turned to look at the girls still clinging onto me. Now they all sported large Adams apples and could have done with a shave. Jesus Christ! I had been set up! This whole dream had been a feminazi trap of some kind. Somehow, they had managed to penetrate my subconscious!

I tried to extricate myself from the stool but the "girls" were strong as hell.

Then suddenly I felt hands under my shoulders and felt myself roughly and abruptly jerked up off of my stool. Two huge black bouncers dragged me toward the door. "Fuck you doin' jive-assin' up here in Harlem, anyway, white boy? Draggin' your goofy white ass around these parts ain't smart. It ain't healthy."

"Harlem!" I said. "There must be some mistake!"

The bartender yelled to me. "Yeah, and you made it, honky."

I looked back and saw that the bartender was now a Mike Tyson lookalike and the "girls" were now black transvestites. Then suddenly I was flying through the air and landed on the sidewalk outside the bar door hard on my back. My head hurt. Nearby birds made strange sounds.

I woke up. I had a hangover. My head still hurt. The neighbor's damn macaws were jabbering away excitedly about something.

I had just been thrown out of a bar in my own damn dream; a dream which showed me that feminazis were attacking me even in my sleep. And now I had to start another day in Bangkok. Jesus Christ!

The Making of:
Thailand: Land of Beautiful Women

Over two decades ago when, in many ways, I was a much younger man, I enjoyed living in Hong Kong and, once a month, traveling to Thailand. I would give the blueprint of the next *Sawasdee* inflight magazine to the people in the head office of Thai Airways International to check for cultural and other errors, and while those good people made certain I did not place a pretty girl's picture above a monk or commit some such typical *farang* editor abomination, for several days I would head out across the country, photographing temples, children, the elderly, rural scenes, *klongs*, fishermen, ricefields and, yes, women.

It wasn't long before I noticed that although I had quite a collection of Thailand shots, I also noticed that the majority were on, yes, women. It was my belief that — whatever their occupations — the women of Thailand were lovely, graceful, charming, etc., etc., and wasn't it a shame that no one was doing anything to pass that message on? Also, I suspected that someday some fool was going to do a book on Thai women and, as I later explained to the photographer extraordinare, Khun Shrimp, (slightly miffed because I had beaten him to the punch) I wanted to be that fool. I was. I am.

And so it was born: a 144-page, full color photobook entitled, *The Girls of Thailand.* I loved it, the girls loved it, men loved it, my mother and stepfather loved it. Uh oh, acclaim was not to be universal: *khunyings* and *feminazis* detested it. Sweetheart of a guy that I am, with the publication of this book, I had nevertheless become the anti-Christ. And while Singapore Airlines was creating arguably the most successful airline ad campaign in history — Singapore Girl: You're a Great Way to Fly, I was told by stern-faced Western women that "there are no *girls* in Asia, Mr. Barrett!" Right, whatever.

The book sold well but one day I noticed in shops at Hong Kong's old Kai Tak airport it was shrink-wrapped so no one could open it. This was strange, thought I, because there was no nudity in it. And certainly no obscenity. And then I understood: the vendors had shrink-wrapped it precisely *because* there was no nudity in it. And so *The Girls of Thailand* attained legend status (duly mentioned in *Publishers Weekly*) as the only book in publishing history to have been shrink-wrapped not because it was a dirty book but precisely because it *wasn't*.

Fast forward more than twenty-one years. 2000 A.D. After 14 years living in Manhattan as a novelist and playwright, I returned to Thailand. No one asked me about my novels or plays or musical or ballads. No one seemed interested in my more "serious" work. The only thing I kept getting asked was, "Hey, when you gonna do another *Girls of Thailand* book?" And finally I gave in: OK, give the public what it wants. Besides, I realized there is a whole new generation of feminazis who know nothing about *The Girls of Thailand* book and the least I could do was to give them someone to focus their anger on.

My film agent in L.A. warned me that if I did books like *The Girls of Thailand* it was possible no one would take my other work seriously. But who, I thought, is taking it seriously now?

And so I abandoned my "serious" novels and non-fiction and off I went rewriting and updating the old texts, adding new material, and photographing like mad. And, before too long, the 160-page, full color photobook, *Thailand: Land of Beautiful Women* was born. (Astute readers will not fail to notice I even changed the title from "Girls" to "Women." Who says men living in Bangkok don't have the capacity to change?)

I assured a local distributor (who still retained less than happy memories of the flak surrounding the first book) that there would be no nudity and just a few nightlife pages in the back of the book. Well, actually, there are more than a few: 80 pages to be exact, but, hey, who's counting?

And the book appeared! And the book disappeared! Apparently, after seeing photographs of the dominatrixes and the ladyboys and the construction workers — not to mention the venerable former *Bangkok Post* nightlife columnist Bernard Trink, someone in officialdom felt it wasn't the right image for Thailand. But then the book (in some places) reappeared! (In his review, Trink complained there were no stewardesses in the book. But I had replaced the stewardesses in the old book with dominatrixes in this one; from plane to pain, so to speak.)

The Girls of Thailand appeared in 1980, *Thailand: Land of Beautiful Women* in 2001. It is my intention to come out with the next one 21 years from now, and the final one 21 years after that at which point I will be exactly 100 years old, and can look back and feel good about having fulfilled what was obviously meant to be my life's mission.

Top Secret!

The attractive young Thai woman was fully dressed. She had short hair which was exactly right for the shape of her face, cute dimples, and an infectious smile. We were chatting a bit at the bar and at some point I bought her a drink. Nothing unusual about this scenario except for the fact that the year was 1966 and it was my first time inside a bar in Thailand.

I had arrived with the American military during March and, not being used to the country's heat and humidity, within three days I had ended up in a local hospital with heat exhaustion. The medical profession is only too aware that GI's don't come down with things like unstable angina or osteoporosis or erectile disfunction and that if a military unit has sent a GI to a hospital in Bangkok then said GI most likely has VD. Of course I hadn't done anything or been anywhere and didn't have VD. (Yet.) So after treating me for VD (and curing me of that which I hadn't had), I was sent back to my unit.

A fellow GI took pity on me and suggested what I needed was air conditioning. In the Bangkok of 1966, not many places had air conditioning — not taxis, not buses, and certainly not my army barracks. So when I asked where I would find air conditioning I was told: "The bars on Patpong Road."

And off I went. In those days there were not many bars on Patpong Road and of course there was no go go dancing. Talk about a hardship post! I must confess those of us stationed in Bangkok were not the most popular people with the Bangkok bargirls because they knew that GI's on R&R from Vietnam, not knowing if they would last out the war or not, would spend their savings freely and without regret. Seri Court GI's, on the other hand, were stationed in Bangkok and we dared to presume we would be around for quite some time. Hence, we were less likely to buy a bargirl lots of drinks or to overlook a padded bill. If I recall correctly, the endearing, descriptive terms they favored us with was: "Number ten, *mai dee* (no good), piss-shit, cheap Charlie, Seri Court GI's."

Anyway, I wandered into one of the bars, maybe it was the Amor, maybe the Roma, I'm not sure. I sat up at the counter and within a minute or two I had both a cold beer to quench my thirst and a lovely girl to talk with. *And* air conditioning.

Things were going along smoothly and she was asking the usual questions about where was I staying, where was I from, that kind of thing, and I had visions of the two of us enjoying the rest of the night over a quiet, smelly *klong* in some rickety, wobbly, non-air-conditioned wooden shack which was the likely nocturnal journey's end in those days for GI's, and then she asked a question which made quite an impression on me. It still does. She smiled and said, "So, you truck driver or cipher?"

You have to understand I had arrived in Bangkok as a Chinese linguist with the Army Security Agency, was cleared top secret, cryptographic, and was assigned to a radio research and special operations unit. No one was supposed to even know we were there, let alone what we did. In fact, our usual response to any queries about our mission in Thailand was something to the effect that we were freelance typewriter repairmen temporarily attached to the 34th Mess Kit Repair Squadron — we unbent spoons, realigned fork tines and sharpened knives.

So, to say the least, I found her question disconcerting. I jerked my head back and did my best to keep a pleasant smile on my face, and said, "Excuse me?"

She then repeated the question, except this time she employed gestures as well. She made the motion of driving a truck and said, "You know, truck driver." And then she made the motion of slipping earphones over her head and tapping out Morse code and said, "cipher."

And I remember thinking to myself, Jesus Christ, we are going to lose this fucking war.

Delightfully Tacky Yet Unrefined

Gulliver's is a cavernous, gargantuan, pub that opened on Bangkok's Sukhumvit Road, *soi* 5. Smack dab in the action area for nightlife. True, there aren't many Russian women hanging around the lanes there anymore to give the Thai women competition but it's still a lively area.

Inside Gulliver's are large bar areas usually packed with young Thai women who, to say the least, are not opposed to meeting foreign men, and there are lots of pool tables usually occupied by still more Thai women and the pub has various games also popular with Thai women. The walls are covered with television sets and several neon signs forming a blush-pink Marilyn Monroe, a goldenrod-yellow Elvis, and you-name-it signs about food and beer and music. And a flashy red 1950's Chevy is at the center of everything above the main bar slowly turning around in a circle like a drunkard who forgot his way home but who refuses to give up trying.

It was raining the last time I was in Gulliver's and maybe that's why it reminded me of when I had been in another huge place with lots of women. It had been in Milwaukee, smack dab in America's Midwest.

To escape the downpour, I had dashed into a restaurant called Hooters. For the one or two people on the planet who haven't gotten the word, Hooters is a restaurant chain with voluptuous young waitresses in politically incorrect short shorts with the slogan "delightfully tacky yet unrefined" on their tank tops.

One of the waitresses was the stereotype of the sweet, young, impossibly wholesome, apple-cheeked, corn-fed Midwestern lovely. Of course, she was less than half my age (everyone is these days) but it has always been my most tenaciously held belief that nothing is more deadening to the human spirit than emotional maturity, and I try to avoid it at all costs. She said she was a model who was hoping to get to Manhattan and become an actress in live theater. As I was living in Manhattan at the time as a playwright, I figured if I played my cards right I was on a roll.

Even at that time I had already lived in Asia for many years, so that may be why a lot of my countrymen's customs were strange to me. In a café where curvaceous, voluptuous, succulent waitresses were walking about in tank top and short shorts, the male customers were engrossed in watching large wall screens and TV sets in which other males were catching, throwing, batting or kicking balls about. And every so often these customers would let out fervent shouts, raucous cheers and roars of excitement.

With the exception of boxing, nothing bores me more than sports and I seemed to be the only one in the room paying attention to the women. I remember thinking: Am I sick? Do I need help? Should I wait for the authorities to pick me up or simply turn myself in?

I mention this because the last time I was in Gulliver's, I sat toward the rear and there was a huge screen against the rear wall on which was a soccer game. And, once again, despite the presence of gorgeous (and available) women, all of the men around me were watching and sometimes cheering hideously overpaid, half-men, half-boy jocks running madly about destroying a perfectly good lawn while attempting to kick balls into nets. And, of course, once a ball was actually kicked into a net, the men watching the game acted as if they'd had their first orgasm in years.

Yes, I do realize I am a bit oversexed, and I do understand that bars like Gulliver's are sports bars, but even so I find it difficult to understand men who value sports events so highly and the company of women so lightly.

Well, the nearest Thai police station is not far from my apartment, so I guess I'll go turn myself in now and confess to my disdain for watching sports and to my shameful cravings and unnatural urges regarding members of the opposite sex. I suppose the charge will be something like "Favoring Female Company in the Flesh in preference to Viewing Sports Events on Screens."

To the Person in Colorado whose Fax Message Woke Me up at 2:38 a.m. this Sunday Morning

1. Writers, especially those living in Thailand, very often have their offices inside their homes.

2. In Bangkok, a "home" for a writer is most likely a one-bedroom apartment.

3. That means when the phone rings, wherever it and the fax machine are placed, it will wake up anyone in the apartment.

4. You woke up Lek and her sister.

5. Lek and her sister are pissed.

6. Unlike China, much of the world has something called time zones. When it is 2:38 p.m. in Colorado, it is the following morning 2:38 a.m. in Bangkok.

7. When a person is woken up early Sunday morning by a faxed advertisement "Final Reminder — Sale — Western-Style Clothing — Don't Be Left Out!" that person is not likely to ever purchase your product or service anywhere at anytime for any reason.

8. After I have one or two cups of Irish coffee, I will no doubt feel more kindly toward you, but if you do it again, I will

teach you why my Hong Kong novel is named *Hangman's Point.*

9. Many Thais say people living in Bangkok are not as polite as those living in the countryside; but that is because we are the victims of sleep-deprivation from being faxed at all hours by people from other countries. People like you.

10. Surely there is something better to do in Colorado than hang about the fax machine harassing people in other countries. Don't you still have square dancing at yo-downs, go-downs, ho-downs, or whatever they're called? Or maybe you could sit around like the four bimbos on *Sex and the City* and babble in a self-pitying, self-centered, self-absorbed, self-indulgent way about "relationships, commitment and communication"?

11. If you are a beautiful woman who looks great in a Stetson hat, colorful bandana, fancy western blouse with brocade and floral embroidery, rhinestone-studded pockets and lots of piping along the collars and sleeves, and pearlized snap buttons and caballero cuffs, and body-hugging, concho-trimmed, stonewashed jeans, huge silver-plated belt buckle, and Western hand-tooled caramel leather boots, ignore points one through ten and fax me again but with a more interesting proposal.

Thank you for your kind attention to this matter.

Sincerely,

Dean Barrett

The Ghost who Loved Me (kind of)

The Bangkok of the *farang* (foreigner) is always full of unsubstantiated rumors and unconfirmed reports and unverifiable scandal; most pass by without drawing undue attention. However, persistent reports from Rumor-Control Headquarters had it that a young Englishman was making a Thai film. A ghost film, no less. And that they needed *farang* males as extras hanging about in a go go bar. Having done exactly that kind of hanging about for decades it seemed to me I would be the perfect candidate.

And so it came to pass that at seven in the morning I found myself in a gutted nightclub several miles to the north of downtown Bangkok (assuming there is a "downtown Bangkok," which seems to exist only in novels and guidebooks written by those who rarely visit Bangkok).

Anyway, the Phoenix had been a pretty popular club in its day until someone — a bit intoxicated perhaps — had studiously and unwisely ignored the sign about not taking weapons into the club and before you could say "Duck yo' haid!" three guys were shot dead. After which the building was closed and at some point completely trashed and gutted, all fixtures including air conditioners simply ripped from the walls.

When I arrived I found Thai camera crews setting up and Thai actresses sleeping about on a debris-covered floor. Although "debris" is much too polite a term for the horrible condition of what once had been a nightclub. And "floor" conjures up far too much comfort for what was actually left to lie or walk on. It really looked as if the place had been bombed and looted by several armies at once.

However, thanks to the valiant efforts of the film crew, one of the rooms had been miraculously and very realistically transformed into a go go bar complete with Cambodian décor and a stage. Each of us, i.e., the foreign male extras, was to sit about and chat with one of the bikini-clad, young actresses playing bargirls while watching a show on the stage. This was great: after 38 years of paying to do this, I was now actually *getting paid* to do this!

Everything was so real it was hard to believe it was not a go go bar with real dancers, especially since the actress-dancers were being trained by the woman who trains go go dancers at the famous Long Gun bar on *Soi* Cowboy. And also because we were supposed to act as if we were in a real bar.

And so while chatting in Thai with the very beautiful girl beside me I learned that she did in fact already have a Thai boyfriend. So I pointed to myself and said she now also had a *farang* boyfriend. To which she gave me a friendly, don't-be-silly, smile, an affectionate pat on the arm, and said in English: "Grandfa*ther*!"

Oh. Ok, I see now how the game is played. These actresses pretending to be bargirls are Bangkok girls from financially stable families as opposed to *real* bargirls from northeast Thailand from impoverished families. In other words, actresses posing as bargirls wouldn't have quite the same alacrity to jump into bed with me as real bargirls sometimes did. OK. I didn't just fall off the durian cart yesterday. But I could handle the situation: Bangkok girls would simply be more of a challenge, that's all.

After the camera panned the room, I was selected to sit at the end of the stage and stare at the bikini-clad leading actress as she danced erotically and then got down on all fours and crawled toward me, long, jet-black hair covering one eye. She then turned onto her back, arched herself, placed her hands on her breasts and stared up at me, her perfect lips just inches away. Using either method acting or simply being myself — whichever — I think I managed to stare back at her with undisguised lust.

I must have done a reasonable acting job as a man with lust in his heart because I got a call from the director a few days later asking if I would like to be in a bed scene and a shower scene with the leading actress. How much would I have to pay? No, saith the director, *they would pay me*! God, I love film people. He mentioned that there was a slight catch.

Me: "A catch?"

Director: "Well, remember the name of the film is *Pii Borb*."

Me: *Pii* means "ghost," right?"

Director: "Yes, and a *pii borb* is the kind of ghost which will eat your heart and liver. She kills you in the shower, actually."

Me: "But I get to go to bed with her first, right?"

Director: "Yes."

Me: "Hell, I've given my heart away to lots of Thai women so that's no big deal. And as for livers I can always get another one of those on the Cambodian black market, right?"

So once again, at seven in the morning, I found myself out at the OK Corral of gutted nightclubs cum film studios. The go go bar was completely gone and now replaced by a small area serving as a shower.

The director had explained how the girl and I would be in the shower but the camera would be on the other side of the shower curtain. So our silhouettes would be seen coming together in profile.

What he didn't say when describing my profile was whether or not he wanted me to have an erection. If so, I thought maybe I should pop a Viagra. With a leading actress as beautiful as she was I figured I shouldn't need it but after all it would be seven in the morning and those film lights get hot. I didn't want to screw up his film but I decided to trust my own instinctive reactions and left the Viagra in the drawer.

As it turned out, the shower scene had been changed a bit. But anyway I was in only my underwear and the actress was in a kind of short body stocking. Even by Western standards of hirsute, I am quite hairy, but seeing a hairy Westerner in his underwear didn't seem to faze her. She simply rehearsed coming up behind me causing me to turn and speak to her. After which I acted out my role by realizing something was seriously strange about her and screamed. Too late. I grabbed the shower curtain, pulling it down with me as I fell to the bathroom floor. Dead.

Then a tube was placed in my mouth, the "blood" was pumped in and out and I found myself covered with fake blood, eyes open, dead. Once the scene was successfully completed, I stood around in my underwear while someone went off to a 7-Eleven to buy some soap.

Wearing absolutely nothing but my underwear and covered in blood, I was led though an open, public area to a building where I was told there was a shower. Apparently, people in a nearby restaurant had not been briefed about the making of a movie, and I received stares I had never received in all my years in Asia.

Inside the building and up the concrete stairs and inside a small bathroom. The "shower" consisted of a ceramic urn, i.e., a *klong* jar with a plastic bucket, a tiny towel, and without a place to hang the trousers I was holding gingerly in my hand. The blood was very difficult to wash off so I decided to try to get it off my face and ears and hair so at least a taxi driver might be willing to stop and take me home where I could have a real shower. Needless to say, this was not the "shower scene" I had envisioned with the leading actress but I remained confident that things would go sexier the following week when they would shoot the bedroom scene.

I confess to always having had a passion for beautiful Asian women with supernatural powers. In my youth, in Hong Kong, I would watch Chinese swordfighting movies, particularly the historical ones involving young Chinese women with bushy tails known as *hu-li ching* or "fox fairies."

These women were actually foxes who assumed the disguise of a beautiful maiden who attempted to seduce men, particularly scholars, but who sometimes neglected to complete their transformation, hence, a bushy tail was still attached to a gorgeous woman, which she of course tried to hide. Fox fairies were a kind of succulent succubus irresistible to men. I always thought of a sexy woman with a bushy tail as a plus not a minus although what Freud would say about that I'm not certain. But I'm a writer and writers are weird.

The day arrived for my last performance. Once again I wasn't certain how much cinema verite would be involved here but because it was a bedroom scene I decided to bring along a condom. After all, hope springs eternal, if not in the human breast, then certainly in the little brain of Everyman.

This time the setting was in a luxury apartment in a completely different area of Bangkok. Swimming pools, hot and cold running water, a beautiful balcony, wow! So once again I stripped down to my underwear and got under the sheet and lay beside the gorgeous leading lady who had been taped up a bit in front so as not to reveal too much.

It had been my oh-so-clever intention to suggest to everyone in the room that the actress and I should be left alone for an hour or so, so that we could practice our lines. I figured if anything interesting was going to happen it would be then. Unfortunately, I only had four Thai words to speak (rough English translation: "How about we do it again?" wink, wink, nudge, nudge) and it is pretty difficult to ask for an hour of practice for only four words — even in a foreign language.

In many films, as in this one, scenes are shot out of sequence, so in the previous shower scene the ghost-actress had already killed me thereby making me, I suppose, a ghost as well. So now we were two ghosts lying side by side in bed one of which had perfect brown skin, a beautiful face and lovely black hair fanned out against a white pillowcase and one of which was getting horny as hell.

And then it happened. For the first time ever! The actress did what no woman had done in bed with me before — at least not before doing the deed — *She fell asleep*. There I was in bed with this succulent Thai creature and she was apparently so excited by the prospect of being in bed with me, so thrilled at the opportunity, that before you could say "yawn, ho hum" she was out like a light.

Embarrassing to relate, yes. But you must understand that in the bedroom were also eight cameramen setting up cameras and lights; the director was sitting on the bed near the actress talking to the assistant director; the TV was on. But when I leaned over to offer the actress some water, she didn't respond. The director looked down at her and said, "She's out." (Of course, it was the next to last day of filming 12-hour days for over a month, and everyone making the film was exhausted.)

The actress was gently woken and the scene was filmed. Her response to my suggestion that we do "it" again was to suggest I take a shower first and we all know where that led to: Death and dismemberment on a cold bathroom floor.

And that was the end of that. But *Pii Borb* is my third film credit. In the late 60's, I played a thirty second role in a grade C Italian war movie in Bangkok; in the late 70's, I played a twenty second role as an auctioneer in a Hong Kong movie; and now I play a one minute (total maybe) role as a horny foreigner who gets the wrong part of his anatomy gobbled up by a beautiful Thai ghost. Surely with *that* impressive resume, Hollywood agents will be swarming all over me.

Praise for
*Don Quixote in China:
The Search for
Peach Blossom Spring*

"The author speaks Chinese and has lived in Asia for 20 years, so he readily enters the lives of the people he meets, and readers end up feeling as if they have gotten an inside look at the world's most populous country.

Barrett is insightful, knowledgeable, compassionate, spontaneous, and humorous, and he has produced an entertaining and perceptive book. Recommended for all libraries with Asian studies or travel collections."

— *Library Journal*

"*Don Quixote in China* is a travel book I won't hesitate to advise you to read. Get Barrett's other books of non-fiction and fiction. You'll be glad you did."

— Bernard Trink, *Bangkok Post*

"If you've been waiting for Bill Bryson to "do" China, here's a book you're sure to enjoy. Dean Barrett expresses admiration for the travel writing of Paul Theroux, but *Don Quixote in China: The Search for Peach Blossom Spring* rather brings Bryson, or even P.J. O'Rourke, to mind.

Don Quixote in China is an enjoyable stumble through the less visited reaches of China's tourist industry. ...a lighthearted read that any fan of travel literature will enjoy."

— *The Asian Review of Books*

"Dean's account of his search is often filled with hilarious episodes leaving the reader longing for more…I found the story entertaining and full of Chinese witticisms. I recommend this book to anyone having an interest in China."
— Roundtablereviews.com

"In *Don Quixote in China*, Dean Barrett sets out to explore 21st Century China with an impossible goal: to find Peach Blossom Spring, an idyllic village described in the famous fourth century poem by T'au Yuan-ming. Of course, the journey quickly turns into something else entirely, and the results are often moving and hilarious and tremendously entertaining. With his empathy, keen eye for the absurd and knowledge of China, Dean Barrett will entertain many, many readers."
— Mia Yun, author, *House of the Winds*

"Dean Barrett's book is as unusual as it is thought-provoking and Mr. Barrett makes a fascinating modern-day Don Quixote as he doggedly searches for an elusive jewel of Chinese literature in the remote mountains and secluded valleys of China."
— Harold Stephens, author, *Take China*

Praise for
Skytrain to Murder

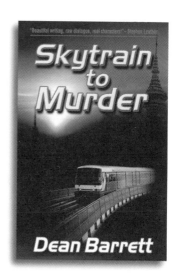

"*Skytrain to Murder* is a brilliantly written novel. The mystery is detailed and intriguing, and will keep readers guessing until the exciting climax....*Skytrain to Murder* is one of the most fascinating mysteries I have read in a long time. The exotic locale coupled with captivating suspense make for a winning combination. I definitely recommend this book for all mystery lovers."
— *All About Murder*

"*Skytrain to Murder*, a noirish mystery steeped in the culture of Thailand, skillfully portrays expatriate life in Asia. Barrett conveys all this with a sure-penned elan that pulls us nonstop from page to page."
— G. Miki Hayden, author and Macavity winner, *Writing the Mystery*

"No one describes the ins and outs of living in the sultry Far East better than Dean Barrett. The beauty of Barrett's writing is that as he takes you along Scott Sterling's voyage of discovery he effortlessly introduces you to dozens of characters, expats and locals, all with their own stories, all with their own insights into surviving in the Land of Smiles.
— Stephen Leather, author, *Tango One*

"Rich in the customs of Thailand, Dean Barrett uses his personal experience living in Asia and brings his readers to this whole other world."
— Roundtablereviews.com

"The author has a gift for creating a detailed world rife with many layered intrigues and immensely personable characters."
— Reviewingtheevidence.com

"Barrett shows a great deal of depth and talent. You don't just get a great mystery but a lot of interesting side stories and great details that make this book a rich and fantastic read."
- Mostlyfiction.com

"This book is a goldmine."
— *Movers and Shakers* magazine

"It rocks! Great stuff! The book is really good! Read it!"
— Stickmanbangkok.com

"*Skytrain to Murder* is as satisfying a read as was Barrett's *Memoirs of a Bangkok Warrior*... *Skytrain to Murder* isn't long enough. Another 50 pages at least would have made it even more pleasurable."
— Bernard Trink, *The Bangkok Post*

"Dean Barrett manages to maintain the pace and the environment all the way through the book...this ability to present real characters in real surroundings gives this book an immediacy and credibility that exhorts you to keep on reading."
— Lang Reid, *Pattaya Mail*

Praise for
Kingdom of Make-Believe

"*Kingdom of Make-Believe* is an exciting thriller that paints a picture of Thailand much different from that of *The King and I*. The story line is filled with non-stop action, graphic details of the country, and an intriguing allure that will hook readers of exotic thrillers. Very highly recommended."
— BookBrowser.com

"A tantalizing taste of a culture, worlds apart from our own. Dean Barrett paints a sharp, clear picture of the reality of life. An excellent account of one man's struggle to find the truth in his existence. Very highly recommended."
— *Under the Covers Book Review*

"An absolutely astounding novel. Its depth and layers of perception will have you fascinated from start to finish. Highly entertaining!"
— *Buzz Review News*

"Barrett spins a tightly packed tale that is part murder mystery, part midlife crisis love story and part travelogue, with vibrant and seductive Thailand in a leading role. This mystery keeps the reader guessing at the next plot twist."
— Today's Librarian

"A gripping mystery documenting Dean Barrett as a writer in full possession of his craft."
— *Midwest Book Review*

"Sharp, often poetic, and pleasantly twisted, *Kingdom of Make-Believe* is a tautly written fictional tour of Thailand. Author Dean Barrett has woven a compelling and believable tale about a country he knows well. Barrett's prose is spare but his images are rich: a winning combination. His obvious intimate knowledge of Thailand combined with a very considerable writing talent make *Kingdom of Make-Believe* a tough book to put down."
— *January* Magazine

"A thrilling page turner. Barrett brilliantly evokes the suffocating fumes of Bangkok traffic, the nauseating stench of morning-after alcohol and smoke in its go-go bars, as well as the lurid lies and deception of washed-up lowlife expats in Thailand. God, I miss that place!"
— Stuart Lloyd, author, *Hardship Posting*

"Barrett has a gift for taking us into cultures worlds apart from our own, displaying a reverence for their exotic and grotesque as well as their beauty and history."
— *Poisoned Pen Reviews*

"Barrett is a powerful storyteller who has a feeling for language that's lacking in many contemporary novels. His dialog is a pleasure to read, and his descriptions from the nightlife in Bangkok to the Thai countryside are vivid."
— *Laughing Bear Newsletter*

Praise for
Hangman's Point

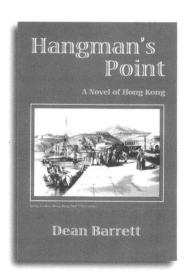

"Setting is more than a backdrop in this fast-paced adventure story of mid-nineteenth-century British colonial Hong Kong....A riveting, action-packed narrative....Chinese scholar, linguist, and author of two previous books, Barrett draws on his vast knowledge of southern China during a time of enormous change and conflict, providing richly fascinating detail of the customs, fashions, ships, and weapons of the times."

— *ALA Booklist*

"An expert on Hong Kong and the turbulent time period portrayed, Dean Barrett has fashioned a swashbuckling adventure which will have both history buffs and thriller readers enthralled from the very first page. An outstanding historical novel."

— *Writers Write Reviews*

"If Patrick O'Brian's Aubrey and Maturin ever got as far as Hong Kong in 1857 on their world travels, the aged sea dogs would feel right at home in China expert Dean Barrett's totally convincing novel of high adventure."

— Dick Adler, *Amazon.com Reviews*

"A great epic of a historical mystery."

— *Bookbrowser Reviews*

"The adventures of this latter-day Indiana Jones will leave him fleeing for his life through the town of Victoria (Hong Kong), bring him face to face with the perils of the pirate-infested waters of the Pearl River, and finally fix him a date with death at *Hangman's Point*....The novel is peppered with well-defined characters from all walks of life....It would be just another potboiler a la James Clavell, but Barrett's extensive research sets this novel apart: as well as a ripping adventure story, it is an intimately drawn historical portrait."
— *South China Morning Post*

"There is adventure and mystery in every corner of this well-researched and well-written historical."
— 1BookStreet.com

"Rich in historical perspective and characters, Barrett's debut is good news for those who love grand scale adventure."
— *The Poisoned Pen Booknews*

"*Hangman's Point* is vastly entertaining, informative and thought-provoking....Dean Barrett weaves an intricate and many-layered tale. Barrett clearly has in-depth knowledge of his field, more so than most Western novelists can command....Barrett offers more than an exciting story. He provides an understanding view of China and the Chinese, guiding readers toward a fuller appreciation of that complex culture."
— *Stuart News*

"*Hangman's Point* is a great historical fiction that, if there is any justice, will enable Dean Barrett to become a household name. Highly Recommended."
— *Under The Covers Book Review*

"Excellently written and steeped in details of the times, all obviously very well researched and accurate."
— *The Midwest Book Review*

"Adams's adventures take him on a thrilling chase, almost an odyssey...*Hangman's Point* is a page-turner that is guaranteed to keep both male and female readers enthralled to the very end. Romance and high adventure."
— *Romantic Times*

A Word About the Author

Dean's novels on Asia include *Kingdom of Make-Believe, Memoirs of a Bangkok Warrior, Hangman's Point, Mistress of the East* and *Skytrain to Murder*. *Murder in China Red* stars a Beijing-born Chinese detective set in New York City.

His humor/travel book, *Don Quixote in China: The Search for Peach Blossom Spring*, caused him to be briefly examined by a panel of psychiatrists who concluded there was nothing to examine.

The Thailand Writers Association voted his detective novel set in Bangkok, *Skytrain to Murder*, as best novel ever written on Thailand with the phrase 'skytrain to murder' in the title.

Hangman's Point was acclaimed by Filipina bargirls in Hong Kong's Wanchai district as the best novel ever written on 19th century Hong Kong by an American living in New York's East Village on 10th Street between 2nd and 3rd Avenues in a lower floor apartment.

Most of Dean's books appear too late for any holiday buying season and die a slow death on dusty, cobwebby, betel-stained, cockroach-infested, ant-preempted, bookshelves in used bookstores along Bangkok's Sukhumvit Road and in the dark, dismal bowels of Manhattan's Strand used bookstore.

There has been a steady and growing demand for Dean's work reflected in the fact that his books now outsell all out-of-print books set in Asia.